FAITH

Also by Linda Calvey

FICTION

The Locksmith
The Game

NON-FICTION

The Black Widow
Life Inside

FAITH

Linda Calvey

MLP

First published in Great Britain in 2024 by Mountain Leopard Press
An Imprint of HEADLINE PUBLISHING GROUP

1

Cataloguing in Publication Data is available from the British Library

ISBN 978 1 8027 9476 2 (Hardback)

Typeset in 13/19 Adobe Caslon Pro by IDSUK (Data Connection) Ltd

Printed and bound in Great Britain by Clays Ltd, Elcograf S.p.A.

Headline's policy is to use papers that are natural, renewable and recyclable
products and made from wood grown in well-managed forests and other
controlled sources. The logging and manufacturing processes are expected to
conform to the environmental regulations of the country of origin.

HEADLINE PUBLISHING GROUP
An Hachette UK Company
Carmelite House
50 Victoria Embankment
London EC4Y 0DZ

www.headline.co.uk
www.hachette.co.uk

This book is dedicated to my siblings who were always there for me in the darkest of times. Terry, Tony, Shelley, Maxine, Hazel, Richard and Karen – I love you all dearly.

And welcome to the world my newest great grandson, Reggie Martin xxx

PROLOGUE

Wakefield, 1964

Poor Annie Wills never really had a chance in life. She knew it, and so did everyone else around her.

In fact, this certainty was such a large part of herself that Annie hardly allowed it to make her depressed any more. There had been moments where she'd hoped for better, but, since she was a young girl, she'd never really doubted that she'd been born having been dealt an impossible hand of cards, with the odds of lasting happiness heavily stacked against her.

And nothing much had changed since then.

Well, Maria had brought in sunshine, of course.

But along with Maria had come a whole new raft of added worries and fears, and so it had all balanced out to the same hideous level of strife and stress as far as Annie Wills was concerned.

'Yer 'ave to, Annie,' Gary screamed at her. 'No ifs and buts – yer just 'ave to, do yer 'ear me? Yer don't 'ave a choice.'

Choice, what's that when it's at home? thought Annie, as she closed her eyes, wishing her husband would shut his mouth.

But he wouldn't.

'If yer don't do it, it'll be the end of me, and then where will you and Maria be? Out on the streets, that's where, and then you'll be doin' it just the same regardless, but without a husband to protect you or a roof over yer 'eads, and where will Maria end up? Top of shit creek without a paddle, that's where,' he ranted.

Annie forced open her eyes and she looked at Gary.

Protection?

He offered protection? That was a joke.

Gary was staring at her, confident now she'd bend to his will as always.

In his imagined triumph over her, he was disregarding the blood-edged nicks showing all over the front of his grubby shirt where the Waltons had, in the last hour, quite literally, driven their point home with repeated jabs at his chest with a flick knife. The wounds were only deep enough to snag the skin but not really wound him, although they'd left Gary, and Annie too, in no doubt that this was the Waltons' first warning, and they'd have no hesitation in taking their threat to the next, possibly fatal outcome, should Gary Wills end up not doing their bidding.

Or, to put it another way, Gary had been left certain there wouldn't be a second warning.

Faith

Annie had seen that Gary was terrified when he'd first made it home, the cuts on his chest oozing, as he'd stank of booze and fag smoke from the boozer, and cheap perfume from God knows who, with the dirt on his trousers and jacket telling his wife that he must have been rolled in the dirt by the Waltons as a final humiliation.

Annie and Maria had been having a cup of tea as they'd sat at the kitchen table this Saturday evening, listening to the new pirate station, Radio Caroline.

They'd recognised the familiar lurch of his drunken steps outside, and Maria had quickly turned off the radio and ran to her room, Annie giving a sigh of relief as she'd heard Maria turn the key in the lock on her bedroom door exactly as Gary had stumbled inside, and immediately squared up to his wife.

Annie had been disgusted by what he'd told her.

But she hadn't been surprised.

She'd long known she had married a stupid man, and these days there was little that Gary could do to surprise her.

Gary's tragedy was that he wore his stupidity on his sleeve so obviously, and this meant that everyone else could see it too, and from there it was only a small step to all and sundry taking advantage. Perhaps if he'd surrounded himself with more decent-minded people he'd have found the world treated him better. But Gary fancied himself a player, and consequently he always sought out the other lowlifes in the belief he'd be able to get one over on them.

And these lowlifes laughed at him, and delighted in thinking up new ways to show him as a fool. And the great lummox fell for it every single, exasperating time.

Illegal gambling, horse- and dog-racing scams, ringer gangs, jump-ups – Gary thought they all sounded wonderful and plunged in, only to fail spectacularly every time, usually upsetting the Waltons, while of course he was no stranger to the Wakefield police either. And as the Waltons had their fat fingers in all the juicy pies in the town, with everything leading back to them in one way or another, even when Gary thought he was getting one over on them, he wasn't really.

And now Annie could see they had well and truly screwed Gary over earlier that evening. Nobody else would have dared to beat him up like that. The Waltons didn't allow unwanted police attention caused by members of their seedy underworld. If violence was needed, they – and only they – were the ones allowed to dole it out. And clearly they were extremely peeved with Gary.

Annie thought her waste-of-space husband must owe the Walton brothers a lot of money, or that he'd done something really daft that the police had twigged, as he'd not been hurt enough to really damage him in a way that announced he wouldn't still be expected to pay. If he had upset them in some other, more terrible way, he'd have been put through the wringer in a different manner.

It was rumoured the Waltons would cut off a fingertip just for the hell of it if someone was setting themselves up in a rival business, and, if that didn't work, kneecapping usually did. Of course, anyone who was kneecapped knew they'd been badly hurt at the same time as they were in effect being given a final warning – and the rumour everyone knew was that there was only one more stage of punishment: death.

She glanced at Gary's fingers. They were all present and correct, so she doubted he'd been running something that would hurt the Waltons' business interests. It had to be money then, money he would have owed them and then ignored their demands for payment.

So just when Annie had thought she'd seen all that Gary could throw at her – the debt-collectors, his other women, his fist-happy treatment of her on a weekend night – it was now clear that somehow he'd managed to bring his family to a new low.

And he was even foolish enough to believe he was cleverer than his wife, to judge by the current glint in his eye that showed he was excited by the idea of Annie getting him out of his latest hole.

As she stared at him with disgust, Gary mistook her look for something else – fear, perhaps? – and he rubbed his chest as he gloated. But he'd forgotten the undressed and open flick-knife cuts on his chest, and his expression quickly became a wincing 'ouch' of pain.

Annie couldn't quite hide her smile over him not remembering the tattoos of shame and dishonour the Waltons had so recently marked him with. She knew they wouldn't treat their dogs with the contempt they'd shown her husband.

Instantly she realised her mistake by allowing Gary to see her smirk, and she prayed their daughter would stay in her room as the inevitable happened.

She'd taught Maria well, however, who was now lying on her bed with a pillow clamped tightly to her ears to drown out the noise.

And Annie just had time to raise her arms to protect her head as best she could as Gary leapt at her, pounding her to the ground with his fists raining down on top of her head, and then kicking her in the belly as he yelled, 'You will do it, my girl. You'll work off my debts with yer body, flat on yer back and for any man that wants yer, that yer will, and you'll do it well, yer mark my words. The Waltons want yer, and they're going to have yer.'

As Annie sank to the floor, she made herself as strong as she could, even if only in her mind, by reminding herself of everything she hated about her husband: his drinking; his gambling; his violence behind closed doors; his foolishness. And how she could see through his stupidity and his vanity, every single time.

This was her tried-and-tested way of making sure he no longer frightened her, and these days it worked every time.

She never retaliated once he was upon her. It was Annie's small act of defiance as she knew how arousing he found it if she fought back, and the day she'd realised this was the day she decided to no longer fight him physically and instead she would suck it up without a scream or a sob or a move away from whatever he had to give, no matter how furious her passivity made him.

Still, this evening, Gary wasn't so dim as to hit Annie around her face. She was a fine-looking woman in spite of her difficult life, and he knew he must take care not to harm what she could earn through having such a pretty face.

Annie made sure not to let out so much as a whimper. She thought of Maria, and the love she had for her daughter, and then she barely felt the pain of what Gary was doing to her.

He pulled her up off the floor and shook her hard in what was now pure rage. Somebody had to pay for all the frustrations he was feeling, and it might as well be Annie.

And as his wife began to lose consciousness, he bellowed at her as loudly as he could, flecks of spittle peppering her cheeks, 'Yer going to be the best tart the Waltons 'ave, there's no two ways about it. Yer going to lie on yer back, and like it, and yer going to have 'em coming back fer more. Do yer 'ear me, Annie, do yer fucking 'ear me?'

Her final thought before merciful oblivion came was that yes, she'd heard, and it was a horrendous thought that her life had come to one of being whored out at the whim of somebody else, although perhaps this wasn't so very different to what had been going on in the marriage bed for the last fifteen years.

Annie wished her situation had been different, and that she and Maria could have survived without Gary.

But she and Gary were Catholics, and she'd always known that divorce was out of the question.

Once, she had tried to have a discussion about the failure of her marriage with the local priest during confession, but he had ducked the question of quite what it was that Annie should do to improve her life at home with a, 'Be guided by your husband and believe in God's will.' Annie didn't know about God, but, as far as being guided by Gary, it was all she could do not to laugh out loud, and then she thought God clearly had never lived with Gary if that was honestly believed to be any sort of a solution. And with no family of her own, who'd help her move away from him; and with no qualifications, realistically what were her choices? Annie had stood up and, without a care for how rude she was being, she'd left the confessional box right in the middle of the priest telling her about the three Hail Marys she should say, and she'd never gone back to the church.

In any case, the Wills family would never have let her go – their women did the men's bidding, and they put up and shut up. Annie had seen their unsympathetic looks when Gary had given her a black eye in the past, looks that told Annie with a depressing finality that they all thought she must have deserved it. As far as they were concerned, for a wife to leave would bring unacceptable public shame on the family name, and no member of the Wills family would be bested by a mere woman – even when they knew their son Gary was a dead loss.

Annie knew she wouldn't like having sex with punters, but she knew too that she wouldn't despise them in the same way as she detested Gary.

And she would remain steadfast for Maria, the only good thing to have come out of her marriage, no matter what this new chapter of her life had to throw at her.

The strength of her hate for Gary would make sure she survived, Annie was sure, and keep her there to give her daughter the choices in her life that she herself had never had.

And then welcome darkness took Annie away from her dingy home and her shabby life, and for a while Gary was foolishly shouting only to himself.

PART ONE

CHAPTER ONE

Sixteen years earlier – Wakefield, 1948

Wakefield was still held fast in the harsh grip of post-World War II austerity when Annie, just fifteen, stared glumly down at the smuts of soot and coal dust on the pavement in front of her, smuts that dampened the colour on everything, even on the brightest summer's day. The local coal mines kept the town alive, Annie knew, but she thought the stench of coal in the air made each breath tangy and strange.

But she wasn't thinking about that just now.

There'd been an almighty bust-up at home and Annie Hooper was half propped on the outside windowsill to their tiny living room on the street side of their terraced cottage as she attempted to compose herself.

She tried to bite back the bitter tears streaming down her face, but she couldn't.

It was no good – her father, John, was adamant she must leave school. She'd always known her father was cruel and selfish, and that this day would come, but she hadn't for a moment had an inkling of just how much it would hurt.

She loved school and she was exceptionally good at her lessons, and it was the very last thing she wanted to do.

Her teacher had just left the house.

Sadly, he'd touched Annie on the arm in sympathy as he'd shut the front door, sneaking a book into her hands as he'd passed.

She'd not been able to do more than manage a small and watery smile of thanks that suggested – as she'd told him already when he'd said to her he'd speak to her parents to persuade them Annie should stay on – that it had been a waste of his breath.

'I know you mean well, sir, but my father doesn't think education is for the likes of me,' Annie had whispered in a shaky voice back then. ''E won't take it well, you talking to 'im. Sir.'

'Likes of you?'

'Girls.'

'He might not realise how clever you are, Annie, and I think he needs to know this. It's such a shame if you leave school now.'

That's as may be but, exactly as Annie had expected, her father didn't care in the slightest that she was bright, and he had told her teacher so, only in much less polite language.

Margaret, Annie's mother, cowered in the background, signalling to Annie with terrified eyes that, although she felt badly about it, there was nothing she could do to help her.

Annie wasn't disappointed in her mother. John Hooper ruled his family with a rod of iron, and Margaret had long ago learned to button her lip.

And as the discussion had ended, nobody was left in any doubt that Annie would be starting work on the packing floor of the biscuit factory within the month.

Annie felt heartbroken as she sat on the windowsill.

She wiped her eyes and looked down at the novel her teacher had given her. It was a well-thumbed library book that presumably had been thought too old and tatty to be lent out any more. It was called *Frankenstein*, and was by a writer named Mary Shelley, and her teacher had whispered as he'd left, 'Annie, this book was written by a woman when she wasn't much older than you. Life can be very difficult sometimes, but remember you are every bit as strong deep down inside as the woman who wrote this.'

She saw the story in the novel was about a monster.

How apt, Annie thought. Well, she knew about monsters – her father had already seen to that, with his total disregard for anyone else in his family.

Annie heard her father open the front door and she quickly hid the book. He didn't hold with girls reading.

'Biscuit factory,' he snapped to rub salt into her wounds as he went past on the way to the pub, and Annie couldn't help but flinch.

He noticed this, and, with a sneer, quickly raised his hand, making her flinch again. He laughed but then decided a drink was what he needed, rather than giving his daughter a clout just to drive home how she had to do what he said.

Once he'd turned the corner at the end of the road, Annie ran her finger over the book's debossed title on its cloth cover, and then she looked to her left, and to her right, to each end of the grimy street.

If this, and biscuits, was all life had to offer her, what was the point? She didn't even like biscuits. And Annie had to struggle not to cry again.

'Penny for them?'

She started as she was so lost in thought.

And then Annie looked up to see a young man she didn't know, sitting on a boneshaker, who'd stopped nearby with one foot on a pedal and the other on the ground, presumably on his way home from a shift somewhere.

'It'd be a poor exchange,' Annie said as she ran a finger under her eyes, which were still damp from her earlier tears.

He laughed, and as she peered at him through her fair fringe, Annie decided that he had a ready smile.

They fell to chatting, and Annie heard herself agreeing to meet him at the same time the following day for a walk around the park.

Years later Annie realised that this very first conversation was probably the happiest she and Gary Wills had ever been in each other's company.

When they'd met, Annie had never so much as kissed a boy.

And if only she knew then what she was later to learn, she would never have gone near Gary Wills with a bargepole.

But just five months after Annie began work at the biscuit factory, she was well and truly in the family way, and she and Gary were being rushed into marriage.

CHAPTER TWO

Annie had realised almost as soon as the wedding ring was on her finger that Gary Wills was hopeless in all respects and, without knowing it, she had neatly slipped an unbreakable noose of her own making securely about her neck.

Yes, Gary was easy enough on the eye if you liked that sort of thing – Annie found she did less and less – and he had a pleasant smile, but only if he felt like making an effort.

At first, when they were walking out, he'd seemed a kinder man than her father, a man ready to listen to what she had to say. He could make her laugh, and the irony – she felt later – was that this had made her want to let Gary go all the way in the park a month after they'd met.

That very first time was when Maria was conceived.

For poor Annie hadn't been told a thing about pregnancy and the way it happened. And she hadn't understood what Gary meant when he said he'd take care of it and that he would pull out. In fact she didn't realise that what they'd done, which she hadn't enjoyed much, could even lead to a baby.

But terrible morning sickness from almost the next day meant her mother had understood all too well exactly what had occurred, and then she had to help Annie hide the pregnancy from her father until Gary could be persuaded to marry Annie.

Gary refused to play ball.

And so Annie had had to tell her father, as her mother was too scared to.

The result was John Hooper marching to the Wills' home, returning home with bloodied knuckles.

'You'll be getting married as soon as, my girl,' he'd told Annie. 'An' then you'll never darken these doors again. Yer not goin' to be welcome in this house after that, do yer 'ear me, you trollop? You've made yer bed. Now yer 'ave to lie in it.'

That was the last time her father ever spoke directly to Annie, and neither set of the couple's parents came to their registry office marriage. Two strangers were asked to be witnesses.

Annie knew that now she was Annie Wills she'd never be able to go to her parents for any help. They were like that. For them, she had ceased to exist, and so had the forthcoming baby. They would never want to see their grandchild.

Annie told herself that her parents had never really been much support to her.

But all the same she felt sad – she was only a week past her sixteenth birthday, and the one person in the world she could call on for help was her new husband. The husband that looked at her now with increasing distaste. It seemed a very big price to pay for a few minutes' fumble close to the park bandstand.

The newlyweds moved into a cramped and dark bedsit at the top of a steep flight of stairs, and unable to hold down any employment for long, Gary began to drink far too much. Actually, Annie realised quickly, he may always have drunk too much and it was only now they were living together that it had become so glaringly obvious.

Of course Gary always had a good reason for why his jobs never worked out. His boss had had it in for him from day one, he was too clever for what they wanted, somebody had stolen some goods and laid the blame on him, and so on.

Annie never believed a word. Her husband was work-shy and often late to his job, and he was generally unreliable and dishonest, as well as unable to follow the simplest instructions a manager could give him. Even in the post-war years, with the endless shortages of strong young men, firms quickly decided to give Gary a wide berth, and Annie couldn't blame them.

The inevitable consequence was that Gary felt increasingly aggravated.

And from there it was only a small step to slaking his anger through pummelling his fists on to Annie whenever he was furious, which was quite often.

One evening when she was heavily pregnant and feeling poorly, he'd said that she hadn't cooked his sausages how he liked. And although she'd apologised profusely as quickly as she could and had taken the plate away, Gary had beaten her badly and then kicked her down the stairs, forcing her into an early labour.

Gary had quickly made himself scarce, and it ended up that a downstairs neighbour had had to ask in the local pub for somebody who could drive Annie to hospital.

She was kept in, and Maria was delivered safely after a traumatic and lengthy labour.

Annie, however, didn't come out of it so well – the injuries Gary had given her had led to an enforced hysterectomy. And not a single doctor or nurse had asked how Annie had come to be so badly hurt.

Once mother and baby were back in the bedsit several weeks later, Annie was relieved to discover that Maria was a quiet baby, seemingly born with the knowledge that she must never cry if her father were there.

Annie loved Maria to distraction.

Gary barely acknowledged his flawless baby daughter.

CHAPTER THREE

Wakefield, 1964

Much to Annie's surprise, becoming a brass for the Waltons' empire wasn't anywhere near as hideous as she'd expected.

Granted, there had been a terrible few minutes when, still feeling very groggy and with a thumping headache from the beating Gary had given her that Saturday night two days earlier, she was accosted on the way to the shops by Ted Walton himself. He was the family patriarch.

'Mrs Wills, 'old up for a minute there. Or may I call yer Annie? Yer 'usband's a fucker, ain't 'e?' said Ted in a companionable, almost soft voice as he got out of his Cortina and leaned against the car's bonnet as he sparked a Player's No. 6 and inhaled deeply, all the while gazing at her with unblinking blue eyes.

Annie didn't think him wrong about Gary, but all the same she couldn't prevent a shudder ratcheting through her body from having such a testosterone-driven man so close to her, which she hoped Ted Walton hadn't clocked.

She realised the fact that the tone of Ted's speech being chummy and almost as if they were old friends was much more terrifying than if he had shouted at her.

Ted stood up then, and stepped back a little to look her up and down appraisingly, as Annie felt almost as if he were looking at her naked, and he nodded as if he liked what he'd seen.

He held the open cigarette pack towards Annie, and she shook her head.

'All right for me to call you Annie?' said Ted, still keeping up his polite veneer.

'Yes, Mr Walton.'

'Ted, please, Annie,' said Ted.

'Ted.'

'Now we're on first-name terms, Annie, I need to talk to yer about a problem I 'ave.'

Annie nodded. She knew what was coming.

'Yer useless pile of shite owes me money. A lot of money, it 'as to be said. We've allowed Gary every chance to make good, and each and every time 'e's taken the mickey. And I don't like people doin' that with me. Know what I mean?' Ted's voice was still silky, but, with each second that passed, Annie grew more scared as she knew that really there was a threat underpinning everything Ted Walton said.

Oozing menace, he moved so close to Annie that when he breathed she could feel the jacket buttons close to his chest nudge against those of her mac, and she had to fight every impulse not to back away.

There were a few seconds of pulsating silence and then at last Ted went on, 'And so I've said to Gary, with the 'elp of my little friend, something 'as to give. And yer know what that something is, Annie?'

Annie heard the crack of herself swallowing at the words 'little friend' – she was pretty certain that Ted was referring to the flick knife that had marked Gary's chest so vividly.

'And do yer know what that something is, Annie?' Ted repeated, an edgy, raspy sound creeping into his voice now.

Annie felt a wave of fear, and had the sensation of blood rushing close to her eardrums.

Ted put his body full-frontal against hers, grabbed her arm and held his lit cigarette so close to one of her eye-balls that Annie could feel its heat.

She squealed but she saw that Ted realised at once that this was because he was holding her around her painfully bruised arm, and not because of what he was doing with the cigarette near to her face.

Ted relaxed his body and stepped back, and then he pulled up her sleeve a couple of inches, before he shook his head angrily as he stared at her mottled skin, and Annie felt this was more that he was cross at what Gary had done to her, than because he was angry with her.

Still, Ted's voice was kind no longer as he brought the cigarette tip even closer to her eyeball.

Annie had no doubt that he would press it against her if he were further riled. 'Gary's debt is now yer own debt, yer understand, and yer going to work for me as an 'ooker until it's all paid off. And if yer don't want to do this, I 'ear tell yer 'ave a good-looking daughter – I don't 'old with young girls plying their trade, but somebody 'as to pay this money, and I'm sure yer would rather it were yer, than yer girl? Wouldn't yer, Annie?'

Annie squeaked out a strangled-sounding 'yes' as she felt an unbidden tear slide down her cheek.

'I won't mention yer daughter to Gary,' Ted's whisper in her ear was loaded with menace, 'as I don't want him to start thinking 'is debt could be paid off double-quick that way. As I say, I think innocence is important when it's a girl, and not to be thrown away. And I think yer smart enough never to allow a pretty young lass like yer girl, all long legs and a trim figure and Bardot hair, to 'ave to pay off 'er father's debt this way, know what I mean?'

Annie nodded furiously to let him know she completely understood, and that Ted would never have to speak to her about this again.

She and Ted held each other's gaze for what felt like an age. And suddenly Annie felt she had moved beyond fear, almost to an out-of-body experience.

Although the street was quite busy with pedestrians, and she could hear the sound of cars driving by, not a single person came to her aid, even though she and Ted Walton were standing like that in broad daylight. The reputation of the Waltons meant nobody dared to challenge what was going on between her and Ted.

Then Ted moved back and took another drag on his fag, and, back to his kind voice, told her, 'I see we're in tune with one another, my gal. That's good – I appreciate it. Take a week or two to get over those bruises, Annie. And tell Gary that if he ever marks yer again, we'll hurt 'im twice as much as what he's done to yer – we'll let 'im know too, although not in the careful words yer'll use. Yer our property now, and we see yer as money on legs – and you and 'e must never forget that. Capeesh?'

'Yer won't 'ave to come looking for me.' Annie was keen to show Ted Walton she would do his bidding, as quickly she added, 'The very minute my bruises are gone, I'll be there at your club, ready and able to work.'

'Atta gal.'

Ted didn't need to say more, as Annie had received the message loud and clear – and he knew she had taken it on board – that if she didn't do his bidding, then he would come calling for Maria. And hell would have to freeze over before Annie would allow that to happen.

And then Ted flipped the cigarette stub into the road and made a show of brushing off the sleeves and the lapel of his jacket as if he'd made it dusty, although Annie understood this was more for dramatic effect than because he needed to.

At last Ted folded himself back into his Cortina and drove off, deliberately gunning the car's engine so that it loudly surged as it screamed away from the kerb, Ted saluting Annie with two fingers to his brow as he did so.

Now that the immediate danger had passed, Annie was left a trembling wreck.

The mix of the quiet reasonableness along with the threatened violence in his words, coupled with the way Ted Walton had accosted her and then taunted her with the lit cigarette, was much, much scarier than Gary kicking off. It suggested so much more simply by relying on her own fevered imagination to do the hard work for him, and Annie knew that she never cared to repeat the experience if she could possibly help it.

Gary could only offer brute violence, and although of course Annie hated this, there wasn't the unknown quality about it that Ted Walton had threatened her – and Maria – with.

Still, however, Ted Walton had given her a silver lining to this particular cloud. By the weekend, Annie realised that although she had never dared to mention her conversation with Ted to Gary, the Waltons must have had a word with him separately, as, although he winched up his verbal abuse of his wife, her husband was much more cautious about keeping his fists under control.

Annie made sure she didn't show she'd noticed Gary's twitches to the face or his clenched jawline, or the jerkiness in his angrily clasped fists as he fought to control himself, and she understood suddenly just how used she had got to him giving her a thump whenever he wanted. But in just a matter of days there'd been a sea-change, and now Gary's body twanged tautly with frustration at this enforced impotence. Once she heard him punching the wall to their outside privy in fury, although the bricks obviously didn't yield in the way that she had, as the thump sound was immediately followed by a pathetic wail of a childish 'Ow'.

She hoped Gary wouldn't forget too soon the Waltons' threat that should he hurt Annie further, then their wrath would descend on him.

But, for now, it seemed that everyone knew that should this happen the net result wouldn't be pretty, and Annie liked it very much that she and Gary seemed to be very much in agreement of the consequences, should he slip up and let one fly at her.

Annie made sure to turn up for work exactly as she had promised Ted Walton, on time and with a pleasant expression that gave no whiff of the 'face like a slapped arse' that Gary had just started accusing her of looking at him with.

As her bruises receded, Annie spent the days before her initial shift trying not to think about working at the Waltons', which proved impossible, and then she found herself fretting endlessly over the course of the next three or four days about precisely what she would be expected to do.

Gary had always been very basic in his sexual demands, and it was always over in a very few minutes, and although this had suited Annie over the years, she was pretty certain there would be a lot of men out there who would be much more adventurous with their sexual demands, although the technicalities of quite what they would be asking her to do to them, she didn't care to imagine.

Then it turned out that that level of anxiety about the future proved impossible to sustain, and thus Annie was pleasantly surprised to discover that by the time she arrived at the illegal drinking den where she'd been told to go, she felt surprisingly resigned to what was going to happen and actually relatively cheerful about spending some time away from the household. However grim it was going to be, it was unlikely to be a patch on what she was going through at home, was Annie's reasoning.

Gary was like a bear with a sore head; the penny had now well and truly dropped in his mind that Annie going to work for the Waltons meant that also, by necessity, she was going to have various men pawing over her.

Although he'd talked the talk before, when he'd said to her she would have to work off his debt as a brass, clearly he hadn't thought through the reality, and now he had, Gary didn't like being set up as a cuckold.

Typical, thought Annie, and then she decided that dealing with Gary was like having a hugely overgrown toddler in the midst of the Terrible Twos every day and with no respite. It certainly didn't make her want to placate him.

Meanwhile, Annie had drilled Maria on not being around her father of an evening if she could help it, and Maria had told Annie in a knowing way that she was about to be having lots of homework, homework that she would do at the small desk in her bedroom rather than at the kitchen table as usual, and then Maria had reminded her mother that, anyway, Gary would have left for the pub by six o'clock and then Maria would be in bed and asleep by the time he staggered back home.

And things got even better for Annie when it turned out that Ted Walton didn't want her as one of the girls the family ran who were expected to work the street corners, standing outside in all weathers, with many of their customers being as rough as rough could be.

Instead, Ted Walton had loftier plans for Annie, as he wanted her to work as someone who almost might be a hostess in one of his family's illegal drinking dens. Almost, but not quite be a hostess, as it was obvious from the start to Annie that although this role showcased brilliantly her looks and excellent figure, no matter how everyone dressed it up, she would still be nothing more than a glorified prostitute.

Still, Annie realised immediately that working in one of Ted's clubs gave her a pretty decent level of physical protection against violent clients, as who was going to want to go up against the Waltons if they could possibly help it? And especially so when punter and brass would be doing the deed on the Waltons' actual premises. Not many men, Annie surmised, and quickly she was proved correct in this reasoning.

Annie felt oddly grateful to Ted for making this decision about her, as at the forefront of her mind was the fact that she must, at all costs, take care of herself as best she could.

She never forgot for a moment that she had Maria to look after, or that Ted Walton might come calling for her one day if Annie didn't do exactly as she was told.

But the more she got to know Ted, the more she believed he had told her the truth that he didn't hold with having in his empire very young girls as brasses, not least as all of the other prostitutes she saw who worked for him were obviously at least twenty. And so slowly Annie relaxed slightly about this as she thought things would have to go terribly wrong for Ted to force Maria into the game, and that this wasn't going to happen on Annie's watch, of that she was determined.

Meanwhile, in the smoky bar of the drinking den, Annie was always warm and dry, while when she was in one of the backrooms where she would see to her clients, she always had the luxury of a big tough bouncer within shouting distance who was ready to come to her assistance upon her call of the special codeword should a john turn nasty.

And thus it wasn't long before Annie had somehow managed to put right to the back of her mind the terrifying moment when Ted had threatened to jab his lit cigarette right in her eye as she got used to the sense of safety that working wholly within the surrounds of the drinking den afforded.

She knew that if she'd been out on the streets it would have been a different matter, and the danger level much higher, and so every moment she spent in the drinking den Annie counted herself lucky that she never had to fear for her life as she would have if she were plying her trade outside, or as Gary had made her feel when he was in a real temper with her.

Ted made it clear that Annie's job as an indoors brass was to look decorative, and as an opening gambit, she needed to make the customers feel special with admiring talk and by her fetching them endless drinks.

Once Annie enquired of the bar staff how much these drinks cost, and she nearly fell over when she learned they were at least ten times the price of pub drinks and often a lot more, although the lure to punters who were happy to pay these extortionate prices was the drinking den remaining open until dawn, which was a long time after the boozers rang for last orders at ten-thirty each evening, and – aside from the lure of sex with good-looking women such as Annie – Ted's clientele could enjoy as much gambling on cards and dice games as anyone could want.

Annie heard whispers of more specialised goings-on in the countryside around Wakefield that the Waltons were engaged in, such as bare-knuckle boxing and dog fighting, where the Waltons would operate a tote after charging sky-high entry fees. Although Annie never saw anything like this herself, she didn't put these rumours past Ted or his brother Frank. If it was illegal and would make them money, she thought it highly probable they'd be involved.

Of course, what was always clear to everyone sitting around one of the green-baize tables or at the bar, was that Annie, although only at a price, was very ready to make a rich man extremely happy indeed for a few minutes – or a bit longer if he were willing to reach into his wallet for a further bundle of notes.

Annie got very good at giving the sort of look at a client that suggested the promise of more, and it became normal for her to be able to charge her punters for the extra session.

All in all, Annie appreciated that the Waltons treated her fairly and that neither Ted nor Frank ever made advances towards her. And she liked it that before her first shift at the tables she had been sent to a clothes shop where the Waltons had an arrangement, in order that she could choose a couple of decent cocktail dresses that would give the impression that the joint had a bit of class, along with some appropriate costume jewellery and expensive stilettoes, none of which she was expected to dip her hand in her own purse for.

Although pantyhose tights were the fashion, Annie was told, as she paraded her new dresses before Ted, she must always wear stockings and suspenders, and they were never to be removed no matter how much a man might beg. Time was of an essence, he added, and so once one trick was finished and she was cleaned up, she needed to be back near the bar ready for her next client. Putting on the stockings and suspenders just wasted time when she could be earning hard cash. She needn't bother with any knickers, Ted added. Some men could have made an instruction like this sound sleazy, but when Ted said it, Annie never thought his comment other than practical.

Indeed, during Annie's first couple of times with punters she was surprised how easy it was to excite the men sitting on the bed just by teasingly revealing a bit of thigh peeping out above her stocking top and then pushing down her the snugly fitting pencil skirt bit of her dress again with a wiggle and a wriggle of her hips until she was demurely covered, perhaps seeming not to notice a minute or two later that she'd allowed the skirt to ride up again.

Men really were very basic, and remarkably similar to one another, Annie couldn't help but think, and sometimes she thought they enjoyed her teasing them every bit as much as – if not more than – the actual sex that inevitably followed.

It went so well and Annie proved such a success that it wasn't long before Ted announced he was putting Annie's prices up. She decided that this was something she wouldn't tell Gary about, as it might be like adding petrol to an already burning fire.

The very best thing about her stints at Ted's drinking den was that Annie was shown the ropes of the trade by Joyce, an older woman who clearly had a heart of gold. Joyce carefully explained to Annie the ins and outs of necessary things, such as how she should douche to get herself ready for her next trick, or try and get a john to wear a rubber, and Annie was really grateful for this freely given advice.

Joyce clearly had once been an amazing beauty and she had been a brass for many years, working her way up through the ranks of the Waltons' organisation to her current privileged position of working for herself as an indoor brass, giving the Waltons a cut of what she earned through her 'private arrangements' with her regulars.

Joyce's clothes were obviously expensive and her copious jewellery real gold, plus she had a new car of her own, and a reputation across the whole of the county it seemed, to judge by the number of men who came to the drinking den just for her services, and so Annie suspected that Joyce's prices were probably sky-high.

There was something incredibly likeable about Joyce, Annie felt, and a generous, wholesome quality too despite what Joyce did for a living; she found very quickly that there'd be a smile on her face should she find herself thinking about this warm and welcoming older woman.

Joyce helped Annie with her make-up and hair, making Annie laugh when she said as she backcombed Annie's hair and showed her how to do her eyes and lipstick, 'There's a trick to making a man think yer've just got out of bed, and can't wait to get back in again with 'im. It's come-to-bed eyes and a painted mouth, and 'air just messy enough for 'im to imagine 'is 'ands in it. Next time, watch me half-close my eyes and run them from his toes slowly up to his face, and then quickly back to his crotch with my mouth slightly open as I look down and I take a big breath. They're putty in my hands at that point, and it'll be the same with you.'

Annie turned out to be a keen pupil in the art of seduction, and she was fascinated by the way in which, with a mere flick of the hand, Joyce would command some punters to come back the next night, saying that she was too tired to see to them that evening, or she just didn't fancy it, and these johns seemed perfectly happy to be bossed about.

At first Annie wondered if Joyce was poorly and was suffering a long-term health condition, seeing how many men were sent away, not that they ever looked frustrated or upset at this turn of events.

Then one evening Joyce winked conspiratorially at Annie behind the back of the retreating client, and Annie realised what Joyce said to these johns was simply a charade and in fact part of the sex, even if the actual sex didn't take place for several days. It was just the way Joyce conducted her affairs and kept her clients eager to come back for more.

'I can't believe how they take it like a lamb when you've just refused them,' confided Annie one evening as she spat on to her black block of mascara and rubbed the bristly brush on it before fanning it across her lashes.

'If I'm honest, it took me a while to learn the trick to it too,' admitted Joyce. 'But they like it even more when they do come back, so much so that often they might not even have time to get their trousers off. Ted's very keen on all his brasses each 'aving their own little speciality, as that way all tastes are accounted for, and this is mine.'

'Really?' said Annie.

'Yes, really. I say I'm going to charge them double if that happens, and then I take my time lifting my skirts or hoicking my top a bit lower at the front, and quite often by then it's all over. I think it's the threat of the double payment I'm going to take that tips them over the edge,' Joyce explained. 'I've one I've only got to call a naughty boy as I let him look down my top as I drop something on the floor – I told him if it 'appens again, it's triple payment. He'll be in later, and it'll be the easiest tenner for not more than two minutes of my time, although I always talk to him for another few minutes so nobody can guess how quickly he goes.'

'I'm shocked,' laughed Annie.

'It's all about reading human nature, and then talking the talk,' Joyce said. 'Yer'll find your own special trick. But for now yer looks and yer figure are all yer need.'

'Does Ted know about you sending them away?'

'This way they visit twice, and will drink at the bar and play some cards, and as I pay over a proportion of my money, the club doesn't lose seeing as 'ow I charge a premium for this. Does Ted know, you ask? I'll let you into a secret – me 'olding back on the punters were 'is idea to begin with!'

And then Joyce and Annie had to think hard about defenceless kittens and puppies getting run over by huge lorries so that they felt sad and therefore weren't at risk of their loud gales of laughter being heard over at the den's bar area.

Every single penny that Annie earned went straight into the pocket of the Waltons, of course. In fact she never saw a glimpse of any of the cash as a punter would pay the bar staff, who would then tip Annie the nod that the money had been received and it was now over to her.

It was always payment in advance, she noted, and if some-body were with her too long, the bouncer would knock at the door to hurry things along.

Gary knew he had to give the Waltons what he could from his wages at his latest job as a cleaner at the steel-works, and so there wasn't much extra cash at home, and certainly this did nothing to put him into a good temper. But Annie didn't mind too much that they had to eat endless jacket potatoes with margarine as she knew the other side of this was that Gary must have used up all the free credit he could get in the local pubs and offies, and so when she wasn't at home he wasn't going to be as pissed as he liked to be, which in turn had to offer Maria a greater sense of protection.

Annie understood from the off that she'd never know the full story of all of Gary's debts and indiscretions with the Waltons, with his silly decisions and multiple gambling dues, and his inability to properly do much of the grunt work they asked of him, although his endlessly sour face told the story of just how far he was in shtuck to them.

Privately, Annie didn't see how Gary would ever be out of the clutches of the Waltons as the way they ran their debts with the spiralling interest payments on top seemed designed that the debtor could never fully clear them. In some ways this suited Annie because Gary still seemed so scared of the Waltons that her home life felt calmer, and this definitely made Maria sunnier too, as it can't ever have been good for her to see Annie always walking on eggshells in an attempt not to rile Gary.

This made her feel secure in a way that she never had before, and it was this unfamiliar sense of security that stopped Annie from being envious of the money that Joyce was making for herself.

For, in her short life, Annie had never had it so good.

CHAPTER FOUR

A lot of how the Waltons kept their stranglehold on the crime community was, by necessity, quite hidden as so much operated on a need-to-know basis, but now and again when she was working, Annie glimpsed how formidable the Waltons were as a feared criminal family.

Although the drinking den had all the trappings of exotic comfort and endless relaxation, occasionally there'd be a harried knock at its unassuming, numberless and nameless front door to the road, and then Annie would hear raised manly voices coming from the den's foyer or, on a couple of occasions, the sound of a woman crying outside.

The Waltons prided themselves on their particular mix of kind-seeming and quiet approach, mixed with sudden bursts of extreme violence. It was very effective, and few people seemed to step out of line, as, if they did, the punishments were harsh.

Despite this, a couple of times something would be said – Annie could never quite hear what, no matter how hard she listened – that would have Ted Walton and his brother Frank suddenly reaching for the sawn-off shotguns in the hidden compartments on the underside of their table in the corner of the room, and then they would rush to front-of-house.

Once Annie had to sponge somebody else's blood and what she thought could well be splatters of brains off of Frank Walton's favourite suit jacket, and she'd felt like gagging.

But a stern look from Joyce told Annie wordlessly not to make a fuss but just get on with what Frank had asked her to do, and not ask questions or look Ted or Frank in the eye for a good while.

And on several other occasions Annie glimpsed either Ted or Frank counting enviable mountains of used bank notes that they stacked into bundles, around which they put rubber bands. There was a very big, heavy metal safe in their office and Annie suspected that at times it must be groaning with the amount of cash it contained.

And thus Annie tried always to act as if she were deaf and dumb both at work and at home, and she took great care never to say a word to Gary about anything she saw or heard at the club, nor about any of the customers she entertained there.

He'd try and wheedle information out of her, but Annie knew her husband was such an idiot that he wouldn't be able to resist trying to use anything she told him for his own ends, and it would likely be herself that'd end up carrying the can when it all went wrong.

Ted Walton never demanded she keep quiet like this, but a couple of times he nodded at Annie in a way that suggested he knew that her lips were sealed and that he appreciated this.

And the fact that neither Ted nor Frank ever expected anything from her other than hard work when she was with the punters gradually won Annie's loyalty, maybe helped a bit by Ted having the sort of looks that were easy on the eye.

The Walton brothers might be crooks, and violent ones at that, but from what Annie could see in the way they did their business, there were distinct lines they wouldn't cross. And they prided themselves on being faithful family men who treated their wives well, and the women who worked for them respectfully.

Annie liked this about them, as it made her feel she knew where she stood. This was a very different experience to anything she had seen in her own life until then.

Meanwhile, there had been a discussion at home over Maria, now fifteen.

Gary wanted her out of school and into work, but Annie was determined not to let history repeat itself and that Maria would be allowed the chances to better herself through as much education as possible, chances Annie had never been allowed but had so longed for.

'Gary, we need to let Maria stay on at grammar school,' Annie said. 'She's smart, and you'll have already thought that this is the way she'll be able to look after you in time, as she'll earn more with a good education behind 'er than she ever will over at the biscuit factory.'

Gary shook his head as if he was going to get his way.

But then Annie played her trump card as she said, 'And then, Gary, just think how *you'll* benefit from those rewards. How easy you'll be able to take it, when Maria is earning well. Putting your feet up, and being a man of leisure. A man at nobody's beck and call.'

Maria took the hint from her mother, and was quick to join in. 'Daddy, if you let me stay at school, it will mean I'll be able to get a job at a bank, and I *promise* I'll make sure yer all right.' As she said 'all right' Maria rubbed together her right thumb against her first two fingers in the time-honoured gesture that suggested cash, just in case her father hadn't got the point she was making.

Gary didn't say anything but he stared at Maria for a while without blinking. Annie thought she could almost hear the cogs of his brain clicking into gear as he weighed up the situation. She bit back a sharp comment. He never had been the sharpest pencil in the case.

And as they were used to dealing with Gary, Annie and Maria knew better than to force the point.

But a few days later Joyce told Annie she had overheard the Waltons laughing about Gary. Apparently he'd been boasting to them that he was going to be a blagger, once Maria was working in a bank and could give him inside gen on setting up a raid on the establishment.

'If that waste of space manages to make himself into a blagger, then I'll eat my hat,' sniggered Joyce. 'I know 'e's yer 'usband, Annie, and I don't mean to offend. But I don't think yer Gary 'as got it in 'im, and neither do the Waltons.'

Annie gave a big sigh as she shook her head.

She didn't for a moment believe Gary had got it in him either.

To pull off any sort of bank robbery would require brains and finesse, neither of which her husband possessed.

On the plus side, Gary thinking he had the nous that being a blagger required meant that, by necessity, Maria had been given the green light for more time at school.

But it meant also that there would be huge pressure on Maria once she had left her education to deliver on this promise to her father.

Joyce guessed what Annie was thinking, and was quick to say reassuringly, 'A lot can change – it'll never get to that point, Annie. You mark my words.'

'I 'ope you're right, Joyce. I 'ate that man sometimes,' said Annie, 'but I 'ate more the thought of what 'e'll do to Maria if she doesn't 'eed 'im.'

'Don't worry, pet,' Joyce told her, 'when the time comes, we'll think of something to make sure Maria never 'as to do anything like that.'

There was something so kind and comforting about Joyce that Annie felt that for the first time ever she had somebody in her life standing in her corner, somebody who believed in her.

It was a good feeling, and she knew that if she wasn't working for the Waltons, she would never have met Joyce.

Joyce in turn enjoyed talking with Annie, finding her funny and quick-witted, saying to her more than once, 'Yer going to make a top brass, Annie, as there's more to yer than most, and this is what'll get yer the top-paying regulars. Just make sure the men never really get to yer, inside yer 'ead, I mean, no matter what they ask of yer, and then it'll be fine.'

Years of living with Gary had already given Annie this skill of shutting out an idiot man, she was pleased to discover, and actually a lot of her punters turned out to be surprisingly decent men. Easily led and with loose morals, no doubt, but kinder and more appreciative of her than her own husband had ever been.

Before she met Joyce, Annie had always felt ashamed that she had never made a proper friend.

During her school years she'd been too embarrassed of her overbearing father and ineffectual mother, never daring back then to ask anyone to her home, as the risk of becoming the butt of anyone's jokes – should her hard home life become public knowledge amongst her classmates – felt too great. Pretty much the same could be said for the whole of her married life too.

It was safer all round never to let anyone become close, Annie had always told herself. Lonely, certainly, but safe.

In fact Annie remained self-conscious over what she secretly put up with at home from Gary, who really had a gob on him these days. Still, if it meant that Maria had a good start in life, then it was all worth it, she kept telling herself.

But there was something about Joyce that made Annie want to let this older woman get closer than she was used to. The truth of it was that Joyce lifted her spirits, and helped her see the good things in life.

And so one day, as they put their make-up on ready for the night ahead, Annie risked saying, 'I wish I'd never set eyes on Gary Wills, Joyce. 'E's a brute, make no mistake, an' a dim one at that.'

'Aren't they all, ducky?' said Joyce in the sort of voice that suggested anyone who thought differently was gravely mistaken, as she stared into the mirror in the room where she and Annie would get themselves ready, and then stuck the pointed end of a styling comb into her blonde beehive and waggled it about a bit to make sure the style had more lift. Joyce added, 'You probably never 'ad much from yer father in the emotional sense. An' when Gary gave yer a bit of attention, 'owever brief, you mistook it for something else, something special.'

Annie realised that in Joyce's thumbnail summing up, what her friend had said perfectly encapsulated what had happened, although Annie had never thought about it herself in quite this way before.

'I'm such a fool,' she said glumly, as she nodded agreement with Joyce's assessment. 'That bit of attention was five minutes in the park as the keeper was ringing the bell for chucking out.'

'That long?' said Joyce with a lifted eyebrow, as she dug her elbow in Annie's ribs.

'You're right. Maybe twenty seconds,' said Annie, and then she looked around quickly to make sure nobody had heard her making a lewd joke.

'Chin up,' said Joyce, once the pair of them had stopped laughing, and had agreed they had a pretty low opinion of nearly all men. 'Yer 'usband's the fool fer not realisin' what 'e's got. Remember that, Annie. 'E's a lucky man to 'ave yer and Maria, but 'e's too stupid to see it.'

CHAPTER FIVE

Maria had never given Annie much trouble. Sadly, this was about to change.

Sure, Annie had worried and fretted about her daughter since the moment she'd been born, but that was all about making sure Gary didn't do anything to harm Maria, or else to do with Annie trying to make sure Maria had the best opportunities that her mother could provide.

Maria had been happy to be at Annie's side at home, and to work hard at school. Even when she was blossoming into a pretty teenager who could turn heads, Maria had never given any sign of being the sort of girl to want to go to youth clubs or talk to boys, and Annie had been grateful for her daughter's quiet and quite solitary nature.

Then one day Maria met a lad called Fred.

It was in the Woolworths on Kirkgate, and drawn in by her good looks and shiny hair, Fred followed Maria around the store, larking about and trying to make her laugh.

Maria ignored him for a long while, but somehow she stayed in Woolies much longer than she'd intended. Then he went around a set of shelves the opposite way to her, and she almost walked straight into him, partly because she was looking behind her, unable not to wonder where he was.

'Surprise!' said Fred.

'Yer'll 'ave to do better than that,' muttered Maria coyly, but unable to stop her eyebrows lifting coquettishly.

Fred offered Maria his arm, which she took.

And then he led her to a milk bar where Maria was bought her very first frothy coffee, which came in a smoked glass cup and saucer she felt was the very height of sophistication. She sipped the unfamiliar drink, not especially enjoying the taste, as Fred did his level best to impress her with talk about his car, and his clothes, and his important job for his father.

Maria couldn't compete with any of this, and she didn't think Fred would be interested in her perfect attendance record at school or her test marks that habitually kept her top of the class. So instead she smiled encouragingly at him, and said 'go on' or 'really?' or 'you must be pleased at that' at appropriate intervals.

By the time they left the coffee bar when it closed, Maria was smitten.

And in turn Fred had appreciated her appreciation of him – indeed it made him feel quite the cock of the walk.

'Yer late,' said Annie when a shiny-eyed and pink-cheeked Maria finally arrived home. 'I'm just dishing up tea.'

Maria had a dreamy expression as she answered, 'I'm sorry fer being late, Mummy. I've been to Woolies and . . .' She stopped what she was saying, and stood there with a goofy smile instead.

'Go on,' said Annie suspiciously, as she passed Maria a fried egg on toast and told her to sit down.

'There was a boy called Fred, and we went for a coffee,' said Maria. 'I've never 'ad coffee before, and it came in a cup made of glass.'

Annie felt her heart bump. She knew a Fred, but she told herself not to jump to conclusions.

'Tell me about this Fred, Maria.'

''E's tall an' dark, an' ever so trendy, an' 'e's a mod with long hair.'

Annie didn't like the sound of this. She had a terrible premonition of what her daughter was about to say.

'An' 'is father is called Ted – Ted an' Fred, can you believe?' said Maria.

Trying to keep a smile on her face as Maria was look-ing at her so intently, but feeling as if she were breaking to smithereens inside, Annie nodded, although hopefully not in a way that would tell Maria that her mother could believe it all too well.

Annie was pretty certain that Fred had to be the oldest son of Ted Walton, who was of course the Walton family patriarch and the very man who'd fallen out with Gary and was now employing Annie as a prostitute in his drinking den, and who had once threatened Annie that if she didn't do his bidding, then Maria would be next in line. Annie hoped against hope that Maria hadn't caught wind of any of this.

She'd never quite said to her daughter what she did at night, and Maria had known better than to question her mother too closely. Gary had made them into that sort of family.

Yes, Maria might have heard that night when Gary was screaming at his wife that she was going to have to be a brass to pay off his debt to the Waltons, but Maria had always seemed such an innocent girl, and Annie had prayed her daughter had never managed to put two and two together as to what being a brass really meant.

Naturally Annie had seen Fred around now and again when she'd been over at the drinking den, and she had always thought that there was something unpredictable and a bit wild about him that had made her careful to give him a wide berth. She certainly hadn't liked anything about him that she had seen.

Fred Walton was always dressed in sharp clothes, a cigarette constantly lit in one hand, and he liked to think he swaggered rather than walked. He had a brand-new Hillman Imp, his pride and joy, and Annie knew that, for him – and he couldn't be older than nineteen or so – he hadn't earned enough to have such a car through working in any legal way. And she'd heard Ted tell his brother Frank that Fred had paid cash for it, and Ted was proud he hadn't been asked by Fred to contribute to the purchase price.

But while Ted Walton made sure that Annie and Joyce were treated with a certain respect by those that worked for him, Annie had seen already that Fred wasn't a chip off this particular old block.

Instead, in Annie's view, it was very obvious that Fred fancied himself a right geezer, a lad about town, and he had a downright lascivious leer when he'd stared at Annie's cleavage when he thought his father wasn't looking at him.

And the fact Fred didn't seem to care a jot if Annie caught him doing this or not, told her that Fred had such a low opinion of women that very likely nothing would ever change his mind to think otherwise, and this made her worry for her daughter.

But Annie was between a rock and a hard place as she wasn't able to warn Fred off, or ask Ted to do so on her behalf.

For Annie knew that, without a doubt, if Fred found out Maria was related to Annie, then it was all very likely to go pear-shaped. In fact, in that scenario, it was impossible for Annie to imagine it going any other way.

And Annie certainly wasn't going to mention Maria to Ted, who had never said anything further to her about her daughter after that time he had threatened to burn her eyeball with his lit No. 6 – in Ted's case, when it came to Maria, out of earshot was out of mind, Annie hoped.

She stared aghast now across the tea things at her daughter as she tried to make sense of this shocking news.

Maria was smiling a secret smile to herself, and was clearly lost in a happy imaginary world of her own.

It was obvious that Maria had been instantly captivated by Fred Walton, Annie could see, and even though Gary had just come in and plonked himself down at the kitchen table, Maria couldn't resist telling her mother and father about Fred having said that he'd be in his car waiting for her outside the school gates the next day when the home-time bell rang.

Annie thought back to when she'd been roughly Maria's age, and she remembered how easily Gary had snared her own attention, and she could see too that Fred had something of a similar James Dean bad-boy look about him that Gary had had all those years earlier. And those looks would be honey for an impressionable teenage girl, especially an inexperienced and innocent one, a girl exactly like Maria.

In fact, Maria was so excited by the afternoon she'd just spent with Fred that she didn't notice her mother's pensive look as Annie glanced at Gary to see how he was taking the news.

Gary normally ignored Maria as he wolfed down some grub before leaving for his nightly sojourn in the pub. But now he gazed at his daughter almost as if he were seeing her for the very first time.

Then he made his feelings on the matter clear, and Annie thought this was the first time in years that finally she agreed with anything her husband said, as he stared Maria straight in the eye and announced, 'That Fred Walton is off limits for yer, my girl. Off. Limits. Do yer 'ear me?'

'Why?' cried Maria, her happy expression giving way at once to one of tremulous confusion. 'I don't understand.'

'Because,' said Gary. 'Just because.' Maria glared at her father as he said this, and then he added in a louder voice, 'Because I say so, Maria, and now there's an end to it.'

Gary pushed his plate of food aside. Then he stood up and grabbed his coat, before slamming the front door as he left for the pub.

Maria stared at where he'd been sitting in puzzlement, and she looked towards her mother, clearly expecting Annie to take her side as normally happened.

'Don't look at me like that, with those big eyes. Gary's right about this, and I agree. Yer going to need to step away from this young man, Maria,' said Annie firmly. 'I'm in agreement with yer father on this. Fred Walton isn't the sort of man we want in yer life. Concentrate on yer school work, an' then in a few years yer'll 'ave the pick of any young man you want, I promise, love.'

'But this is stupid,' wailed Maria, 'it's Fred I want to get to know, an' there's nothin' wrong with 'im. Yer don't know him as I do.'

"E's a crook, Maria, and if 'e isn't yet, it's only a matter of time before 'e will be. Mark my words. 'E'll drag yer down to 'is level and, trust me, Maria, that's not where yer want to end up. It's a life where there's never a moment's peace, and while I might not know much, I do know about that,' said Annie. 'And yer not stayin' on at school for the likes of Fred Walton to make merry with.'

'Like our life 'ere is so much better?' shouted Maria, angry now. 'A father who can't keep a job or stay out of the pub or keep his fists to himself, and yer all dressed up each night, an' what yer wear isn't fer *our* benefit, now is it?'

'I'm doin' my best, Maria,' said Annie. 'It might not seem like it to you, but it is the most I can manage. And it'll be exactly what yer have to look forward to for yerself if yer don't steer clear of the likes of Fred bloody Walton, I promise yer that.'

'If this is your best, then it's not up to much, is it? It's not very good, don't yer know?' Maria shouted, and then she pushed her chair back with a scrape across the kitchen floor that set Annie's teeth on edge, and flounced out of the house, pulling the front door shut behind her as hard as she could.

No, Maria, it's not very good, Annie thought, feeling cut to her core by the first disagreement that she and her daughter had ever had. But, my girl, I'll be damned if I'll let you make the same mistakes that I have, she vowed.

CHAPTER SIX

That evening at work Annie had a second piece of unpleasant news to digest.

After Annie had told Joyce that Maria had met Fred and instantly seemed unbearably smitten, Joyce had tried and mostly failed to bolster Annie's spirits by saying that Annie would do well to remember that young people were flighty, and although Maria might say it's love at first sight now, by next week she'd probably be after someone else.

'I hope you're right, Joyce, really I do,' said Annie. 'But Maria has never seemed that sort of girl. She knows nothing of the ways of the world, and I fear for her. Fred is much worldlier than she is, and I'm sure he'll take advantage. And I worry that Maria's a determined lass, who might right now be talking herself into a daft course of action.'

'Calm down and get a grip, as yer not helping yerself or the situation. If Maria 'as got yer sense and yer brains, she's got a lot going for 'er, remember, Annie, and she'll come to her senses and she won't want a man like her father, or one like Fred,' said Joyce.

Annie didn't have anything to say to that other than a circumspect 'hmmn' sound, and then the two friends sat in silence beside each other, thinking about what had been said as they put their make-up on.

Then Joyce spoke carefully, 'And, meanwhile, I have some news of my own that I need to tell yer, although I am sorry it's coming right on top of what's happened with Maria and Fred.'

Annie looked suspiciously towards Joyce, her wound-up lipstick in a hand that was halted on the way to colouring her lips.

Joyce continued powdering her nose as she stared at herself in the mirror and said, 'I'm goin' to miss you as you've been a great pal, Annie, truly yer 'ave. But I need a change of scenery and I'm not getting any younger, and so I'm leaving Wakefield and moving back down to Stepney in London. Yer know it's where I come from.'

'No!' cried Annie, as she blinked in panic.

For a moment she thought her ears had deceived her, but when she peered at Joyce's face reflected back towards her in the mirror, it was to see that she had heard perfectly well what her friend had just said.

'When are you leaving?' Annie was powerless to stop her voice wobbling uncontrollably, and her eyes became darkly glittery, filled now with a different kind of emotion from how she had just been thinking about the problem of Maria and Fred.

'I'm off at the end of the week,' said Joyce.

'So soon?' whispered a disconsolate Annie, a shaky hand lifted to her throat. 'Why on earth?'

'It's just time,' Joyce told her. 'I need to spread my wings, and, in fact, meeting yer 'as already kept me up here a lot longer than I intended, as when yer started, I'd already promised myself I was just about to go back 'ome.'

Joyce had a look about her that told Annie her friend wasn't open to persuasion. Clearly Joyce had made up her mind it was time to go back to her roots down south, and now nothing was going to hold her back from doing this.

'Whatever am I going to do without you?' Annie wailed, unable to stem a flood of tears. To lose her staunchest ally and to argue with her daughter on the same night felt simply devastating.

'What does Ted say about it?' she sobbed then, hoping that Ted Walton would prevent happening what Joyce had said.

'Now 'e's got yer, 'e's not that bothered about losing me, to be honest. Yer the icing on 'is cake,' said Joyce. 'There's always a job with 'im 'ere if I need it, 'e says, but I can go with 'is goodwill.'

'But I'll not be able to manage without you,' howled Annie, and then she gave in to another bout of tears as she put her head on her now folded arms.

Joyce put a hand on Annie's shoulder as a gesture of support, but Annie shrugged her off.

'Aw Annie, don't take on so,' comforted Joyce. 'If you ever leave Gary, then you join me in London, an' together you an' me can be the best brasses that city's ever seen, the bee's knees. Maria can come too an' work in a bank down there, in the Smoke. Is that a deal?'

'Gary'll never let me go,' hiccupped Annie sadly, shaking her head as she wiped her eyes.

'I'll always let you know where I am, just in case,' Joyce promised. 'I'll never not be there if you need me, Annie. You remember that always, you promise me?'

Annie felt too down in the dumps to think of anything to say back to her friend.

Joyce looked in the mirror, undoing another button at the neckline of her form-fitting leopard-print blouse and pulling in the black leather belt at her slender waist another notch, and then put her hands on either side of her chest to give her bosoms a little shake.

Annie watched her, and she realised that although there had never been anything sexual between them, Joyce was the love of her life after Maria.

And now she was on the brink of losing them both. It felt almost more than she could bear.

Naturally, Maria took no notice of anything her parents had said to her regarding Fred Walton, and, naturally, it was only a matter of time before it all went to hell in a handcart.

Almost from the minute she had first seen him in Woolworths, Maria believed herself to be one with Fred Walton.

In fact by the time she saw him the second time, Maria had elevated Fred in her mind almost to the status of a demi-god.

And Fred quickly took note of Maria's adoring eyes and, predictably, did nothing to dissuade her of his near god-like status.

CHAPTER SEVEN

Over the next couple of months Annie's life took several further turns for the worse, and it was hard for her to be cheerful, even though Joyce stuck to her promise and telephoned the drinking den one evening when she knew Annie would be dolling herself up, so that she could pass on her London address, which she made Annie memorise while she was on the phone, with the instructions not to write it down, 'just in case'.

Annie made herself not think about any 'just in case' scenarios, for to do so would be depressing, and, frankly, she had enough on her plate to deal with right then.

For Maria, defiantly, flat-out refused to stop seeing Fred. Annie hated this.

And she hated it even more when Fred discovered who Maria's mother was, and the way immediately he took to making inappropriate sexual gestures to Annie when he saw her at the den to rub salt into her wounds.

Annie wished that Ted would catch him at it, as were his father's wrath to come tumbling down upon his son, it was probably the only thing that would stop Fred's taunts.

But Fred was too wily to act up if Ted was anywhere near, and Annie had to steel herself not to give any sign to Fred that she found his actions repugnant as she knew if he got wind of that, he'd double his efforts in trying to rankle her.

She was also careful to no longer speak badly of him to Maria.

She'd said her bit as best she could already, Annie felt, and to say more risked making Fred hugely attractive in her daughter's eyes in a way that really spelled danger.

Gary wasn't happy about the situation with Fred either, but he was caught in his old bind of not being able overtly to criticise anything the Waltons did, not even in this case, as he couldn't risk them getting wind of how bad it made him feel in case they used it against him. And so, predictably, Gary's response was to spend more time at the boozer, and several times Annie caught him going through her coat pockets and purse looking for any stray coppers.

After the second time, Annie told Maria to make sure she hid her piggy bank well, and later that same evening on a rare night that Annie wasn't working, Maria said to Annie she had put it in the linen cupboard under the folded sheets, as Gary was never going to change anyone's bed linen, not even his own, and Annie couldn't help wishing she had Joyce to tell what Maria had just said, as she knew Joyce would have made a pithy comment back that would have made Annie laugh.

Indeed Maria seemed surprised that her parents didn't have further comments to make on the matter of her now having a boyfriend.

But if she tried to bring up Fred, Annie usually just responded by mildly reminding Maria not to let her schoolwork suffer, while Gary would look at her with a frown on his face, although his eyes would narrow as he sent silent daggers in his daughter's direction.

Then something dreadful happened that really soured the atmosphere at the Wills' house.

Gary took a nasty fall on the way home from the pub when steaming drunk one Saturday night, completely wrecking his back.

At first it wasn't so bad as Gary was carted off to hospital in an ambulance, and he ended up spending a fortnight on a ward there, leaving Annie and Maria to enjoy the new quiet of the house while he was being treated.

But this was only the calm before the storm, as then Gary was dropped back home in his pyjamas by an ambulance. He looked, thought Annie, as if he were in all respects a broken man.

And this turned out to be the literal truth because Gary's injury had caused permanent damage and he could no longer leave the house, and in fact he could barely make it from room to room, even with the help of a stick, and there was no way he could hold down a job.

Luckily their house was so small that he could just about hobble to their outside privy and it was clear to all that Gary was pretty much reduced to living and sleeping in the sitting room as the stairs were too much for him.

There was an advantage in that Annie no longer needed to share a bed with Gary. But if she had found her husband a bad-tempered, hideous wretch before his injury, it was nothing to how he behaved now. He was rude, surly and thoroughly unpleasant every single moment he was awake, and he took to endlessly taunting Annie about her work at the Waltons'.

Annie tried to tell herself that 'sticks and stones can break my bones but words can never hurt me', but the endless jibes thrown her way, of 'fat bitch' and 'cock-sucking fucker', began to take their toll, and Annie couldn't help but feel continually worn down by the drudgery of her home life.

She thought about the years stretching ahead of her, and all she could imagine coming her way was an endless stream at work of sweaty men opening her up and pawing her as if she were a Christmas present they had to unwrap, alternating with a depressing home life of revolting barbs and insults thrown daily her way by Gary, and the empty space in her heart that had once been filled by the close and affectionate nature of the relationship she had shared with her daughter.

Joyce's absence made things infinitely worse.

Annie felt as if a part of her had been ripped away, a part that couldn't heal. There was a huge Joyce-shaped hole in her chest that was impossible to ignore, and although Maria was still around and seemed happier than she ever had, the Joyce-shaped hole stood next to one the previously innocent Maria had occupied.

It all combined to make Annie feel a mere shell compared to the strong woman she had been just a few months earlier, and she berated herself for thinking back then that she deserved a bit of luck going her way.

The reality was, Annie firmly believed, she was destined to always remain a downtrodden, unfortunate woman.

And once she was in this mindset, each shift at the drinking den required a Herculean effort of will by Annie to appear serene and companionable, and so she found herself walking around in a continual state of exhaustion.

The only slightly positive aspect to the whole situation was that Maria was out with Fred so much, or was so full of daydreams on the rare occasions when she was at home, that she didn't seem to notice Gary's worsening temper.

As positive aspects go, Maria's wasn't to last very long.

Yes, she and Fred had a great time driving around in his Hillman Imp, with her making him laugh, and him making her heart beat unbearably fast when he'd parked in a secluded lane and they'd climbed into the back seat of the car.

Maria was every bit as sexually ignorant as Annie had been those sixteen years earlier, Annie having found she didn't have the heart to explain anything about sex or babies to her daughter at any point since then.

This was because it felt too close to what Annie did of an evening over at the Waltons' drinking den, behaviour that she felt really uncomfortable talking about to anyone, even to someone as wise and experienced and close to her as Joyce had been, and especially so when it came now to her daughter.

Annie knew she should say something, even if only about ways of not getting caught out, but no matter how much she tried to cajole herself to speak to Maria, each time she steeled herself, she found she just couldn't follow through.

It wasn't long before Maria found herself pregnant.

She chose not to tell her mother yet, promising herself that she would the very moment she and Fred had agreed the date for their nuptials.

In comparison to how scared Annie had felt when she'd discovered she was going to have Gary's child, Maria felt happy, and as if she had in her belly the ultimate gift that she could give Fred. She was sure that he would be as delighted as she.

How wrong Maria was.

For Fred saw it all very differently.

He was simply livid. And the first time Maria mentioned it, in his fury he pushed her out of the Hillman Imp even though he was driving at the time.

He hadn't been going fast and Maria wasn't too badly hurt in the physical sense, but it was nasty all the same. Anxiously she checked her knickers to see if she would lose the baby, but all seemed to be fine in that respect.

Maria told herself firmly that Fred had only behaved that way because he'd had a shock over her announcement, and this had led to him over-reacting, and in her mind Maria quickly forgave him.

Subsequently ignoring his silence, she allowed what she felt was enough time to pass for him to get used to the idea that he was about to be a father.

And then Maria went to the drinking den early one evening.

Once she had sweet-talked the doorman into letting her inside, she stood in the bar in front of Fred with a big smile, certain he was going to take her in his arms and say he was sorry.

Instead he laughed in her face.

'Yer just skirt,' he told her, 'good fer a fuck and a tumble, Maria, but nothing else.'

'Come on, Fred, don't be like that,' Maria pleaded. 'I know that now you've had chance to let things sink in, you'll want to marry me, and we can be a family. Think how nice that will be.'

'Married! Yer out of yer mind, yer silly bitch! Lads like me don't marry daughters of tarts like you are!' he told her.

And then Fred laughed so much that his father Ted came out of his office to see what all the noise was about.

Ted guessed immediately what had happened when he saw Maria's crestfallen face and the too-tight waistband on her skirt. 'Go home, Maria, go home,' Ted said to her. 'There's nothing fer you 'ere. Fred'll never marry you. 'Ave the baby adopted and you'll be all right. Gary and Annie won't say anything, and I can 'elp yer with a little money if yer short.'

Annie walked in at that moment, having just arrived for her evening's work. She had no idea that her daughter was pregnant.

'What won't I say anything about?' she asked. 'And why might Maria need money?'

Nobody answered Annie.

'Fred? FRED!' yelled an anguished Maria at the top of her voice. 'I'm having yer baby, don't yer understand? Yer *baby*!'

'Yeah,' said Fred. 'I 'eard. Get rid of it, or keep it. I don't care. Babies aren't for me. Anyways, we've had our fun now, Maria, and that's it. There's nothing for yer 'ere now.'

Maria ran towards Fred as if that would make him change his mind. Annie screamed and took a step forward as if to wrench her daughter away with a, 'No, Maria, leave him be.'

Maria was deaf to Annie's words.

And as Maria tried to throw her arms around Fred Walton, as if that were going to make any difference, he brought up the back of his hand and whacked it with full force against her face, and then he whacked it back the other way, and then back again and kept the frenzy of whacks going for far too long in spite of Annie trying to wrench his arm away from her daughter.

Finally Ted stepped in and grabbed Fred's arm, and held it aloft as a panting Fred stood there, spent with the effort.

A dazed Maria crouched down, and then she put her hand up to her cheek and drew it away and stared at her blood, dark and shiny on each of her fingers.

And Annie saw that Maria's skin across the whole of one side of her face was erupting with blood bursting through the gashes of the slashes that Fred had inflicted.

There was a horrifying maze of cuts that went from the outside edge of her eye down to the corner of her lips, intersected across the width of her cheek by myriad lacerations, horizontal this time from nostril to ear.

Annie screamed as she looked at her beautiful daughter's spoiled face, and even Ted yelled at his son, 'Fer fuck's sake, Fred, that fuckin' ring of yers! Get it out of my sight.'

Annie realised that Fred must have had his signet ring customised with an embedded razor blade tip for exactly this sort of purpose. She'd heard about this sort of thing before, but she hadn't for a moment thought Fred would want one of these rings.

There had been many times in her life she thought she loathed Gary beyond all measure, but in an instant Annie realised that she abhorred Fred even more, so strongly and with such a passion that it made her feel faint with fury.

Fred stepped back with an uncertain look on his face, half pleased with himself and half worried about the reaction of his father, who was looking at him furiously while muttering a string of disgusted 'fuckin' 'ell's.

Fred didn't look sorry in the slightest for the carnage he had just caused.

Annie realised that Ted wasn't cross so much about Fred impregnating or maiming a lovely girl, but more that Maria's blood was now cascading freely to the floor and making a mess that needed cleaning up when it was only minutes to go until the drinking den was due to open.

Ted gave Fred a hefty shove in the chest that almost pushed him over, hissing, 'Mop and bucket, Fred. Now!'

And then Ted grabbed a stack of clean tea towels and thrust them at Annie, as he rather roughly shepherded her and Maria out of the back door to the establishment and bundled them into the back seat of the ancient and battered Ford Popular that he always kept right outside.

Annie remembered Joyce telling her, when Annie had wondered once why ever the Waltons kept such an old and rusted jalopy alongside their newer and much smarter cars, 'It's for when they have a bleeder they need to deal with. They don't want to spoil their nicer cars, but they don't care what happens in that old Ford Popular and so that back seat is hard with the dried blood when they need to get rid of somebody from the den.'

As they set off, Annie wondered what was going to happen next, now they were in the car for bleeders.

Would Ted go as far as killing her and Maria so that there could be no comeback on Fred?

Although she felt they had had a decent working relationship, Annie wouldn't put it past Ted Walton, whom Joyce said always loved to tie up all the loose ends to any situation as he didn't like any chance of comeback.

Annie knew that while Ted liked her personally as she was honest and hard-working, he wouldn't hesitate to kill her and Maria if he felt he should.

Ted Walton would take the view that family was family, and so he would do his best to protect Fred, and in some ways Annie couldn't really blame him for that.

She looked into the rear-view mirror, and Ted glanced at her. His face was expressionless, and Annie could only pull Maria to her as she thought the very worst was about to happen.

But in fact Ted drove mother and daughter to the home of a crooked doctor he had on his payroll for precisely this sort of occasion, for Maria to be patched up.

And by the time Annie and Ted had got the shaking Maria out of the car at the doctor's, and she had been taken away by him so that she could be attended to, every single one of those tea towels was sopping wet with Maria's blood, and Annie's clothes were drenched too.

Ted and Annie stared at each other, and then Ted shrugged and shook his head, before he got back into the Popular and drove away without giving Annie a second look.

He hadn't said a single word directly to her that day.

CHAPTER EIGHT

'Maria, can you hear me?' said Annie several hours later.

Her daughter groaned in reply to her mother's voice, and the doctor gave her an injection.

Maria lay now on a ratty sofa against the back wall of the doctor's garage, the whole of one side of her face swathed in bandages, in stark contrast to her perfect, luminous face on the other side.

She'd had to have over ninety stitches to close all the wounds, and she had been lucky not to lose an eye, the doctor had said. It was a shame on such a young, beautiful girl but the muscles beneath her upper dermal layer had been damaged irrevocably and this was likely to affect her ability to make facial expressions on that side once the wounds healed as the ring had caused so much damage, he'd warned.

And then he'd added that Maria was going to have extensive scarring too on her top layer and this would show as puckering, and this was even though he had done what he could.

If she were really unlucky her eye might have to be removed at some point, but he thought it highly unlikely it would get that far. She should expect that her recuperation would be long and painful, and she must make every effort not to get any infections as some of the wounds were close to her nose, which was a quick route to the brain and really serious outcomes.

On the plus side, the baby's heartbeat was strong and regular, and so he was hopeful that the pregnancy would continue as normal.

Annie and Maria were both in tears at what he'd said. What a desperate situation.

The doctor wasn't totally without heart, and he told Maria that she should think of her baby, who would need a mother.

'Babies need love and security,' he said. 'They don't care about a few scars.'

Maria was crying too hard to take in what he said.

The doctor went to fetch some old but clean clothes belonging to his wife for Annie and Maria to dress in, and after he'd passed the bundle over, he pressed four crisp ten-pound notes into Annie's hand, after which he looked at Annie with raised eyebrows.

Annie gave the tiniest of nods. She understood what the doctor was trying to tell her, even though he hadn't used any words.

While she and Maria dressed in the clean clothes, leaving their soiled ones in a pile for the doctor to burn as they were all saturated in blood, he telephoned for a taxi.

Annie heard the doctor say to the taxi driver when he pulled up outside that they must be taken wherever they wanted to go and the cost of the taxi put wholly on the Waltons' tab, and he would take it as a personal favour if the taxi driver kept quiet about wherever the drop-off was.

Annie didn't think for a moment that the taxi driver would do this should Ted Walton lean on him, but she appreciated the kind thought of the doctor, and she hoped that he wouldn't get any unpleasant comeback from the Waltons for going beyond what Ted had asked him to do.

It took some time to get Maria into the taxi, as she whimpered and winced with pain at each step.

'We want to go to Doncaster train station,' said Annie as the taxi drove away. Annie was clutching a small brown glass bottle of aspirin the doctor had given her for Maria.

She saw Maria's uncovered eye blinking at her mother in surprise at the words 'Doncaster train station', and Annie put a finger to her lips to quiet her.

At Doncaster they got out of the taxi and made their way to the station concourse where they found a wooden bench to sit on.

It was too late at night for them to get a train, but when a policeman came to ask them to move on, he took pity on them after he saw Maria's face and the way she couldn't stop trembling, and he found a station worker who could be persuaded to unlock the waiting room so that they could go inside. And then the policeman told the worker to make sure they were fetched a cup of tea.

When they were alone, Annie whispered quietly in Maria's ear, 'We're going to London. We'll find Joyce, and we'll make a new life there, away from all of this. And no one will know where we are.'

Maria made a strangulated noise, and Annie realised that she was having difficulty speaking.

'Don't yer try to talk, Maria. And don't worry. I said Doncaster station as lots of trains go through here, and so no one will know for certain the train we take will be going either south or north, or maybe east or west. If we'd gone to a train station in Wakefield, we'd have been too easy to find,' Annie told her daughter.

She didn't want to worry Maria further, but Annie knew that Ted Walton would be furious about her running away with Maria.

Now that Joyce had gone and she was Ted's top girl, he'd feel that she'd left him in the lurch, both in terms of the punters and because Gary's debt was still unpaid.

Ted would want her back if she stayed around and he would expect her to carry on in spite of what Fred had done. It was just how he did business.

But as Annie looked sadly at Maria, she felt that working for Ted Walton was the last thing in the world that she wanted. And the result of this was that, whatever the future held, she knew without a doubt that she could never go back to her place at the Waltons' drinking den, the centre of their empire, as that was part of Fred's territory and she couldn't bear to set eyes on him again.

Annie didn't feel bad about running out on Ted. She'd worked honestly for him and he had made a lot of money through what she had brought in.

She thought he'd get over it in time. Immediately Ted would find another woman to take her place, and before long there would be a bit of him that fairly quickly accepted that Fred had gone too far in what he had done to Maria, and that all Annie was trying to do was be a good mother and look after her girl. And eventually Ted would come to believe that Annie had done the right thing by taking Maria and running away from Wakefield, of that Annie was hopeful.

Meanwhile, Annie didn't care a jot about leaving Gary behind. In fact she had hardly thought of nor considered her husband at all that evening, and had never for a moment felt she should ask the doctor if Gary could be fetched as Maria was so badly hurt.

To Annie's mind, Gary was an odious man and they'd all be better off apart from one another. Their Catholic marriage vows aside, he had parents who could take care of him now that she and Maria were no longer around, she was sure, and so there was no danger of him being unable to go on in one way or another, although what the Waltons would do about him concerning his debt and his inability to work, Annie had no idea. There were precious few belongings that Gary could sell, and they'd always rented their house.

If she were honest, Annie didn't really care much what the outcome was.

Gary should never have treated her as he did, and as she looked again at Maria, without a moment's guilt over whether she was doing the right thing, Annie decided she would never think about her waste of space husband again if she could possibly help it.

The railway worker came back with a freshly made thermos and a couple of tatty old blankets, and said there'd be a mail train leaving for London in half an hour, and if they didn't mind slumming it by sitting on upturned wooden crates, he would sneak them inside so they could travel as stowaways in one of the mail coaches alongside the sacks of post, and nobody would know they were there.

Annie smiled and said that would suit them just fine.

'Our secret,' said the man with a wink, as he pressed a couple of florins into Annie's hand.

'Our secret, and thank you,' she agreed, as she put the coins in her pocket, thinking it would save her having to break a note when they needed to catch a bus to where Joyce lived.

*

Faith

The train was bumpy, uncomfortable and chilly, and Annie and Maria held each other tight for comfort and warmth as they huddled under the grey blankets they'd been given, and listened to the sounds of the envelopes and parcels settling in the hessian mail sacks and the click-clack of the train's wheels on the metal tracks as it bore them southwards. Neither slept a wink the whole night long.

And by six o'clock the following morning, mother and daughter were at King's Cross station in London, standing in its entrance, exhausted by the shock of all that had happened the previous night, and blinking owlishly at each other in the weak shafts of dawn sunlight.

But exhausted and spent as they were, nothing could dull the relief Annie and Maria felt at having left their old lives behind, even though they only had the forty pounds between them, and the few florins, as well as the clothes they stood up in, and two thin blankets.

It wasn't much for a new start, and it might be tough for them.

But it certainly wasn't a disaster either.

Annie felt she had faced worse before, and she was equal to the challenges she and Maria would find in London.

Although grateful never to have to see Fred again, understandably Maria didn't feel as confident.

Tentatively, she raised a hand to touch the waistband on her skirt and felt underneath the still-small swell of her pregnancy. Then she touched gently the bandages and dressings obscuring the whole of one side of her face, and on which her blood had spotted through the gauze. She breathed in sharply, as her wounds and their stitches were sore.

Annie noticed her daughter's good eye well with tears, as Maria realised anew how badly she had been hurt and how her looks had been compromised for ever by the need-less actions of a selfish and hideous man, a man she had foolishly believed cared for her when he'd whispered those sweet nothings in her ear. And all the while he'd only been interested in what was inside her underwear and very ready to say whatever he had to in order to get what he wanted.

'Look at me,' said Annie gently. 'Yer beautiful, Maria, in my eyes, and nothing can change that. Yer always 'ave been and yer always will be. A man is never going to dim that beauty, come what may, no matter 'ow your face 'eals. I hope you know that right now. But if yer don't, one day yer will, I'm sure.'

'I will try to believe it, Mummy, really I will, but it will be 'ard. I wish I'd listened when yer warned me about Fred. I know 'ow 'ard you tried to look after me, and I am sorry I messed up so badly,' said Maria.

'You have *nothing* to be sorry about, my darling. It is – and always will be – my privilege to look after yer, and so try to remember that. What I feel for yer is love, and it's exactly as yer will feel about yer own baby, when 'e or she arrives, I promise,' Annie told her daughter as she felt her own eyes brim with tears. 'That little one is going to be very lucky to 'ave yer as a mother,' Annie added.

'Really? You think so?' Maria's voice was tremulous, telling Annie that this was a difficult thing for her daughter to take on board, even though she longed to do so.

'I do,' Annie replied as firmly as she could. 'Yer baby is the luckiest little mite in the world, I promise. And 'e or she will see you as the most beautiful woman who 'as ever lived.'

Maria stood there, blinking rapidly, and Annie had to fight to hold back her own tears when she saw how very much Maria wanted to believe her, and she rubbed her daughter's arm in comfort.

And then, in the early light of dawn, mother and daughter calmed themselves so that they could share smiles that were resolute despite being watery (even though Maria's was hampered by her stitches and bandages) as they reached for each other's hands.

They had each other to turn to and to love, and it was this that made them strong.

And as they turned away then from each other to look about them at a grimy London that was just starting to rouse itself for the coming day, both could sense a new beginning stretching before them – a future – with neither having any intention of throwing away the second chance their arrival in the city had brought them.

'Let's find Joyce,' said Annie as she pulled Maria close to her in a final hug.

'Yes, let's,' her daughter agreed as she laid her head briefly on Annie's shoulder, and the two women stayed standing close together for a little longer as they felt the beat of the other's heart.

And then they pulled away with determined expressions on their faces and stepped on to their first London pavement as the sounds of a new day bustled around them.

PART TWO

CHAPTER NINE

Stepney, East London, 1965

Later that day, Annie stared agog towards the checked cotton cloth covering the kitchen table in Joyce's downstairs back room, off which the scullery led, as she watched lodger Sean reach into his landlady's dresser-larder cupboard to retrieve the best china crockery and then turn his attentions towards making a pot of tea for Annie and Maria, while his brother Paddy nipped to the corner shop to get some biscuits.

Sean took great care to warm the teapot with a swoosh of boiling water, and then spoon in the tea after he'd tipped the water out before filling it properly from the steaming kettle, and then he poured the milk into a dainty china jug without spilling so much as a drop, and for a moment Annie felt tears threatening once more, provoked by the sight of his simple kindness.

Mother and daughter couldn't help then exchanging confused looks – they had never experienced a man offer to make themselves useful in the way these brothers just had. But Sean and Paddy seemed for all the world as if it were their pleasure to do something like this for these two women they had never met before, and in fact as if it were the most normal and everyday thing for young men about town as they were, to offer to do.

Annie felt especially full of gratitude towards them both as they had each made a point of not staring unduly at the bandages covering one side of Maria's face, but neither had they shirked looking at Maria either.

Instead they treated her like someone who'd had a nasty experience, but that it wasn't anything for a stranger to make too much of a fuss about, and Annie felt grateful that this was Maria's first experience of young men after the traumas of the previous evening.

'Men are not all like Ted and Fred, yer know, and Sean and Paddy are good lads who understand 'ow to be respectful and 'elpful. Their mother 'as brought them up well, and they've lots of sisters who've kept them in line when they were growing up in Dublin, and I wouldn't want them 'ere if they weren't kind and always polite, and keen to go to church on a Sunday,' said Joyce, a warm smile for the lads evident in her voice.

Sean stopped what he was doing and leaned over with a huge twinkle in his eye to say in a stage whisper to Annie and Maria, 'Lucky she and Father O'Reilly don't see us swearing like navvies on the building site then, or pushing the others out o' the way to grab the best boxes to sit on when it's time fer our snap.'

'Get on with yer, Sean,' laughed Joyce.

And then Joyce lit an Embassy with one hand as she pulled an ashtray across the table so that it was in front of her as she flicked her match into it, sucking the cigarette's smoke deep into her lungs with a satisfied sigh, as she added much more seriously, 'My lodgers are not like that waste of space, Gary, who wouldn't be able to tell the difference between a please or a thank you, and 'is own backside. I wouldn't 'ave them 'ere in my 'ouse if they were, and Sean and Paddy know right from wrong, and when not to cross the line. I know Gary's yer dad, Maria, and I don't like speaking ill of anybody who's not around to defend themselves, but . . . Well, that Gary Wills was a useless streak of piss as an 'usband, and probably not much better as a father, and I very much doubt yer can say otherwise.'

Annie noticed how Joyce already regarded Gary as a part of Annie's past and as if he no longer needed to be taken account of. She glanced quickly at Maria to see how her daughter would take the blunt words Joyce had spoken.

There'd been an awful lot of brushing things under the carpet in the Wills household, Annie accepted with a sigh of disappointment directed at herself as she saw Maria looking circumspect.

Gary's hair-trigger temper had meant Annie tended to keep her head down and just get on with things, trying always not to rile her husband unnecessarily, in case for once he took his fists away from her and turned his violent attentions towards Maria. As far as Annie knew, Gary never had laid a finger on his daughter in temper, but she'd never believed that he wouldn't at some point. And if Gary did turn on Maria, it didn't take a genius to guess that his story would be that whatever happened had completely been Annie or Maria's fault and certainly not his.

But now Annie thought perhaps she hadn't done the best by Maria, and instead her own behaviour had only made the subject of Gary pretty much a no-go area when it came to talking with her daughter. Certainly, she had never moaned to Maria about Gary's terrible attitude, or taken Maria into her confidence about other, darker things she had never seen that had gone on between the couple, as Annie had never wanted to depress her or force her into taking sides. In return, Maria had never said anything about her father – either for good or bad – back to Annie.

As finally Maria dipped her head as if she were being held in a dream, and then began to nod sadly in agreement with Joyce's terse words about her father, Annie couldn't help but wonder if she had made a huge mistake by being so reticent over the years.

Perhaps if she had talked more about Gary being the unpleasant man that he undoubtedly was, and encouraged Maria to speak up about her own feelings for her father, then Annie would have been able to head off what had happened later with Fred Walton. Perhaps Maria could have seen the similarities in the way her father thought acceptable to carry on, and how Fred did too.

Annie would never know the truth of it; if mother and daughter had managed to be more open with each other about the way a certain type of men carried on, thinking they were perfectly within their God-given rights to behave this way, then it might have made Maria more cautious regarding those she encouraged into her life, and much less naive.

But it was difficult to talk ill of a father to his daughter, Annie had found, as happiness was so hard to come by that she wholeheartedly believed no child needed to learn upsetting things to do with their father that nobody could alter. Dear Maria hadn't chosen Gary and Annie for her parents, and Annie felt very guilty that she and her husband hadn't been able to make a better stab of things.

Joyce guessed pretty much what Annie was thinking.

Paddy had returned clutching a brown paper bag of Garibaldis that he quickly arranged in a circle on a gold-rimmed side plate, while Sean poured the cups of tea. As the brothers made themselves scarce by clomping upstairs to get ready for work, Joyce said wisely, 'Just remember, Maria, men like Fred Walton, and your dad Gary, they're their own worst enemy – they don't know it, but they are.

'They grow up thinking they're The Man, but in the end they'll be suffering more than they can ever make us women 'urt – you mark my words, ducky. I know it's bad for yer right now, but someone will come looking for Fred one day with murder in their 'eart, and 'e's a coward, and 'e'll die quaking in 'is boots with fear, and Gary will probably end up just the same. What Fred 'as done to yer is a tragedy, anyone can see, and I'm not trying to belittle that, Maria love, not in the slightest. But what I know too deep down in my 'eart is that what's happened to you at Fred's hand is also something that will make yer strong and, in time, you'll become a woman who can cope with whatever 'appens to 'er, good or ill, during the 'ighs and lows life throws yer way. Yer just 'ave to believe it, Maria, but time'll 'elp with that, I promise. And no daughter of Annie's isn't going to be strong, now is she? Like mother, like daughter, I always say. And the good news is that yer Annie is the strongest woman I've ever met . . .'

'I don't know about me being strong, Joyce. I blame myself,' Annie interrupted in a small voice. 'I should have told yer more about what I thought Fred was like, Maria. I'd seen him around, and I could see he was bad news. I am more sorry than I can say that I didn't come clean with yer.'

'Don't take on so, Annie,' said Joyce, briefly patting her friend's arm. 'Once Fred was in the picture, this was going to 'appen to Maria, sooner or later, and there were nothing you or anyone else could do to stop it. And at least now it's 'appened before the baby comes as Fred might 'ave 'ad a change of 'eart once that baby's arrived if it turns out to be a boy, and he might then 'ave wanted 'im fer 'is own. And it's led to you two being down in the Smoke, and a new start, and *that's* what's important.'

'Auntie Joyce . . .' began Maria.

'Just Joyce, please, dearie.'

'Joyce then,' said Maria, 'I know you and me, we don't really know each other and I'm not sure I deserve it, but thank you for being so kind to me.' She turned towards Annie, adding, 'And Mummy, it really isn't your fault – none of this is, and I know that.'

'It's nothing to do with kindness on my part, Maria,' Joyce told her quickly as Annie had her mouth open as if she were about to apologise again, 'but only what anyone with an 'eart would do. And, in any case, I feel I know you – Annie 'as told me such a lot about yer and what a clever girl you are. She's always been so proud of yer, and I've loved 'earing it. Any daughter of Annie's is a pal of mine already, and if ever I'd 'ad a daughter, if she were 'alf as good as you, then I'd be made up. Now, drink your tea, 'ave a biscuit or two and take some aspirin, then Annie can change your dressing, and afterwards you can 'ave a nap on the settee in the parlour – I'll fetch you an eiderdown.'

At the mention of a nap and there being a couch she could rest on, Maria's eyelids began to flicker and her shoulders slumped as she slid down a little in her chair, and quickly Annie reached for the first-aid tin Joyce was passing her way as it was obvious that Maria was completely done in, and Annie realised she was worn out too.

And when Annie gently peeled the top dressing back a little, both she and Joyce had to fight very hard not to cry out in horror at the livid sight of the terrible havoc Fred Walton had wreaked across one side of Maria's beautiful face.

'You'll stay 'ere tonight, of course,' said Joyce, speaking softly to Annie half an hour later so they wouldn't disturb Maria in the next room. 'The boys can sleep downstairs – they'll manage fine – and you two take their bedroom,' Joyce added.

'We don't want to put you or your lodgers out, as they are paying you good money to have a proper bed each night,' answered Annie. 'We can find a room somewhere, but earlier we came 'ere as it was just I wanted you to know we're down 'ere in the Smoke now, and that we shan't be going back to Wakefield, and yer know I don't really 'old with using telephones and so I didn't want to ring the pub to go and fetch yer to take my call. And I needed sight of a friendly face, just for a little while.'

The two women looked at each other. They'd each experienced such a lot in their lives that they knew the value of a friendly face.

'Maria needs 'er rest, and as well as the outside privy down here, I've got a proper upstairs bathroom too, and she's welcome to a long soak later as I expect every bit of her body is 'urting,' said Joyce. 'And tomorrow we'll dose her up with aspirin and then go to the church and get a recommendation from Father O'Reilly, who's very obliging, for the Social – it's the best way, as then the Social can 'ouse you all. If the Social gets wind that I own this house, which I do, with not a penny owing to anyone, it'll only be a short step until they talk themselves into thinking that I can take yer both in. And that means they won't give you somewhere to live, or at least not for a long time, and while I'd love to 'ave yer 'ere with me, that's not right long-term fer yer and Maria. And this way the Social will really quickly sort yer out with somewhere to live. Yer own place where only you can say who comes in and who stays out, and it'll be just what yer need, in order for you and Maria to get back on to yer feet, and to get ready to welcome that little one 'ere in a few months.'

'Do yer think? I don't want us beholden to anyone, or taking 'andouts, you know, Joyce,' said Annie dubiously, and then she realised that she had never had a dip in a bath that had taps to run the hot water in, and that was inside somebody's house. And she really wanted to try it. A tin bath filled by kettles and saucepans in the kitchen was all Annie and Maria had known until now, or the public bath house.

Pitiful, she thought, but she refused to allow herself to feel sad about this.

'Get over yerself, Annie. If anyone deserves a leg-up, it's yer both. It's not charity and it'll only be until yer both get on yer feet. And Maria's face will look worse tomorrow as the bruises will be coming through and the scabs will have formed, and she's showing too now with the baby, and so that's all to the good as the Social will know a man is behind the woes of all this. I just 'ope it's nearby where they put yer both,' Joyce told Annie. 'And you must have a bath 'ere too, with one of my Dubarry-scented cubes that I got given for Christmas.'

'That sounds very tempting, I admit, Joyce. But is Maria showing already? I 'adn't noticed – and in fact up until Fred went for her last night, I 'ad no idea that she was even in the family way, I'm embarrassed to say. I was sick from morning to night when I was carrying 'er, but she's never let on. If anyone should have seen it though, I should have. I don't know how far along she is even.'

Joyce lit another cigarette. Then she said, 'I bet my bottom dollar yer Maria is close on six months gone, if not more. I suppose the shock she went through with Fred and that damn ring of 'is 'as allowed the baby to pop itself forward, or else it was once you knew, Maria just gave up on trying to 'old it in. She'll 'ave wanted to keep it secret until Fred did the right thing. 'Ave a look at 'er when she wakes up and you'll see, as it was the first thing I noticed. After her face, of course. Maria is only a young lass after all, so don't be nagging 'er, Annie, as there's not one of us with tits and a fanny who's not fallen for a bit of sweet talk and canoodling at one time or another.'

'You're right – I know that. It breaks my 'eart though. The whole thing is tragic. 'Anging would be too good for Fred Walton, and Ted's turned out not much better when push comes to shove. I'd bloody flay that Fred alive if I could get my 'ands on 'im. Whatever is going to come of us all?' Annie's voice cracked with emotion as Joyce stared at her sympathetically, and as she realised that Joyce was always going to do the best she could by them, she smiled at her friend as she managed to croak out a, 'I'm never going to be able to repay yer, I 'ope yer know that.'

'Rubbish!' Joyce joked in a deliberately funny way, and once Annie smiled, Joyce poured her a fresh cup of tea.

And then Joyce turned serious once again as she said, 'This isn't about payback, yer know that, don't yer, Annie? And now you've had yer gripe regarding Ted and Fred, it's time to stop it now. It were right you said it to me, and let all the hate out yer have in yer heart fer what the Waltons have caused. But yer've left it all behind now, and now yer need to think differently about it all.'

'I'm not sure I'm fully getting what yer meaning, Joyce?' said Annie.

She couldn't imagine not loathing Fred Walton. Or Gary, come to that.

Joyce turned a bit more towards Annie and leaned forward a little in order to make her meaning very clear. 'I've seen a lot over the years, and now I am telling yer, Annie, to choose this moment to start looking forward and not backwards, and this is the time for yer to get it into yer noggin that this talk between us needs to be the last time yer ever spout off like this against Fred and Ted.

'Yer owe it to yerself and Maria to instead say that Fred is a git and Ted is a father trying to look after him, and that they are now nothing more than a part of your pasts, but they are *nothing* to do with your futures. Repeat it again and again, until yer've talked yerself into believing it, and then do the same about Gary too. Don't let thoughts of them and the bad that's happened turn into the sort of bitterness that eats away inside of you like a cancer and taints this new start that yer fought so hard for. Yer deserve the best, and Fred, Ted and Gary aren't that, remember, Annie.

'I'm not saying it's a thing that'll be easy fer yer, but do yer very best not to allow that bitterness in yer 'eart to remain, as it'll only cost yer, and it'll be a high price yer will end up paying. And the truth of it is that what's gone on will never 'arm Fred and Ted in any way or set them back, and they'd just think yer'd be daft for suffering so when it's all done and dusted, and they're getting off scot-free. In a perfect world, the police would step in, but we all know Ted Walton has the law in the palm of 'is hand, and so yer on yer own, but this isn't a surprise.'

Annie nodded at this.

Joyce wasn't finished yet. 'Maria will have the baby to lighten her mood up, and she'll probably end up being much stronger than yer expecting. But yer'll be looking at 'er poor face each day and be made to feel bad as yer'll be constantly reminded of Fred Walton and that damn blade in 'is blasted ring. And my advice is, don't let Fred inside yer 'ead or allow yerself to think 'ow much yer 'ate 'im, as if you do, he'll always be a measure against which you compare things, good or bad. Don't give Fred Walton that power, Annie, please. Nor Ted or Frank, nor Gary. Yer strength will lie in this, and finding yer power will lie in refusing to give them the time of day. Yer weren't, neither of yer, 'appy in the past. But yer both can be in the future. So put the past to bed, and look to the future, and I'm sure yer won't go wrong.'

'Put the past to bed, and look to the future,' echoed Annie.

What Joyce had told her felt an important, and wise, lesson.

Those words, and the rest of Joyce's sentiments, made her feel strong and almost invincible.

And Annie vowed that she would do just as Joyce suggested, if she possibly could.

CHAPTER TEN

On his way to work, lodger Paddy had, off his own bat, gone to the rectory of the church he and Sean attended, and mentioned to Father O'Reilly, whose half-shaved face had flecks of shaving foam over it, that Joyce had guests who definitely and urgently needed the Father's help.

The result was that when there was a tap at the front door at four o'clock that afternoon, and Joyce opened it to find Father O'Reilly standing there with a warm smile, clutching a bottle of port in one hand and an old table-cloth knotted around a bulky bundle in the other hand so that he could easily carry whatever was contained inside.

'Have you had divine inspiration?' said Joyce as she took the bottle of port from the Father and then chivvied him down the hallway in the direction of the back room. 'We were coming to see you in the morning,' she added.

'The Lord works in mysterious ways,' Annie heard the Father answer in an affable and lilting Irish brogue. 'In this instance he chose your Paddy as his vessel to inform me that you were in need of assistance.'

'Interesting choice the Lord picked for his vessel,' deadpanned Joyce, 'and how fortunate the Lord remembered how much I enjoy a tipple of port too.'

And as the Father let out a cheery guffaw, Annie realised that Joyce and the Father enjoyed a real camaraderie.

Annie had never met a priest whom she felt did anything other than look down his nose at her with a sense of disgust, and so to hear this easy rapport felt quite strange and more than a little disconcerting.

Not long out of the bath, Maria was sitting at the kitchen table wearing Joyce's dressing gown and some clean pyjamas that presumably belonged to Sean or Paddy, and with her hair still damp, when the Father came into the room, just as Annie had started to change the dressings.

'Let me introduce you to my good friend Annie Wills, and her daughter Maria, Father,' said Joyce. 'And ladies, this is Father O'Reilly. Annie and Maria arrived in London just this morning after tough times, and they're planning on staying 'ere permanently and making it their 'ome.'

'Poor child,' Father O'Reilly said sympathetically when he saw the extent of Maria's injuries. And, quick to notice Maria's pregnant stomach, he added then in a jovial tone that had no hint of disapproval, 'And a baby on the way – how excellent. Well, this suggests most strongly that a plan of campaign is needed, don't you think? But first, as we're due to have a jumble sale on Saturday, I asked Paddy to describe you both and then I picked out some clothes and shoes – we can blame Paddy if what I've brought across is ridiculous, in which case you can come back with me to have first dibs on the rest of the stuff that's been donated, and the church will not expect payment, as if we can't help people in real need as you are right now, then what on earth are we doing? So, once that dressing is where it needs to be, let's get our thinking caps on regarding where you're going to live and how you're going to achieve that.'

This was exactly what Annie and Maria needed to hear as the Father made it sound as if what they needed had a real chance of being achieved, and mother and daughter smiled at each other.

'And after we've got our plan of action ready and are raring to go, and have had a glass of port to celebrate, what say you that I run to the chippie and get cod and chips for us all, and for Sean and Paddy too?' Father O'Reilly said then, and both Annie and Maria found their mouths watering as their weekly budget back in Wakefield hadn't allowed for this sort of luxury for a very long time.

For a moment, Annie wondered if she was actually in the midst of a dream, and a glimpse of Maria's slightly dazed face suggested her daughter felt similarly.

The next morning Father O'Reilly drove Annie and Maria over to the housing department. Joyce stayed behind so that there would be no inkling as far as the Social were concerned of her being anywhere in the background.

In the car's boot was a tatty old cardboard box into which had been stuffed two ancient pillows, two sheets and another couple of blankets to go with the ones from the mail train that Annie had made sure to keep hold of, and an old and very dented saucepan, two small chipped plates, two cups, and two each of knives, forks and tea-spoons, all harvested from the jumble donations.

On top of the box was a change of clothes for each of them, the shoes they had worn to London, and some hankies and a green-and-white roll of Izal toilet paper that was hard and medicated, and a very small bar of face soap.

Those four pristine ten-pound notes the Wakefield doctor had pressed into Annie's hand were still folded and safely tucked into the top of her roll-on girdle as Joyce had suggested this was the safest place.

'Yer not joking,' said Annie. 'No one's going near my girdle for a very long time . . .'

'That's the ticket,' said Joyce.

Neither of them really believed this as, although they hadn't admitted as much to each other, the truth of it was that they both knew that Annie had a real skill as a brass. With no qualifications or experience of working as any-thing else, aside from that short stint when she was on the shop floor of the biscuit factory, undoubtedly she would earn more through selling her body than she could any other way, which would become a real factor when she had three mouths under her roof to feed and take care of.

But now wasn't the time to think or talk about this, both Annie and Joyce knew. There were more pressing things to sort out first, such as getting a roof over Annie and Maria's heads.

The clothes and shoes the Father had brought with him to Joyce's house were mostly a good fit, and while not quite what either Annie and Maria would have chosen for themselves, they were clean and Joyce had got up at the crack of dawn to iron the dresses and clean the shoes, and so mother and daughter looked more than presentable if a bit wayward in the colour and fabrics of their clothes compared to how many East End women dressed.

As they drove along some narrow side streets, Annie and Maria could see that the East End of London was every bit as run down as the worst areas of Wakefield, although a lot of the women they saw walking about were decidedly glam while some of the men wore sharp-looking suits.

There had clearly been more intense bomb damage to this area during the war than Wakefield had suffered, and, although nearly twenty years had passed since the war had ended, there were still a few gappy, open spaces where houses and shops had once been.

Annie noticed that there were also quite a lot of grey and brooding blocks of brutalist flats made from what looked like concrete slabs that, she presumed, had been recently built for families who would rent from the council and who had had to move because of the loss of their previous homes. It seemed as if high-rises were the preferred option now over re-building the old-fashioned terraced streets. Once Annie had heard a couple of men at the dice table at the drinking den talking about the profits to be made from modern housing developments for local councils, and now she could see what they had been describing.

There was something about the sight of all these flats that made Annie feel spooked and unsettled, although she told herself off for being so daft, and she looked at Maria to see if she had noticed her mother's unease.

Fortunately, Maria seemed lost in a world of her own as she stared silent and unblinking out of the car window at her right shoulder as she gently and rhythmically stroked her swelling belly.

Then, in the older streets that hadn't been bombed, Annie realised that there had sprung up a host of lodging houses aimed, she supposed, at a wave of labourers just like Sean and Paddy, who had come to London to exploit the ready opportunities for building work.

Many of the old red-brick terraced houses looked as if their owners offered the space to one or two lodgers in each of their rooms, in order to jam-pack each dwelling, although it was shocking to see time and again signs propped in the windows that shouted harshly 'No Coloureds, No Irish, No Dogs'.

Annie wondered where those people ended up living. Joyce had said Sean and Paddy had been suggested to her as good lodgers by Father O'Reilly, but Annie suspected that there weren't that many Joyces around who would be happy to rent a room to Irish labourers or, if it came to it, blacks who had been lured to Britain by the Government from the Caribbean on ships like HMT *Empire Windrush*.

Father O'Reilly saw Annie's taken-aback expression as they passed sign after similar sign, propped in the ground-floor windows, and he told her, 'It's not a facet of human nature that I like at all, Annie. But many of these landlords and landladies are incredibly poor, and I think this attitude of thoughtless dislike is partly those people needing to know there's someone lower down the 'eap than they are, although that's not to say they don't 'ave about their 'earts an element of hate for Indians, blacks or paddies. It's true, though, that without all these new people coming to London, the building work that is supporting the local community would stop, and the hospitals would grind to a halt too and there'd be a shortage of bus drivers, but the people who write these signs don't see it like that. Anyway, you need to prepare yerself for being put in a flat with perhaps a Jamaican family in a flat on one side and an Irish family on the other – would that be a problem for yer both, as if it is, it's best I know now, before the Social put yer on the spot about it?'

Annie and Maria looked at each other, and shook their heads.

'It's no bother to us. We've seen the worst of human behaviour, and it was white and British,' said Annie firmly.

Father O'Reilly gave an unhappy sigh as if he were considering what he imagined they'd been through, and then he said, 'So that yer know the drill, what the Social will likely do first is put yer both up in an emergency 'ostel fer the 'omeless, and yer two will be expected to share a single room, although there won't be anyone else in with you, and yer'll 'ave use of the bathroom and kitchen, but this will be shared by everyone. It'll be noisy and there might be some strange folk, or some drinkers, and so be prepared fer that. Anyways, with Maria so far along and Stepney Council wanting as many little ones resident in the borough as possible, I doubt it will be long before yer all housed properly together. And once yer 'ave the 'ostel address, yer can get to a doctor's surgery, as I expect yer've not yet seen a doc during the pregnancy, Maria?'

Father O'Reilly obviously knew how young girls in the family way tended to carry on, thought Annie.

Maria wouldn't look at her mother, as she whispered as if embarrassed, 'No, Father, I'm afraid I haven't seen any-one. When my face was stitched up, a doctor listened to my heartbeat, and then the baby's, but I don't even know that he were a proper doctor as it was late at night and at 'is 'ouse, and I almost can't remember much about it already.'

'Be quiet about that now, Maria. It's safer I don't know anything about yer past, and I would urge yer both to keep very silent about everything that 'as 'appened to yer, as although yer've come down to the Smoke from a long way away, one never knows who knows who, and the world can be very small sometimes. And so the least said, the more yer protecting yerselves,' said the Father. 'The story that I will say to the Social about why I 'ave brought you there is that I found yer in the church after Mass this morning, and from what I can tell, yer have no money and know nobody in London, and yer too scared to say any-thing about where yer come from or who did this to yer. And then I'm going to stare very hard at yer face, Maria, to really drive the message 'ome that yer 'ave good reason to be frightened fer yer life, and so don't be put out when I do this. And then I'll say yer've told me very firmly, and I believe yer, that yer both 'ave no intention of returning to where yer came from, and yer need the Social to step in and 'elp out.'

'Isn't lying a sin?' said Annie. 'We feel awful for put-ting yer in this position, especially if it means making yer stretch the truth on our behalf.'

Father O'Reilly gave a little snort as if he were amused. 'I feel we need to think about it differently – more that my greater sin would be in *not* doing everything in my power to give you two, and that baby as well, the very best chance of a new start. And if that means a fib coming out of my mouth, it means a fib, and in my book a mere fib is not a lie,' said Father O'Reilly as he parked the car and pulled up the handbrake lever. 'Now we're 'ere, so before we get out, I'll run through a few things so it's fresh in yer minds.

'Let me do all the talking, remember – I'll nod at yer, Annie, if yer need to speak, and Maria, yer keep schtum, even when I'm making them stare at yer face. You two just have to look terrified, and rely on the Social remembering that in the wake of the war they are very aware that we need to get that birth rate back up. I 'ad better say it now in case they whisk you away, but one thing to bear in mind, though, if it ends up that you have a choice of bedrooms if you go to a 'ostel, is that if you choose one near to either the kitchen or the toilet, you will constantly have people walking by your door – this position will be a good thing, or not, according to how much you like or need a nearby bog or kettle, and whether or not yer light sleepers.

'Remember too to *never* leave anything of value in yer room – yer just 'ave to take it all with yer wherever yer go, and so don't leave anything precious unattended, not even for a second when you're not there as there'll be those there who are very light-fingered. I'm sure it'll be a nuisance but it's just the way of 'ostel life.

'And yer need to keep the door locked at all times, and to put a chair under the door handle at night, and when yer bring any food back from the kitchen to eat in yer room, never leave a pot on its own on the hob as it'll walk in a trice. And take just enough toilet paper that you'll need – never leave a roll in the bog else somebody will nab it.'

'The terrified bit isn't going to take any acting,' Annie said quietly.

'Mummy, take off my dressings, so they can see my face,' demanded Maria suddenly.

Father O'Reilly turned to look at Maria. 'Are yer sure? I wouldn't expect yer to do it without the dressing, as that's a big thing fer a young girl so recently hurt to do.'

'I'm very sure,' said Maria, the eye that her mother could see bright. 'Take them off, Mummy. I can bear it. We want that hostel bedroom, and this is the best way for us to get it as they will see that I'm not shamming what 'appened to me.'

And Annie realised that Joyce had been spot on in her assessment of how strong Maria was.

She gently removed the gauze and the bandages, and then they got out of the car. The white of the eye near the slashes was deep red all over it.

Taking a deep breath to fortify herself, Annie clasped Maria's hand in hers as the two of them followed Father O'Reilly inside the housing department, Maria walking with her head held high and every single bulky black-cotton stitch, raised scab and fold of puckered and bruised skin clearly on display for anyone to gawp at.

Instead, everyone who saw Maria's face as they made their way to the right department quickly averted their eyes.

Annie felt prouder of her daughter than she had ever been.

And when she caught Father O'Reilly's attention, Annie couldn't help but notice that his eyes were shining at the sight of Maria's bravery, and this made Annie think very kindly of him.

Indeed she was very grateful that the Father hadn't so much as made the tiniest mention of Maria's unmarried status, when she knew her previous priest would have had this firmly foremost in his mind.

And apparently Father O'Reilly didn't have much of a problem turning a blind eye towards how Joyce supported herself too, as she made no secret that she was a brass working in a Soho establishment.

Things really were different down in London, at least so far, Annie concluded. Perhaps it was a place where women really could carve a niche for themselves without having to take too much notice of what men might think.

CHAPTER ELEVEN

Three hours later, Annie and Maria were settling in to a tiny, dark bedroom in a run-down hostel.

There were lumpy-mattressed bunk beds stacked one above the other and a minuscule table with two rickety chairs, as well as a tiny chest of drawers. The room couldn't have been more than ten feet by eight, and there was a roundish section of missing plaster on one wall that revealed the bricks underneath and announced to Annie that this was the spot where someone had punched the wall in temper, while a faint but recognisable smell of urine constantly twitched their noses.

There were no curtains, other than a tatty bit of greyish once-white nylon netting strung across the lower half of a grimy window that had its paint peeling and looked straight out on to a nearby brick wall. And when Father O'Reilly put the cardboard box on the table and stood beside the two women, the room felt full to bursting.

They had already inspected the shared kitchen (ill-equipped and filthy) and the toilet (truly dire, with a seatless pedestal and a sopping, stinky floor), and they'd discovered that someone had stolen the bath from the bathroom, while the hand basin there was lying smashed in two pieces on the floor.

'It feels like a palace,' said Annie, determined not to be downcast.

'It does,' Maria agreed.

Father O'Reilly looked at their faces, expecting one or other of them to follow up with an ironic quip.

But he saw they had meant what they said, and he realised they must have been through some truly terrible times if honestly they thought they were well off here.

'I'll tell Joyce to expect yer both each day for yer tea as catering fer yerselves 'ere clearly isn't going to be easy, and she'll be 'appy for yer both to have a spruce-up in her bathroom each day – Joyce's is only about ten minutes' walk away and I'll draw yer a map. And I'll get a couple of Thermoses so that yer can take a hot drink away from hers to bring back 'ere at night. I'd love to take yer home to the rectory with me, but if I do, it's going to slow down you getting proper housing, so let's think of this as pain now fer gain later,' Father O'Reilly told them. 'Meanwhile, yer will be means-tested fer benefits, but these won't come in as much, and yer'll both find London a more expensive place to live than where yer've come from.'

'Joyce 'as told us 'ow the system works,' said Annie. 'And you've been kind and so considerate, Father O'Reilly, and we couldn't ask fer more. Honestly, we can't thank yer enough. We do appreciate it. Maria and myself 'ave each other, and we'll be fine, I promise.'

Five weeks later, although only seven months pregnant, Maria went into labour.

It was the same day that Annie learned that she and Maria had been allocated a home of their very own.

Luckily Maria was at Joyce's when the drama started, as Annie was over at the Social answering some final questions concerning the means-testing for her benefit payment (it had turned out to be a nightmare having left Wakefield without documents like her and Maria's birth certificates and Annie's National Insurance number that the Social required before doling out any benefits. Father O'Reilly had been kept very busy getting this sorted out without any letters going to Gary's house, and he'd even managed to obtain Maria's NI number now that she was just old enough to have one).

Joyce was asking Maria if she fancied a fried egg for lunch when suddenly Maria bent over double and cried out in pain as she experienced an excruciating cramp. Within minutes her waters had broken and, as her brow dotted with perspiration, it was obvious that the baby was well and truly on the way.

Normally Stepney mothers were allocated midwives who'd then supervise a home birth, but after a home visit a couple of weeks earlier, it had been decided that, because of the unsanitary conditions in the homeless hostel, it would be best for all if Maria gave birth in the unmarried mothers' home.

As Joyce stared in horror at Maria, she swore to herself as she remembered that Father O'Reilly was with a sick parishioner that morning and so couldn't be called upon to help.

This meant Joyce had to run to the nearby pub to use their telephone to call for an ambulance, only to be told there would be a wait of about an hour. Joyce didn't think Maria would last that long, and so she had to beg that anyone who was having a lunchtime tipple in the bar and who owned a car, could they please drive her and Maria over to the home?

While the mostly male clientele looked distinctly squeamish at the thought of this, it was counterbalanced by Joyce being popular locally and one or two of those in the bar being her clients, and so in the face of Joyce's pleading stare, eventually someone agreed to do the run to the unmarried mothers' home with Maria and Joyce, while somebody else offered to go to the Social to try to find Annie.

It was all over by the time Annie arrived at the unmarried mothers' home.

There was good news though.

With very little trouble, Maria had given birth to a healthy baby girl, who, although small at only three and a half pounds in weight, nevertheless had lungs of a sufficient size that she quickly proved she could cry just as loudly as any of the other newborns in the nursery who'd arrived at twice her size.

Annie raced on to the new mothers' ward to see a serene-looking Maria sitting up in bed as she tucked into some toast and a large mug of tea. The only sign that Annie could see of what Maria had been through were some slightly damp hairs around her forehead, presumably through the contractions making her sweat.

A much more ruffled-seeming Joyce was pale and dithery as she sat on a chair at Maria's bedside. Joyce had never had children of her own, and she had once told Annie that this was because she found the mere thought of what a woman's body had to go through to birth a child really upsetting, and actually she had quite a phobia about it.

'I'm fine, Mummy, although a bit sore,' Maria said, once Annie had stopped hugging her to ask how she was.

'I should think so!' laughed Annie. 'Us women should come with a zip in our bellies as standard issue, as it would make the birthing bit so much easier.'

'Your Maria nearly gave me an 'eart attack,' said Joyce. 'There were a moment in the car on our way 'ere when I thought that I was going to have to deliver the baby myself. But we made it – I told Maria to cross her legs, and keep them crossed – and twenty minutes after we got 'ere, the baby shot out, the nurse told me, right into the nurse's arms, and gave a big bellow to announce 'er arrival. Neither mother or baby had any problems, and the little girl is perfect although a bit on the wee side. She's in the nursery at the moment having a wash and brush up, and they've just done the same for Maria, but they'll bring the baby back soon for 'er first feed, the nurse said.'

'You clever girl, Maria!' said Annie who, although she couldn't stop smiling, then came over a bit tearful at the same time, as she felt totally overwhelmed by emotion. 'I'm just so happy,' she gulped at last.

Maria's eyes also began to well up at the sight of Annie, but Joyce interrupted with a, 'Here she is, coming back to us,' and Annie and Maria quickly looked towards the nurse bringing back the baby.

Everybody smiled as the nurse lifted her from the crib in which she'd been wheeled into the ward. She was swaddled in a clean cloth and looked angelic, if a bit pink in the face and peevish about what she had just been through.

As the baby let out a grizzle, the nurse placed her in Maria's arms, and told Maria to see if she could get her to latch on for a feed.

Annie wanted to offer some advice on how to do this and took a breath ready to speak, but quickly Joyce touched her hand in a way to suggest that Annie should

118

allow Maria to try it her way first. 'Granny, let the dog see the rabbit, at least for a while,' said Joyce.

At Joyce calling her 'Granny', Annie felt a warm rush of emotion. Yes, Joyce was right – Annie was a grand-mother! But Maria was the baby's mother, and Annie vowed that she would always respect that. She trusted Maria to do the right thing by her little girl.

This was the right thing to do as Maria proved to be a natural at nursing, instinctively understanding what she had to do, and before too long the baby was feeding, sucking greedily at Maria's breast as she held the small scrap of a thing lovingly in her arms.

The nurse nodded approvingly, and said Maria shouldn't forget to move her to the other side, and she'd be back in a while to return the baby to the nursery so that Maria could have a snooze.

As the nurse walked away, Maria mouthed at Annie and Joyce, 'I'm not tired,' but Annie told her, 'Trust me, Maria, take every moment to rest up now, as once you're up with her doing the night-time feeds, you'll long for every moment of sleep you didn't take advantage of.'

Annie and Joyce watched the young mother with her baby, Maria smiling as the tiny girl clutched her little finger, and then Annie hugged Joyce and whispered in her ear, 'Thank you, my dear Joyce – you've saved the day again. Whatever would we do without you?'

'Give over,' said a puce-cheeked Joyce, and Annie smiled as she decided that she had made Joyce bashful.

'In all the excitement, I nearly forgot. I've got news! We get the keys to a two-bedroom flat on Monday,' said Annie, then. 'Maria, you and yer little one shall both be 'ere for a couple of weeks, and so I'll make sure to have everything shipshape and ready for when you and the little one come 'ome.'

'That's grand news, just grand,' said Father O'Reilly, who had arrived just in time to hear what Annie was saying.

And then a nun bustled over with some official-looking papers in her hand, and Annie caught sight of the word 'Adoption' in a heading at the top of the uppermost page, and she felt her heart lurch and then a stab of panic in case the Social was going to forcibly remove her granddaughter from Maria's and her care.

But Father O'Reilly made the position very clear, as he said sternly, 'We don't need those papers, Sister, and so take them away immediately, and don't you dare bring them back. This is a very *wanted* baby, and she 'as 'er own family eager to love and care for 'er, as you can see. So we'll have no more talk of adoption, do you 'ear?'

The Sister frowned and looked for a moment as if she disagreed, but then, after a final irritated flap of the papers, she capitulated under the forbidding gaze of the Father and without a word withdrew.

'Any problems in this way regarding even the slightest hint that you should put the baby up for adoption, Maria, when we're not with yer, yer make sure to immediately send fer me and I'll sort it out,' said Father O'Reilly, pretending he hadn't noticed the Sister's final huff as she went back to her desk. 'And in the meantime, I'll 'ave a word with the Mother Superior to put an end to any further shenanigans along these adoption lines.'

'Thank you, Father. I'd as soon as die rather than 'and 'er over to anyone else. She's my baby and I want to keep 'er.'

'And so you shall, Maria,' Father O'Reilly said.

'Maria, 'ave you thought of a name fer her yet?' asked Annie, keen to bring the mood back to something happier.

'Faith,' Maria said immediately, smiling as her baby grasped and then held on tight to her little finger, as if her life depended on the unbreakable bond between them.

Maria leaned forward to peer more closely at her daughter's sleepy face with its teeny button nose and cupid's bow mouth, and the pink of her fingernails making them seem so tiny near Maria's own much larger ones, before Maria added with a note of wonder in her voice, 'What else could she be called but Faith?'

Annie thought it a perfect name for a perfect little girl.

While she and Maria had had their difficulties, and the baby had been conceived in unfortunate circumstances, Annie knew that she and Maria had taken the biggest leap of faith that they ever would by running away down to London.

And now baby Faith was here, showing them that with enough faith in each other, there could always be a better future just around the corner.

Faith was something they must all believe in, each and every day, no matter what life had to throw at them along the way.

Maria and Faith were going to remain at the home for unmarried mothers for the normal fortnight after the delivery, which was excellent timing, as the next day Joyce and Annie went to see the flat Annie and Maria had been allocated.

It wasn't amazing at first sight.

Undeniably dingy, with olive-green walls and dark, chipped paintwork throughout, it was on the fifth floor of an already shabby block even though the flats hadn't been built that long ago, and there wasn't a lift.

The shops were a fair step away, over a quarter of a mile, and Annie wondered how she would be able to get their clothes and bedding dry as there wasn't a washing line to peg damp garments on to. And there would be a constant stream of nappies too.

'Look on the bright side, Annie,' said Joyce, who'd seen her hopeful expression fade. 'If you pay your rent, no one can ask you to move. And a lick of paint will work wonders.'

'I know, Joyce,' Annie said, her voice determined. 'That's what I need to think of.'

Joyce had a word with Sean and Paddy, who pulled in favours from some of their pals to help, and their kindly site manager they were all working for donated some paint that had been left over from a previous job.

With so many people helping, within the space of three nights, once the lads had finished work for the day, the flat had been transformed, its walls now a sunny light-yellow throughout that contrasted cheerily with sparkling new white paintwork, and the floorboards painted a mid-brown colour everywhere, so that although there were no carpets, all the rooms looked spick and span and as if they belonged to one another. And each bedroom turned out to have a useful built-in cupboard that Annie hadn't noticed when she'd first seen the flat, which the lads painted inside as well as out.

While the painting was going on, Annie and Joyce gave the kitchen and bathroom a really thorough seeing-to with Vim and bleach, which, although the cooker put up a manful fight not to give up its grime, really helped brighten those rooms up.

Meanwhile, Annie agreed to a never-never loan and by the next weekend had managed to find two fairly decent second-hand mattresses for her and Maria to sleep on, and a Formica-topped table and two chairs for the kitchen, plus a settee that had seen better days but was surprisingly comfy that would go into the lounge, all coming from a shop that sold on furniture from house clearances.

Joyce managed to charm the salesman so that he delivered everything for free, and put it exactly where Annie told him to, in spite of all the stairs up to the flat, up which the furniture had to be heaved.

The next day, Annie made up a makeshift cot for Faith in an old wooden drawer one of her new neighbours lent her.

Then she went to the corner shop to get some tea and some broken biscuits as a treat for when Maria and Faith arrived home later that day, and there she saw a white postcard pinned up on the shop's door offering for sale a second-hand yellow-painted wooden cot with a drop-down side.

The price on the card was ten shillings, and Annie had exactly ten shillings in her purse.

So she said to the woman behind the counter that she'd come back for the biscuits and tea later as the cot had to be the priority just then.

'Pop them in your basket, dear – I'll start you a page in my book, and you can pay on Friday. Now get your skates on and get that cot,' Annie was told.

Annie went to the address on the card, apologising profusely for turning up as she had.

'My daughter comes home today,' Annie said to the rather harassed woman who opened the door, 'and the council have only just given us the flat. I have a drawer that someone gave us ready for baby Faith. But then I saw your card about the cot.'

As two toddlers clung to her skirt, the woman led Annie through to the parlour, where the cot had been dismantled. She said it had done good service for all her eight children but she had taken care to treat it well over the years and it had been responsible for many happy memories.

Annie smiled at this, and said she was sure those good times had more than made up for all the broken nights the cot owner must have had with all those babies.

And when the woman saw the genuine warmth in that smile and noticed the threadbare sleeve-edge of Annie's coat, she quickly put two and two together, and said she knew Annie and her daughter would make their own treasure box of reminiscences around the cot too, before refusing to take any money for it, even sending Annie away with the promise of her husband dropping it off after he'd finished work.

That evening he delivered and put the cot together. And then he nipped down to his car to collect an eiderdown for the cot and a huge pile of terry nappies and some baby clothes that his wife had insisted he bring, leaving Annie choked up over how kind some people could be.

At the weekend, Joyce took Annie, Sean and Paddy to the Whitechapel Road market, and Annie broke into a ten-pound note to buy some bedding, towels, cookware and a kettle, crockery and cutlery, and a washing-up bowl and a bucket for the nappies to soak in, which the lads put into some roomy string shopping bags they had been carrying for just this purpose.

When Joyce caught Annie's envious but brief glance at some warm winter coats on a stall, she insisted on buying one each for Annie and Maria, saying they'd be glad of them once the cold weather came in a few months and these would be her early Christmas presents to them. Then Joyce bought Annie a tartan shopping trolley too, saying it would really help with those stairs up to the flat and bringing potatoes back from the shop.

And when they got back to the flat, it was to find that Father O'Reilly had popped a note through the letterbox about a scheme the church was running that would loan them a pram for an affordable fee, the pram to be returned once it was no longer needed.

Once everyone had left, Annie put all the new things carefully away, and then she went to the corner shop with her new shopping trolley to stock up on cupboard staples like flour and lard, as she wondered how she could possibly repay everyone's kindnesses.

Later, Annie counted up her money, reserving some for Friday to pay for all the groceries she had had.

She made a careful list of expenditure, and what she and Maria had in hand.

It wasn't happy reading.

Even with the subsistence money from the Social, at best there was going to be a bare five pounds a week coming in, with expenses going out totalling over four pounds a week as the never-never deal wasn't cheap, and those figures she'd totted up didn't include a penny budgeted for food or washing powder or face soap, or any heating in the flat, which was fine as the weather was still warm, but that wouldn't last, or if she or Maria ever needed to catch a bus, and Annie knew that both she and Maria could do with getting some slippers to wear at home.

Paddy had told her that he and Sean both earned seventeen pounds ten shillings each week, and they tried to send their mother twenty-eight pounds of their joint earnings per week. Annie was pleased the lads were so good to their mother in Dublin, but she realised just how stretched she was going to be in the financial sense and that she just didn't have a safety net behind her as some other families did.

It didn't feel at all fair that women like Annie and Maria had to scrimp and save to get by on such a pitiful income, but it was reality, and Annie knew that, actually, there were many other women who had it much worse off than they did.

Still, it didn't help either that she and Maria really needed additional household items such as a dustpan and brush, and a mop, and a folding clothes rack for drying the nappies, while Annie would also love to get a standard lamp, and a lampshade for the central light in the living room as the bare light bulb hanging from the centre of the ceiling gave off an uncompromising glare in the evening that wasn't relaxing. She'd also like a little wireless, as it was very quiet in the flat without one.

Annie sighed, and decided she must join a library as, without any money to buy a book, how else would she be able to entertain herself in the evening?

She remembered fondly her teacher's gift of *Frankenstein* all those years ago; she had read it so often while she'd been breastfeeding Maria in the middle of the night that it had become an old friend that she had come to know word for word. She was sorry she'd not been able to go home and pick it up before she and Maria left Wakefield, as it held huge sentimental value for her, being one of the very few gifts she had ever received.

Then she told herself not to be sentimental, as it was only a book after all.

Annie sat at her kitchen table and looked about her.

Their possessions were scant; there was no way of thinking of them differently. And what she and Maria and little Faith needed still seemed only the forerunners of what very probably was an endless list of wants.

She tried to buck up her spirits by reminding herself of all the things that had changed for the better since she and Maria had been in London.

But although this did make her feel a little better, especially when she thought of little Faith, Annie couldn't quite forget that in view of how kind everyone had been already and the many ways in which Joyce and her new friends had all really helped with the burden of getting her and Maria set up, Annie knew that she was never going to be able to say to Joyce or her lodgers, or to Father O'Reilly, that she was very frightened now about precisely how she and Maria were going to manage.

For, aside from some coins in her purse, Annie was down to just having the one ten-pound note left of the four the doctor had given her. Father O'Reilly hadn't been joking when he'd told her that living in London was very expensive, she thought ruefully.

She hid her precious remaining ten-pound note deep inside the cupboard in her bedroom. She had decided that this note needed to be kept for as long as possible as rainy-day money, and thus only to be called upon in a grade-one emergency.

And Annie had decided too that she needed to get out to work.

She knew Joyce had regular clients, but that these days she worked out of a rented room in Soho, and her regulars would visit her there. But Annie also knew that, although Joyce would willingly introduce Annie to the Soho set-up, the reality was that this would be too expensive an option for Annie, as she simply couldn't afford to borrow more money to cover the cost of the room or the smart clothes or make-up that she would need in order to charge top dollar, nor the cost of the maid that came with it. Plus she'd also have to build in the travelling time to the West End when Maria might have need of her mother's help. This had an emotional cost to it too.

And she would as soon cut her tongue out as allow Joyce to help financially. Joyce was a dear friend who had gone above and beyond in oh so many ways already, and Annie was determined that she and Maria wouldn't become a burden any more than they already had.

Annie's head started to thump painfully at the thought of her limited choices, and she felt very agitated.

She was cross with herself that she had been so focused on getting a flat for herself and Maria, and on getting Maria's baby born safely, that she hadn't really thought until now beyond what would happen once those two things had been achieved.

But now she did.

And she didn't like what she was faced with.

CHAPTER TWELVE

The next morning was a fortnight to the day after the birth, and Maria and Faith were coming home.

They were driven back from the unmarried mothers' home by Father O'Reilly, and Annie smiled as she showed Maria around, revelling in the joy of holding a sleeping Faith in her arms as she did so.

She had made up Maria's bed, with the cot placed nearby, and sunlight was pouring into the living room, and so the flat was looking its very best. Maria couldn't stop grinning either as she kept saying how lovely it all was.

Annie made them egg on toast as Maria fed Faith, and then Maria put her down in the cot for nap-time.

'Mummy, I know what you will be planning on doing to make money,' said Maria as she joined her mother on the sofa after they'd had their lunch, passing Annie a welcome cup of tea. 'My face means I'll never be able to work in a shop or a bar or a bank. I've decided that I'm going to work alongside you doing business, and we can look after each other out on the streets, and Joyce said she'd help organise the babysitting.'

Annie hated what Maria was suggesting, as she had wanted so much more for Maria's future than her having to end up as a brass just like she had had to become. However, while it took several weeks for Maria to talk Annie into it, this was inevitably what mother and daughter ended up doing.

They needed to eat and to pay their rent, and their options were extremely limited. And with Faith to care for, it was an easy decision to make in the end, they discovered.

They took to wheeling Faith in her pram over to Joyce's house after tea so that Paddy and Sean could look after her while Joyce was working up West, allowing Maria and Annie to ply their trade on the streets nearby.

Finding a spot where they could stand wasn't easy, as the best places with lots of johns looking for trade were jealously guarded by the pimps who ran the other streetwalkers.

It was tough and it was dangerous, but somehow Annie and Maria managed to scrape by, just about, although they had a couple of run-ins with pimps who wanted them to work on their patch of land.

They had to do some favours for free with the local police so the pimps were warned off.

And few of their clients could afford a car, and so Annie and Maria were pretty much limited to some uncomfortable humping in various alleys, standing up against a wall, and they'd be unable to clean themselves properly between johns.

Maria's badly damaged face proved no barrier, and in fact some men paid extra.

And, just as Annie had found at the drinking den, her own good looks and figure ensured a busy night each time she worked.

It wasn't long before they began to get their regulars, and some weeks they found they had made enough money that they could even save a little cash.

But both Annie and Maria made one huge mistake.

They believed the old wives' tale that a woman couldn't get pregnant while breastfeeding.

And so, eleven months after Faith had arrived, Maria found herself in labour once again at just seven months pregnant, although this time a midwife who attended home births oversaw the delivery in Maria's bedroom in the flat.

Annie tried to entertain a fractious Faith on a hot Sunday afternoon in the July of 1966, but the little girl couldn't understand why her mother was somewhere in the flat as she could definitely hear something going on, but somehow Maria didn't seem to want to come and play with her or feed her.

Yet again Joyce was nearby when the contractions began, but as Joyce said to Annie afterwards, it didn't get any better the second time around and she'd been very grateful not to have had to stick around for the end bit.

Annie told her friend she knew exactly what Joyce meant.

For, this time, Maria didn't just give birth to one baby, but instead she produced two miniature but nonetheless beautiful twin girls, each healthy despite being so small and blessed with lungs every bit as powerful as Faith's had been as a newborn.

Of course Maria named her twins Hope and Charity.

And of course Annie bit her nails to the quick once again as she wondered how on earth she was now to manage looking after all five of them.

PART THREE

CHAPTER THIRTEEN

Stepney, East London, 1969

'Go on, Maria – you be the first one of us inside,' said Annie, passing her daughter the key to the front door of their new home.

Not paying any attention to the several people who'd stopped to watch the street's new residents make themselves at home, Maria gave a big smile at her mother, and then lifted up Faith so that the little girl could put the key in the lock, which Maria then turned, although not until after she'd made a happy grimace towards Annie to let her know that Faith was heavy now to do this sort of thing with.

'The last one out to the yard at the back is a ninny,' said Maria to the children once Annie had shepherded the twins inside the hall, and right in the way of herself and Faith. And then Maria let Faith lead the stampede of small feet charging down the corridor, as Hope and Charity gave chase to their big sister, their Start-Rite shoes making a reverberating hullaballoo on the bare wooden boards of the hallway, and Faith's light brown hair contrasting with the blonde hair of the twins.

Annie was left at the front door to direct Liam and Conor about how she and Maria had labelled the tea chest containing all their worldly possessions, and where they should be put after they had been taken inside from the back of the open-topped builder's truck that had transported everything over from the flat.

Liam and Conor were another set of Irish brothers and they had replaced Sean and Paddy as Joyce's lodgers once those lads had returned to Dublin to get married in a joint ceremony nearly two years previously. Now, both Sean and Paddy were each the proud parent of a little girl, with their wives already pregnant again.

Liam and Conor were just as pleasant and obliging as Sean and Paddy had been, although they found London very big and strange as they had grown up in a seaside town called Ballyconneely that was on the Errismore Peninsular in Connemara, far away from what they felt was the metropolis of Dublin and over on the windswept west coast of Ireland, and they had arrived across the Irish Channel much less worldly-wise than Sean and Paddy had, which had made Joyce and Annie feel very motherly towards them.

Joyce and Father O'Reilly would be coming to visit the new house later, once Annie and Maria had had chance to settle in a little and acclimatise the children to their new home, and, meanwhile, Liam and Conor had been volunteered by Joyce to help with the move.

Faith

The new home was a rather dilapidated three-bedroomed Victorian terrace house in Stepney that the council had finally allocated to Annie and Maria.

The children would share the large bedroom at the front, and Annie had insisted that Maria have the next largest bedroom, saying she, Annie, would be perfectly happy in the tiny box room as it was so cosy and would keep her as snug as a bug in a rug, and Maria mustn't give it a second thought.

For almost four years previous to this, the flights of stairs to their first proper home in London had been a real hurdle to get over every day, and particularly so when the twins were tiny and Faith was only one.

The result was that Annie and Maria had ended up with enviably flat stomachs, muscular arms and firm thighs through manhandling the heavy pram up and down the eight sets of steps.

It had been especially hard work when the newborn twins were top-and-tailed in the pram, and Faith was only just beginning to walk as this meant she usually had to be plonked in the pram by the third floor on their way up to their home as both women were needed to haul the pram upwards, one at the front end and one at the push-bar end and no one could carry the affronted toddler. Faith's unceremonious arrival in the pram usually led to all three children bawling by the time the flat's front door was reached, leaving the breathless Annie and Maria longing for earplugs.

And what felt like endless journeys out with the shopping trolley as Annie or Maria collected their groceries only added to everyone's frustration.

Eventually Father O'Reilly had had to strong-arm a council officer from the housing department into coming and seeing for himself what a fifth-floor dwelling actually meant for two women looking after three children under five, and there being no garden or balcony to hang washing out in nor a lift.

Purely by chance the housing officer arrived as both Hope and Charity were having a tantrum just inside the main ground-floor entrance to the flats over them each wanting to be carried upstairs while Faith could be heard running around noisily on a floor or two above, as Maria was trying to heft the sheets and towels she'd just lugged back from the launderette up the first flight of stairs, and Annie was dealing with a shopping trolley bulging with tins and potatoes as well as a second shopping bag containing two white sliced loaves and a giant cabbage.

When the housing officer offered to help, Maria hadn't needed asking twice. She dumped the heavy bag of laundry into his arms, and had run up the stairs in the wake of Faith, while, yet to get to even the first step upstairs, Hope and Charity egged each other on to lie down on the ground of the foyer and scream that their legs were tired. Helpfully, they were impervious to Annie's cajoling to show the nice man what big girls they were now that they were three years old, and why didn't they show him how quickly they could run up the stairs?

By the time he was at the front door to the flat, the housing officer was sweating and out of breath from the effort of getting to the top floor of the block of flats, and behind his back Maria and Annie exchanged an unsympathetic look as if to say that really this was just part and parcel of their everyday lives, and they often had it much worse than this.

The offer of the Senrab Street house was made in less than a week.

In the intervening years since the family had first moved into the flat, Annie had begun to bleach and backcomb her hair, and each morning she did her make-up with heavy pan-stick, applied a chalky pale-pink lipstick, and smudged the outline of her eyes with lots of eyeliner and mascara. With gusto, she had adopted miniskirts once she'd discovered her punters found this look very convenient. It wasn't that great during the winter months as Annie's thighs would goosebump pitifully in the icy weather, but it seemed to go with the territory these days and so she didn't fight against that.

Maria told her mother that she was turning herself into a younger version of Joyce, to which Annie replied proudly, 'There is no greater compliment anyone could pay me.'

Maria knew exactly what her mother meant. There were many bad things in the world to be compared to, and Joyce certainly wasn't one of them.

Meanwhile, Maria's facial scars had, very gradually, lost a little of their initial lividity, although her skin remained dreadfully puckered and dented with folds and bumps, while her eyelid function on the scarred side of her face was definitely impaired. The lid was stuck at being constantly half-open, giving all of her expressions a distinctly wonky look.

Still only twenty, Maria compensated by wearing even shorter skirts than Annie's, nearly always teamed with shiny white kinky-boots to draw attention to her shapely legs, and she styled her hair carefully so that a thick sweep fell over her injury. This she would set with so much hairspray that it made her hair crispy and caused her to cough each time she got herself ready to go outside as the aerosol belted out its spray.

Maria rarely spoke about what had happened with Fred, or its devastating cost to her looks.

But occasionally when they got home after work and the next-door neighbour who babysat the children had left (the reciprocal arrangement being that they would look after her two Yorkshire terriers during the day when she worked), Annie would notice her daughter carefully massaging in a little Vaseline to soften the raised flesh of her scars. Maria's wincing expression as she did this told

Annie that, while to the naked eye Maria's injuries were slowly healing, they still remained angry and painful as far as her daughter was concerned.

Nevertheless, both Annie and Maria had heeded Joyce's advice of never thinking about Fred Walton if they could possibly help it, instead digging deep to focus on moving forward in their lives in the belief that this would make the good things happen, instead of allowing themselves to look back and dwell on the unhappiness from the past.

They had a lot to be really grateful for, they both recognised.

Somehow they had built new lives for themselves, and all five in the family were strong and healthy. With more than a bit of luck, Annie and Maria had managed to avoid running foul of dangerous punters, always working together in a way that meant they were able to look after each other. And as they'd got used to the hustle and bustle of London life, their experience grew of the types of men they should be nervous of, with the result that slowly they began to feel a little safer.

Faith, Hope and Charity were each as bright as buttons, and real chatterboxes. It was hard not to feel optimistic about the future with such energetic little girls in the household.

Naturally Joyce remained the family's fairy godmother who they all loved to have in their lives, being wise, kind and always ready to stick on the kettle and chat over a cup of tea.

In fact, it had become increasingly difficult for Annie and Maria to recall quite how bedraggled and beaten down they had felt when they'd first arrived in London.

Life had definitely improved all round, and to remind herself of this, Annie still kept safely tucked away that last precious ten-pound note that the Wakefield doctor had given her to aid their new start.

After all of their hard work, and their careful budgeting, and scrimping and saving, Annie and Maria had now a handful of notes in their rainy-day kitty, but this last one of the four of their first notes was by far the most special as to Annie it symbolised that even in life's darkest moments a chink of unexpected kindness was never far away. And when Annie looked at Faith, she was always reminded of why her granddaughter had been given this name.

CHAPTER FOURTEEN

On the day of the move to Senrab Street in Stepney, Annie instructed Liam and Conor as to what needed to go where while Maria allowed herself a moment of relaxation as she stood in the small backyard of their new home. The girls let off steam by running furiously around her legs as they shouted their heads off in excitement.

'Mummy, come and join me fer a fag – we deserve a moment to ourselves,' Maria called to Annie, as she enjoyed standing in a shaft of warm sunlight on a patch of ground that, although currently rather sooty and cracked concrete, was at last a little bit of 'outside' they could call their own. Maria added, 'I'm sure Conor and Liam can manage without you for a moment.'

Annie came outside and, used to not paying much attention to the racket the girls were making, the two women then stood companionably side by side, looking up at the back of their new house.

The outside paintwork on the windows and the back door was a bit shabbier than the houses on either side, but nothing that couldn't be fixed with a couple of coats of paint.

'We can tart that up, and also doll up the inside of the fence on our side,' said Annie with a nod towards the windows, as then she turned to inspect the yard's brick wall that had wooden fencing on top to separate their yard from the others on either side and to the back of them. 'We can give the yard a good sweep and sluice-off so the girls aren't treading all the grime back inside. Actually, Liam and Conor might be able to do the sweeping and the sluicing fer us before they go, while you and me get to unpacking and putting things away, Maria. Now we're standing 'ere, I think maybe we should splash out on a rotary washing line, rather than simply stringing a line across?'

'Whatever yer say, as I really don't mind. You just tell me what to do or what yer want, and I know it will all be perfect. But all the space inside the house and out 'ere just fer us, and don't it look wonderful,' said Maria. 'We're going to be rattling about in it, aren't we?'

Annie sucked at her cigarette. 'You just wait, Maria – when yer girls get big, they'll seem to fill every inch.'

Maria laughed in a way she hadn't for years, and the sound of this transported Annie back to the days long before Fred Walton.

'But right now, it feels good, doesn't it, Mummy?' asked Maria.

'Yes, very good,' agreed Annie. 'It's hard to believe how far we've come.'

Maria added, 'Well, we've had our moments, but look, 'ere we are, all well and happy.'

Mother and daughter were grinning at each other, when the moment was suddenly trampled upon by the sound of a voice coming from, it sounded like, the inside of a kitchen that would be overlooking the yard next door, just like theirs was.

This voice made its way to them through what must be an open window, so that simultaneously it sounded a trifle muffled yet very close. Its owner was clearly male and Stepney-bred through and through.

'Yer'll never believe it, Lisa,' it said in a way that suggested the speaker had no idea that what he was saying wasn't part of a private conversation, 'but I've just seen we've two right old tarts moved in next door. Cheap as chips, and as slutty as 'ell. One's a cut-price Diana Dors, and the other, well, she's not a bad looker when yer first glance, but then 'er face on one side . . . Anyways, she'd be one to chuck a bag over it if yer 'ad to do the dirty with 'er, that's fer certain, and still yer'd get change from a tanner. Both of them with skirts right up round their fannies, and their tits more or less fully on display.'

'What! A couple of cheap old brasses? Next door? Fucking 'ell, Dan. And it won't be long before the council will be wanting to put our rent up, even though they'll have put these right old slappers 'ere alongside us, you mark my words. It's a blooming disgrace, that's what it is,' answered a petulant female voice.

Annie gasped as she heard this, and quickly she glanced at Maria, who'd looked so content just a moment earlier, but was now standing there as if all her stuffing had been knocked out, looking as if somebody had punched her that second very hard in the gut, which in a way Annie supposed that they had.

Maria's knees buckled slightly and then she put her hand out to grab at the wall, and for a moment Annie thought her daughter was about to faint with the shock of the cruel jibe that she'd just heard.

Annie couldn't bear to see Maria so wounded.

Normally mild mannered, considerate and pragmatic, Annie threw all of that out of the window as in a trice she, quite literally, saw red.

'Right! We'll see about that!' she said in temper. 'Stay 'ere, Maria, and keep quiet. I'm going to 'ave a word about this and put them right on a few things. They're not going to get away with it. Over my dead body, just you see . . .'

Maria barely took in what her mother was saying, plunged as she was in to the depths of instant despair.

This house in Senrab Street had promised so much, but in the very few minutes since she'd turned the key in the front door, it was already sullied and dirty as far as she was concerned.

As Annie furiously marched across the yard, suddenly Maria realised what her mother was about to do, and wailed, 'Mummy, don't! Yer'll make it worse. Let it lie. *Please.*'

But Annie was so angry that she didn't hear Maria. Or, even if she had, she didn't care to take any notice.

Maria listened to Annie's enraged footsteps pound out to the front of the house, and then the sound of rapping on the front door of the neighbours' property.

'Fuck me, what's that about?' Maria heard the man say through next door's kitchen window.

'Don't answer it, Dan,' the woman told him. 'It'll only be some rubbish yer don't want to be bothered with.'

Then there was a cacophony of thumping sounds that were even louder and Maria realised that Annie must be kicking the front door.

'Sod it,' said the male voice, angry now.

And at the same time, Annie bellowed at the top of her voice, loud enough for the whole street to hear over the scrape of the neighbours' front doors opening, 'Don't you ever dare talk about my daughter like that again, d'you 'ear me?'

There was no danger of any of Senrab Street's residents not hearing, Maria thought, as she buried her face in her hands.

'I don't care what you say about me, as I'm a trollop and that's that, so do yer worst. But my daughter is a gem. A total *gem.* Yes, her face is scarred, but a brute did that to 'er fer no reason other than 'e felt like it. Yers 'ave no idea what my girl's been through, nor how brave she's been nor what a flipping *fantastic* mother she is. And now all she wants is to earn a little honest cash to look after 'er kiddies. And yer dare to say out loud that she needs to keep 'er face 'idden. After what she's been through? Shame on yer.'

Annie moved back to her own front door, and still standing in the street, she screamed a final, 'SHAME ON YER!' at the offending giant of a man who was now on his doorstep, before coming back inside and slamming the front door as hard as she could.

And then Annie stood with her back against it as she panted with temper, with a hand clutching at that bit of her tight top lying directly over her heart.

With panicked expressions, Liam and Conor looked at Maria through the scullery window, before quickly making themselves scarce as they shepherded the children upstairs, while, in different parts of their new home, Annie and Maria each gave in to tears of pain that were of such intensity that their shoulders heaved and their chests shuddered.

Two hours later, there was a timid rap on the front door, and with a depressed sigh, Maria trudged down the hall to open it.

Since Liam and Conor had left she'd sat slumped in a chair at the kitchen table, watching a cup of tea go cold.

On the doorstep stood a petite woman with bouncy dyed hair and swathes of gold bracelets above her wrists and a clutch of rings on her fingers, holding out a large paper carrier bag that had Harrods stamped across one side.

'Peace offering,' the woman said as she thrust the bag towards Maria. 'Me and my Big Danny spoke out of turn, and we know we did. We want to make it up to yer both.'

Maria looked stonily at the woman without saying a word, and then she lifted the swathe of hair across the scarred side of her face and jutted this cheek in challenge towards the woman.

'Oh my,' the woman said in a shocked voice, and when Maria stared at her again, it was to see this woman's eyes glistening with sympathy.

Then, dropping the carrier to the pavement, she stepped forward and folded Maria into her arms in a tight embrace as she said, 'You poor, *poor*, dear girl.'

Although stiff and unyielding at first, somehow Maria found herself hugging this woman back as she laid her head on her shoulder and inhaled her expensive perfume, feeling the release of her pent-up emotion, her body softening around this woman's curves.

By now Annie had come to the door to see who Maria was talking to, and stood there hovering in indecision as to what she should say or do.

The woman took her arms away from Maria, and grabbed one of Annie's hands. 'I'm Lisa. And me and my

Danny are truly sorry for what we said. It was wrong and unfair of us. Can you find it within your hearts to start again? A clean slate . . .'

'I don't think so,' said Annie, as she sharply yanked her hand back. 'What you said about my Maria was unforgiveable.'

And then Annie pulled a surprised Maria back from where she was standing in the street and wrenched her into the passageway behind her.

Maria discovered she was sorry she wasn't in the woman's embrace any longer; it had felt safe and warm and comforting, all qualities that had been lacking in much of her life.

Annie quickly pulled the door to, although not before the Harrods bag was chucked inside the house, where it slithered down the hall, narrowly missing their legs and feet.

'That wasn't a no,' called the woman through the door. 'Really nowhere near a no.'

There was something about the resolutely upbeat way she said this that made Maria and Annie shrug in a bemused way at each other.

Later they looked inside the paper carrier bag to find it contained four luxurious bath sheets that were fluffy, heavy and extravagant beyond anything that either Annie or Maria had ever touched.

Gingerly they took out the ruby-coloured towels and shook them from their folds, marvelling at their generous size and inspecting the label that proudly announced Harrods as where they had come from. They ran their hands over their deep pile, and then they held the bath sheets to their noses and breathed in – these towels that rich people used had a very distinctive smell.

Annie tried to work out what it was, and after a while she realised it was the scent of money and a pampered life that she and Maria could hardly begin to imagine.

After a while, both Annie and Maria dared to fancy what it might be like actually wrapping one of these towels around themselves when they stepped from the bath.

Maria felt her skin shiver at the thought of being so cosseted.

Annie realised what her daughter was thinking and, not for the first time, wished she could spoil Maria just now and again. If ever a daughter deserved one or two of the nice things that life had to offer, it had to be Maria.

Then the towels were carefully refolded and placed once more in their carrier bag, and the carrier bag placed high on a shelf in the cupboard in Annie's bedroom.

Such swish things weren't for the likes of her and Maria was the tacit understanding between mother and daughter.

All the same, as apologies go, it was a hell of a peace offering.

CHAPTER FIFTEEN

Almost a week went by, and the dust began to settle on the dicey start the family had had to their new lives in Senrab Street.

Keen not to be seen by all their new neighbours as the sort of women who were routinely out to make trouble or to be screaming in the street like fishwives, neither Annie nor Maria ventured out as they concentrated on unpacking and making everything shipshape. As they got the house organised, the children were happy to amuse themselves inside as they acclimatised to their unfamiliar surroundings.

But this couldn't go on indefinitely. And while it had been good to have some time away from their johns on the streets and enjoy some undivided time with the children while they sorted their new home, Annie and Maria knew they'd have to get back to work soon.

But, before this happened, one morning Maria had to take Faith to the doctor as Faith had bumped her head hard against the kitchen table while chasing the twins around, causing the bread board and knife to clatter jarringly to the floor. Although Faith had seemed fine after letting out some loud wails, she'd been left with an egg-sized bump on her forehead and Maria wanted to double-check that all was well.

Once Maria and Faith had left and the house was quieter, Annie gave the twins their breakfast and then she nipped upstairs to make the beds.

When she came downstairs again, she had to bite back some sharp words as she looked around at the chaos in the kitchen.

For, more than a bit stir-crazy at having been kept inside for so long, both Hope and Charity had been naughty, poking their fingers in their cereal bowls when Annie wasn't watching them in order to find Sugar Puffs that they then had thrown at each other. They had upended the pile of dirty laundry Annie was just about to hand wash, and were now running riot all over the house with knickers on their heads as they giggled wildly, refusing to come back to Annie when she called them.

And the final straw was Annie discovering the twins had poured down the outside drain the pail of hot water that she had got ready to soak the tea towels made grubby by being used as oven gloves, which Annie wouldn't have minded so much had she not put a generous shake of Omo into the water ready to dunk the tea towels into. They got through a lot of washing powder, and it was very expensive.

'Right, we're going out,' Annie announced.

Lighting a cigarette to calm her nerves, Annie decided that what they all needed was a visit to nearby St Dunstan's playground. It was only a couple of streets away, and came with recommendations from Joyce, who'd told Annie it was great for children and that many moons ago Joyce had even enjoyed her first kiss while sitting on a bench there. There was lots of space, and the twins could run around and let off some steam, while it would be a nice space for Annie to have a little time for herself and calm down.

Getting a pair of over-tired but under-exercised three-year-olds to stand still while she passed a damp flannel over their faces and hands, proved very testing. The short summer nights meant the girls didn't want to go to sleep when put to bed, and then they were waking up not long after the sun had risen.

'Pack it in, you two,' said Annie sharply. At last her final shred of patience wore thin as, after a series of shenanigans, Hope tried to duck away so that her grandmother couldn't reach her chops, while, at the same time, Charity bellowed out a tuneless rendition of 'Puff the Magic Dragon' very loudly and far too close to Annie's ear now she was bending down to wield the flannel.

Normally extremely patient (other than when hearing Maria being bad-mouthed), Annie very nearly shouted at Charity when she then tried to make off playfully with the flannel and hide it after insisting she knew how to clean her face herself and wanted to show Grammy. Annie had been foolish enough to actually pass it to her, even though Charity had a very naughty glint in her eye.

'Lord, give me strength,' Annie muttered to herself when finally the three of them were standing on the pavement outside as she turned to lock the door, the kitchen still a tumble of disorder inside. But at least Hope and Charity were now out of their nighties and wearing reasonably clean summer dresses and white ankle socks, as Annie turned the deadlock. It was only just nine o'clock but already she felt quite worn out.

Still, Annie wasn't so tired or jaded that when she spied from the corner of her eye a flash of colour racing past her that was the same lemon shade as the dress Charity was wearing, she couldn't immediately shoot out a hand to foil the escape as she grabbed a handful of cotton and hung on tight.

And it was just as well she did as suddenly a car came from nowhere and sped by, its horn blaring loudly and its engine screaming.

Somebody was in a terrible hurry, Annie thought, her heart lurching as she knew that with someone driving at that speed, it could have ended up a very nasty accident. The car's driver hadn't been on the lookout for small children running into the road, that was for certain.

Then Annie noticed Hope and Charity standing side by side nearby, staring up at her in confusion.

And if they were there, who on earth was Annie holding on to for grim life?

Annie looked down to see the cheeky grin of an impish small boy gazing back up at her as he wriggled about, apparently not perturbed in the slightest that a total stranger had him firmly in her grasp with the collar of his short-sleeved shirt rucked right up under his ear because of how Annie had seized him.

'There you are! I told you not to open the door. You little devil of a monkey!' cried a relieved voice behind her that Annie recognised as belonging to the rude neighbour with all the bracelets and the big hair who'd tried to make amends for her cruel comments about Maria with the gift of the bath sheets.

Embarrassed at possibly looking as if she were man-handling the lad, Annie dropped the handful of shirt she had in her hand as if it were hot, and said, 'He's only small, but he can run.'

'He's a little tinker, that's what he is,' said the woman. 'I didn't know he could open the front door. But the moment I was on the telephone, he took a stool from the kitchen and stood on it to release the snick. Didn't you, Little Danny? And then I heard the car, and you don't want to know what I thought . . .'

The full horror of what could have happened hit home, Annie noticed, as her neighbour's face suddenly blanched pale.

Little Danny threw back his head and gave an almighty chuckle, clearly not at all sorry over how much he'd scared his mother.

The woman rolled her eyes in a deliberately dramatic way, sighed loudly, and then said to Annie, 'Takes after his daddy, that one. Never one fer rules.'

She leaned forward and grasped Annie's hand to shake it, adding, 'Lisa. I did say my name when we first met, but I dare say that weren't the best time fer introductions. We got off on the wrong foot previously, didn't we? And me and Big Danny are sorry. Really we are. And now yer've stopped Little Danny coming to any harm, and my Danny will never forget that after I tell him. Can yerself and yer daughter find it in yer hearts to begin again, do yer think?'

For an instant Annie remembered how furious she had been when she had overheard what Lisa and Big Danny had said about Maria.

But now as she looked at Lisa, who was anxiously fiddling with her multitude of gold bracelets, Annie could see Lisa also had something of Little Danny's happy-go-lucky impish attitude too, and somehow this made it incredibly hard to remain cross with her.

So Annie listened to herself saying, 'I give in! I'm Annie, and these two ruffians 'ere are my twin granddaughters 'Ope and Charity. I can't say that my Maria will be all right over accepting yer apology though, so fer now it's just me, yer understand?'

'Understood,' nodded Lisa.

Annie wasn't sure what to say next as she really wasn't at all used to chatting with women. She'd never had a friend other than Joyce, and although she and Maria were always polite to the other working girls they ran into, it never went beyond mere passing of the day.

But as Little Danny walked over to Charity, and firmly grasped her hand with his much grimier one, the two youngers stood close together, transfixed at the sight of each other's faces at such close quarters as they still clasped hands. As the children tilted their heads from side to side as they tried to get a better look at each other, Annie suddenly said, 'I don't suppose you and Little Danny feel like coming over to St Dunstan's playground with us, Lisa?'

'I 'oped yer'd say that!' came the cheery reply. 'But you might want to remove that Sugar Puff from your cheek before we meet any other women there with their kiddies. It's sweet, but not *that* sweet. Anyways, 'ow are yer all settling in?'

At the mention of the Sugar Puff, what could Annie do but give an amused honk at her own inability to look in the mirror that was now hanging in the hall to see if she were presentable?

This made Lisa laugh, and then the children joined in, even though they weren't too sure what it was that the grown-ups were finding so funny.

The five of them set off, being very cautious about any passing cars, with Hope constantly giving her grandmother bemused glances over her shoulder at the way her sister seemed equally as captivated with Little Danny as he was with her, both seemingly still unable to tear their eyes away from the other. Charity's lemon sundress and Little Danny's yellow and white check shirt, and their fair hair, made the pair look like the twins out of the trio of children.

Hope's exasperated expression announced she simply didn't understand why her sister would find anything the slightest bit interesting about a *boy*, and Annie had more than a little sympathy with that opinion herself.

Lisa pointed out how similar Charity and Little Danny were in their colouring and the way they were exactly matching each other step for step, adding in a stage whisper, 'Little Danny can't have noticed your Charity is a girl, as he can't stand girls.'

At that precise moment Little Danny looked over at his mother, nodded towards Charity and then gave his mother a cheeky thumbs up.

'Yes, I can see yer lad's obviously *not* a fan of the female of the species,' Annie said in an ironic voice, and this made Lisa laugh again.

And then Annie thanked her for the towels, adding they were far too nice to actually use, to which Lisa replied with a wink and a nod of the head, saying, 'Give over, yer daft 'a'p'orth, and just enjoy them. There's plenty more where they came from, girl, don't yer know.'

Annie thought the towels must be either shoplifted or had fallen off the back of a lorry or were knock-offs from the market.

Then she remembered just how thick and heavy they were, and realised they had very likely come from a display on a Harrods sales floor. They definitely weren't cheap copies of the real thing.

Annie had never been to a department store, let alone one with the reputation of Harrods.

But while working at the Waltons' drinking den, she'd heard a punter tell his pal that seconds from batches of linens or clothes that would ordinarily go to posh shops, but which had small manufacturer's imperfections, always had a small nick cut out of their labels so that the seconds wouldn't get confused with the perfect goods. All four labels of the towels were perfectly intact.

And these towels had been shaken out to fluffy gloriousness before being folded and so hadn't recently been squashed together in any sort of factory packing box.

And Annie knew that nobody in their right mind would have bought four bath sheets at full price from Harrods, and then simply passed them on a whim to Annie and Maria.

By the laws of deduction, this told Annie the towels had been hoisted.

Although scrupulously honest herself, Annie knew the ways of the world, and that there wasn't any point in making a fuss or getting on her high horse about where the blessed towels had come from. They were very lovely and plush, after all, and so Annie decided that she and Maria would enjoy them in the way that clearly Lisa hoped they would.

Lisa nudged her with a playful elbow and gave her a quick thumbs up, and Annie couldn't help but grin as Lisa explained, 'I always go kiting up west with a few empty store bags, and dress posh, and nobody ever dares to ask. I don't do it round 'ere – you can't get the quality. And so what's the point if it's not the best?'

'Ah,' replied Annie.

'Ah, indeed,' said Lisa, raising her eyebrows. 'My Big Danny told me about the trap with the bags, and it works a treat.'

Annie couldn't think of anything to say other than, 'Right.'

'We all have tricks of our trade up our sleeves, yeah?' said Lisa.

'I suppose we do,' Annie agreed.

They looked at each other with serious expressions for a moment, and Annie realised they were still having a conversation even though they weren't saying anything.

'Sorted then?' asked Lisa.

And Annie knew without a shadow of doubt that what Lisa was really suggesting was that if she, Lisa, never made another disparaging comment about the way Annie and Maria earned their money, then in return it was a given that what Lisa, and presumably Big Danny too, did for their own living, would also be accepted by Annie and Maria without comment.

Annie looked at Lisa for what felt like several heart-beats and then carefully she nodded agreement, after which the two women continued to gaze at each other for a very still-seeming moment before they both blinked, and then gave in to shy smiles.

The air seemed to shift somehow, and the colours of everything Annie could see looked brighter.

And just like that she understood she had made her very first friend.

Aside from Joyce that was. Nobody could ever take the place of Joyce in Annie's heart, and she had long known that she would readily lay down her life if ever Joyce needed her to.

But Joyce and Annie had become friends through working for the Waltons, and back then it had been to their mutual safety and advantage that they had sought out the good things about each other. This had always made Annie feel – only a tiny bit, but it was a bit of her that couldn't be denied – that she and Joyce had become buddies in large part because of being thrown together and having to put their make-up on in a tiny cubicle of the illegal drinking den before they would go out and charm the punters, and then make sure during the evenings that they always watched out for each other's safety.

Those early days of turning tricks for the Waltons, long before Maria had been so badly hurt, felt a lifetime ago now, Annie realised, with the Annie of Senrab Street feeling now very much ready for yet another new chapter in her life to begin.

And as Lisa slipped her arm through hers in an easy way, Annie felt this new friendship would be very different to what she had with dear Joyce.

Not better, but definitely different. And it felt nice. Really quite exceptionally nice indeed.

It was because Lisa and Annie had no reason to like each other, Annie understood, especially following their rocky start and the disparaging comments Lisa and Big Danny had made about Annie and Maria being brasses and Maria's scarred face, and then there had been Annie's furious reaction that had told the whole of Senrab Street what had happened.

Because of this, the fact that now Annie and Lisa seemed to be finding a genuine connection together was what made it feel distinctly special.

For the first time in her life, Annie recognised she felt chosen just for herself, rather than through being a victim of circumstance and through just being *there*, and she felt very happy that Lisa hadn't given up on getting to know her when previously Annie had sent her packing with harsh words.

Meanwhile, the fact Lisa knew exactly how Annie and Maria earned their money – and now Annie knew Lisa was a hoister – didn't seem to matter in the slightest.

'I like her. I didn't expect to, but I confess that I do,' Annie told Maria later, as they shared the washing-up after lunch as the now-clean clothes were drying on the clothes line in the yard and the kitchen was once more tidy.

At the kitchen table, the three children bickered good-naturedly over who'd have the pink wax crayon to draw on the back of an unused few feet of an old roll of wallpaper.

Maria went over and shook out the other crayons from their box, saying, 'Thank goodness no one is using my favourite.'

Her daughters looked at her expectantly, and so Maria said, 'The green.' Hope grabbed it at once, and then Maria added, 'Or is my favourite the blue?' and quickly Charity made sure that was hers, leaving Faith with the coveted pink one.

Now peace reigned at the kitchen table, Maria glanced at her mother and asked in what was supposed to be a casual way, not that Annie was fooled for a moment, 'Go on then. What's this Lisa like?'

'Fun, or at least she makes me both feel fun and feel also that I'm funny. And it's obvious Lisa adores 'er Big Danny as she calls him. Little Danny, 'er nipper, is exactly the same age as Charity and 'Ope – their birthdays are the same day, can you believe – and Little Danny and Charity took a real shine to one another, much to the disgust of our 'Ope,' said Annie. 'Lisa insisted we must use those bath sheets, by the way – I'm certain she 'oisted them, not that she said it in so many words.'

'Really?' said Maria. 'So not quite as squeaky clean as she led us to believe that first day. Daring, though . . .'

'Yes, I 'ad the impression that not much gets her down or gets in 'er way. That Little Danny seems very like 'er from what I could see, although she swears Little Danny takes after Big Danny, who from all accounts is also a chancer.'

Annie said carefully then, 'I know you didn't get off to the best of starts, but I think you might get on well if you gave 'er the benefit of the doubt. A chance . . .'

'I'll think about it,' said Maria, understanding where her mother was leading the conversation.

Annie knew her daughter's firm tone of voice well enough not to push it further, saying instead, 'Cuppa?'

And Maria nodded as she inspected the scribble Charity was drawing with such concentration that her tongue was sticking out.

'What are you drawing?' she asked her daughter.

Charity gave her mother the sort of look that suggested as only a three-year-old can that her mother was being very dim. 'Little Danny,' she said, as if it was obvious from the mishmash of blue squiggles.

Hope stuck out her tongue behind Charity's back to show her mother what she thought of that.

CHAPTER SIXTEEN

Lisa was irrepressible though.

She must have kept an eye on the place, as Annie can't have been gone for more than a couple of minutes just after six o'clock that same day, off out to fetch some fish and chips for their tea, when Lisa knocked at the door, immediately placing a brand-new Mary Quant lipstick in Maria's hand.

'Just a little something I saw at the weekend, and thought of you as I am sorry over 'ow rude I was,' Lisa said. And before Maria could say anything in reply, Lisa went on, 'And my Little Danny won't give me a moment's peace, as everything now is Charity-this and Charity-that . . .'

There was the sound of small feet running behind Maria's back, and she turned to see Charity proudly holding her drawing of Little Danny, which she waved at Lisa in a way that made her study the drawing.

She looked at Maria for a clue as to what it might be, and Maria said, 'Charity, tell Lisa who this is.'

'Little Danny!' all three of them said together.

'It's exactly like our Little Danny,' Lisa said to Charity as she crouched down to her height. 'I'd 'ave known 'im any- where. Can I give it to 'im? 'E'll be chuffed to smithereens.'

Charity's big grin at Lisa's words told Maria what her own childhood had missed. Small pleasures, but pleasures nonetheless, and Maria felt for a moment as if she had a lump in her throat.

By the time Annie turned the corner back into Senrab Street, clutching a package wrapped in newspaper, it had been agreed that Lisa would come over the next morning so that Little Danny could play with the girls.

This proved such a success that Annie offered to look after all four children the following day, so that Lisa and Maria could go on their own to Watney Street market, with Annie saying to Maria she mustn't feel she needed to hurry back.

Hearing Lisa and Maria chat as their children played in the lounge told Annie how rarely she'd heard her daughter speak in a natural way to any woman other than Joyce, let alone someone reasonably close to her own age.

Lisa was twenty-eight, so right in the middle of Maria's twenty, and Annie's thirty-six.

But Annie knew that her and her daughter's self- imposed isolation had been because of the tense situation at home when they'd lived with Gary, that it was due to this that Maria had never allowed herself to make friends, and since then most of the women she and Maria had run into in London were other brasses. As Annie and Maria avoided working for pimps, they never fell into the sort of camaraderie those other girls seemed to enjoy together as they shared a fag or joked about their punters.

Like mother, like daughter, Annie thought to herself grimly as she considered how starved of female companionship she and Maria had been all their lives. Family was important, of course, but so were friends, and this was where they had both suffered.

Those men in Wakefield had found so many ways to hurt them.

Maria's scars were the obvious consequence, and while Annie wouldn't say or do anything to devalue her acknowledgement of the extreme pain Maria had been through over what had happened to her face, perhaps, she wondered, the really crucifying wounds both of them were still enduring lurked far deeper and beneath their skin, and therefore were much harder to deal with.

Over the coming months the two households got to know each other well.

Lisa recommended a reliable teenage girl she knew who'd left school and whose father owed Big Danny a favour. She'd keep the house ticking over each evening and watched the children while Annie and Maria worked in a much more hands-on manner than the neighbour to their previous flat had been comfortable with. It saved a whole lot of running around and time-watching by Annie and Maria, and made all three children better tempered now they could have an unwavering routine and be put to bed in their own beds and be able to stay there the whole night long.

And during this period, as they got used to life in Senrab Street, Big Danny turned out to be much more decent than they had first given him credit for.

One teatime, Annie and Maria stood by the window in their living room, hiding behind the curtains as they heard Big Danny right outside, giving some teenage lads a thorough telling off for knocking on their own front door and running away. Once the lads realised this was the house where two brasses lived, they had thought there was fun to be had at Annie and Maria's expense, and now Big Danny was making sure the lads knew this was a bad call.

'I know where yer all come from, yer best remember, and if yer try this again, or if anybody else does similar, I'll come looking fer yer all, so make sure *nobody* bothers next door,' said Big Danny as he stood close to their front door, speaking in the sort of stern voice that left the lads in no doubt he would follow through if they didn't heed his warning.

Big Danny was aptly named as he was tall and broad, which made Lisa look all the smaller when she was beside him, and as the lads realised quite how huge and strong he was as they looked up at him, their faces fell in the realisation that they had been messing with the wrong household.

Maria and Annie listened silently, and then Maria nodded when Annie laid a hand above her chest to show she agreed that she was touched by Danny standing up for them.

It was the first time a man had ever done anything like this to make their lives a bit easier, they realised.

Soon Lisa was happy to tell Annie and Maria that Big Danny made his living with jump-ups on goods lorries, and then selling on what had been found on board.

But, according to Lisa, her husband had a strict code of conduct – no violence if at all possible, and he had no holding with things like drugs or girlie mags. He would threaten to get his way, and of course he looked the part of an East End gangster with his heavy-linked gold wristwatch and his many gold rings, Lisa said, but she was yet to know him act in anger and cause anybody real harm.

'Big Danny just tells people what 'e wants, and then they give it to him with no fuss,' Lisa boasted to Maria, who could see how that would be, as although now Maria thought increasingly of him as a softie, he had been an intimidating sight at first, that was for certain.

And actually Maria didn't really buy into Lisa's assertions of the 'no violence' bit.

Big Danny commanded such respect locally, according to the local grapevine, that Maria was convinced that now and again he would have to put on display the muscle behind his words, in order that it kept on being the case that what Big Danny said, went. And those that disagreed with him should find the mere idea of getting on his wrong side needed thinking about very seriously indeed.

Maria had seen no sign that Big Danny was habitually fist-happy, but she had noticed several scars on his knuckles and she thought these lent credence to the fact he would lay down the law at opportune times.

Not paying any attention to Maria's slightly dubious expression, Lisa added, 'There's rarely any trouble, and on the odd time anyone looks chippy, once 'e makes a show of reaching into 'is trouser pocket, they give in. They probably think he's reaching for knuckle-dusters or a blade or a lock in a sock. He's got a lot of respect locally, but of course my Big Danny don't take liberties, and 'e's always mindful not to go back and strike again too often from the same people or firms.

'Everyone's got to make a living, 'e says, and I think 'e is looked up to fer recognising that. A bit of skimming is one thing, but taking away everything someone 'as worked 'ard fer and letting the well run dry is too much, my Big Danny always says. He thinks it's good business to be thinking of their well-being too, as it keeps everyone going fer longer. And we get the benefit, as yer 'ouse, and mine . . . well, no one's ever going to take the risk and rob either of them.'

Maria thought Lisa was probably right that they were never going to be burgled.

And she was never in doubt that Big Danny always treated Lisa like a queen – in fact they quite often heard him calling her Princess – and he was extremely patient with Little Danny too, from what they could tell, even though Little Danny could be a right handful; qualities that were hard not to like.

And now Big Danny had got over the shock of having two brasses next door, he was never less than respectful and kind to everyone in the house next door to his, and so gradually he won over Annie and Maria by being gentle and reliable, and just by being *there*, very much as if he had their backs should their luck turn bad once more.

One crisp autumn morning, Annie was standing in the street, cleaning the outside of the window to their lounge with a twist of newspaper doused in vinegar, when a couple of bobbies in uniform knocked at Lisa and Big Danny's front door, and demanded to see upstairs.

They were looking for someone who'd escaped from custody, Annie heard them say.

Big Danny was out, but Lisa caught Annie's eye for an instant, and Annie understood immediately.

The minute the constables had plodded inside, Annie trotted through the house to her own backyard, and in a second or two Little Danny was poking something wrapped in a towel through the hole in the fence that divided their yards, which had been made so that Charity and he could talk to each other.

Quickly, Annie grabbed the bundle, thinking it oddly heavy, and then she snatched some washing off the line so that, should one of the bobbies glance out of the window from upstairs next door and see Annie outside, it looked like she had a reason to be there.

In the kitchen she lifted the corner of the towel and saw the unmistakeable shape of the black barrel of a pistol.

Thank the lord that Maria had taken the girls to the greengrocers, Annie thought, as she hated the idea of a shooter in the house.

However, this didn't mean she was going to dob in Big Danny to the law so, quick as a flash, Annie rammed the gun into their open cornflakes packet and made sure the cereal covered the gun, and then she returned the box to the top shelf of the turquoise-painted kitchen dresser and closed the cupboard door on it, the cornflakes box in clear view through the glass front to the cabinet.

Annie folded the two skirts she'd brought in from the yard and put them on the back of a chair.

And then she nipped back to cleaning her outside downstairs window out in the street.

A minute later a Rover P6 2000 drew up outside and a fresh-faced young man in fashionable civvies got out, and Annie could tell immediately he was a copper.

Frankly he looked a bit of a wideboy, but she heard him yell with authority to the bobbies from the hall they were in the wrong house, and they should be over in Dunelm Street instead.

Sheepishly, the two PCs left the house, not daring to look their plain-clothed colleague in the eye, and the young man looked a bit awkward. Annie supposed he must be a detective as he wasn't in uniform, although she thought then that he might be not yet at work that day if he were a uniformed constable or sergeant. He had a few whispered words with a relieved-looking Lisa before he got in his car and drove away.

'False alarm,' Lisa said. 'But best 'ang on to *it* for a wee while, just in case. If you don't mind, that is.'

Annie knew that 'it' was the gun.

When Big Danny got home, it was only a few minutes before he came around, saying to Annie, 'Girl, I'm in yer debt. Anything, just ask. Now, or a year from now, or ten years, I never forget a good turn, doll.'

And right in front of the children and Maria, a cool and collected Annie reached into the dresser's top cabinet and reached for the box of cornflakes, passing the whole box to Big Danny, watched by the children, who were having their egg-on-toast tea, and a bemused Maria.

Big Danny chuckled as he clutched the box to his chest, saying, 'Now *that's* a brekker!' and then he headed back down the hall to go home to Lisa and Little Danny.

'Don't ask,' said Annie to Maria, after she'd made sure the front door was closed and bolted now that Big Danny had left.

Maria knew enough to do as her mother had instructed, and that she should distract the puzzled children by asking what stories they wanted reading in bed after their bath.

CHAPTER SEVENTEEN

By the time the days had shortened and Christmas was looming, Charity and Little Danny were inseparable, and there were tantrums if they were parted for too long.

It threw Hope and Faith together in a way that hadn't happened before, and their jealousy caused by Charity obviously not feeling the same way about them meant that sometimes the two sisters were mean to her, and wouldn't let her join in when they were playing with their Barbie dolls. Charity wasn't allowed to sleep in the ancient double bed that Faith and Hope shared, and Maria had to buy a second-hand single for Charity to sleep in that she somehow shoe-horned into the bedroom too.

Annie and Maria kept saying to Hope and Faith that although Charity liked Little Danny, it didn't for a moment mean that she liked *them* any less, but the hard looks the two youngsters gave their grandmother and mother when they said this announced very clearly that Faith and Hope were not convinced in the slightest, and that they didn't feel the same way about Little Danny that Charity did.

Trying to cut down on the squabbles, Maria had several conversations with Charity about being a bit more obviously nice to her sisters, but although Charity would nod at the time, it didn't really make much difference.

To keep the peace, Lisa often had Charity in to hers to play with Little Danny as she said to Maria that this was actually easier for her as they'd amuse themselves, and there was only so much playing with Little Danny's extensive collection of Corgi cars that she, the princess, could stand when mother and son were alone together.

Maria laughed at the thought of the glamorous Lisa kneeling on the floor and going brmm-brmm as she pushed the small metal cars around as Little Danny directed.

'I know what you mean – once the girls had mastered 'opscotch, it drove me mad as I thought they'd play it quietly together and I'd be let off the 'ook. How wrong I was! Turns out I 'ave to judge every game and see again and again their "special" skips,' added Maria.

'Little Danny 'as never shown any interest in 'opscotch,' Lisa said.

'Keep it that way,' replied Maria.

It wasn't long before Charity began to call next door 'Other Home'.

Maria and Annie were convinced that Charity and Little Danny's devotion to one another was just a stage they were going through and it would probably fizzle out before too long, and so they tried not to make too much of it.

Until, that is, the day that Charity, still not yet four, came back and announced that she and Little Danny were going to be married.

Faith noticed that Charity was hiding a small object in her hand, and said, 'Mummy, what's she got?'

Immediately Hope shot her big sister an approving look for possibly having got Charity into trouble.

Ignoring them, now that Faith had drawn Maria's attention to it, she noticed too the glint of something even though Charity was doing her best trying to hide what it was, so she asked, 'Yes, Charity, what 'ave you got there? Show me your 'and, please.'

Obediently, Charity held out a hand palm-up to show there was nothing there, but Maria was wise to this. 'The *other* 'and,' she said, as Faith and Hope grinned at each other.

With a sigh, very reluctantly Charity lifted that hand to the table top, and slowly opened it. And there, shining on the flat of her palm, was laid a delicate gold ring with a huge cluster of shiny stones.

'Did Little Danny give you this?' asked Maria suspiciously.

'Yes. When 'e asked me to marry 'im,' Charity told her. 'And I said I would.'

'Of course you did. May I?' Annie asked Charity, and as the little girl nodded that Annie could pick the ring up, Annie brought it nearer to the window for a closer look.

'Lordy,' she said then in a shocked voice, 'Little Danny has only gone and given 'er a real diamond ring. 'E must have been in Lisa's jewellery box, the little devil.'

Annie passed it to Maria, who said, 'Oh, whatever next. This must be worth a fortune! Charity, I know it was a lovely thing fer Little Danny to do, but this wasn't 'is ring to give yer, and we're going to have to take it back to Lisa, as it belongs to 'er.'

'No!' screamed Charity. 'Nooooooo! It's mine.'

Charity's anguished cry brought Faith and Hope to her side of the table to comfort her, and then the three girls looked up at their mother crossly.

'You take the damn ring back where it belongs, and I'll deal with this,' said Maria, and as Annie went down the hall she could hear tempers rising behind her and raised voices.

Annie knocked at the Other Home, as they had now all taken to calling Lisa and Big Danny's house, and Big Danny came to the door.

She held up the ring, and Big Danny smiled and said fondly, 'Aww, I gave that to my Lisa when I went down on bended knee and asked her to marry me. Not sure why yer've got it, but you'd better come in. She made me wait fer an answer, yer know.'

Annie said as she followed him to the kitchen, 'The apple's not fallen far from the tree then as Little Danny 'as just given it to Charity, asking 'er to marry 'im. She said yes at once, apparently.'

'The monkey!' said Big Danny.

'Monkey?' Little Danny said as he looked at Annie in a way that clearly said he hoped she had a live monkey with her.

Big Danny said, 'Well, I think you did something this morning . . .'

'Me and Charity are going to be married,' announced Little Danny.

'And did you give her anything while you sorted this out?'

'A ring.'

'Mummy's ring?'

Little Danny nodded as if he'd been very clever.

Big Danny opened his huge mitt to show it now looking very small in comparison.

'That's *my* ring. My engagement ring!' cried Lisa. 'What the flipping 'eck!'

'I'm sorry . . .' Annie began.

And then through the kitchen window, although closed, they could clearly hear Charity yell as loudly as she could through the hole in the garden fence, 'I'm still going to marry yer!' before she let out a livid screech as presumably Maria picked her up to haul her back inside.

And Little Danny beamed with such happiness at Charity's shout to him that it was hard not to smile, and

Lisa could only say as she stared askance at her son, 'That's as maybe, and I can see you're chuffed, Little Danny. But you and I are going to have a serious talk about respecting what belongs to others.'

Which, thought Annie with a chuckle as she returned home, was quite ironic, seeing as how Lisa and Big Danny made their living.

PART FOUR

CHAPTER EIGHTEEN

Stepney, East London, 1980

Everyone was still pretty much as they had been eleven years previously. Older, of course, but still the same somehow.

Faith, Hope and Charity had all proved very bright and each had sailed through the eleven-plus at school with high marks.

Faith and Hope were now doing really well at grammar school and excellent grades were predicted for their forthcoming O levels, which Faith would take a year earlier than her sisters.

Faith had already announced that she wanted a career in law and would therefore definitely be going to university, while Hope remained undecided about what she wanted to do, although she hadn't rejected the idea of also attending college.

Annie and Maria didn't actually know anyone who had gone on to further education, and it felt incredible to them that their hard work out on the streets had given the girls such a springboard to what would hopefully be very different lives. Neither Faith nor Hope seemed terribly interested in the opposite sex, something Annie and Maria were pleased to see.

The previous Christmas, Faith had asked for a contribution from her mother and grandmother for some elocution lessons, saying that no one would take her seriously if in court in the years to come she talked with her Stepney accent, and as there was obviously some truth in this, Annie and Maria had obliged and they'd given her enough for ten lessons. Faith had kept her elocution lessons going since then, working as a Saturday girl in a shop to make sure she could continue to pay for them.

The twins had long given up laughing at Faith as she practised her vocal exercises. Hope and Charity thought she sounded daft, but Faith looked at them so intently if they ribbed her that the fun had long gone from teasing her.

Meanwhile, Charity and Little Danny were still thick as thieves, and were more or less glued together at the hip.

Charity had only lasted two days at grammar school before flatly refusing to go there again, even though her sisters loved it, insisting she would only be happy at the comprehensive where Little Danny was, as he'd not passed the selection exam for the grammar school.

And so that was what happened, with Charity exchanging schools with Maria's eventual agreement, and actually proving a good influence as she made Little

Danny work hard so that they could be in the same class and sit next to each other, and this in turn lifted his grades as Little Danny wasn't going to risk having Charity sitting next to anyone else, in case it was a boy she might end up fancying.

Indeed Charity seemed on course for good exam results too, with her year head telling Maria at the most recent parents' evening that all her teachers had very high hopes for her indeed.

Charity always pooh-poohed the idea that her exams could help her get a good job, saying that she and Little Danny wouldn't need her to work in an office. But, she reassured her mother, she found exams easy and fun to do, and so was quite happy to get a decent number of O levels under her belt just to prove to her family she was every bit as brainy as her sisters, even if university or A levels were never going to be right for her.

An early marriage was still very much on the cards it seemed, as Little Danny never missed an opportunity to say that he would look after Charity in exactly the same way he'd seen his father make Lisa a total princess in the Other Home, and Charity would joke she expected nothing less, although actually she wanted promoting to queen status.

Behind Charity's back, Faith and Hope had taken to calling her M'Lady in the voice that Parker used to Lady Penelope from *Thunderbirds* that they'd enjoyed on the telly when they were small, but they didn't dare try this in front of her as Charity could be both very touchy and extremely intimidating if she felt like it.

Lisa and Big Danny seemed to have remained more or less untouched by the passing of time, Lisa still doing her kiting visits to the West End, and Big Danny his jump-ups.

The Rover-driving detective continued to make the occasional visit next door, Annie and Maria noticed, but unobtrusively so and usually late at night. Over the years they'd commented on the way he'd replace his Rover with a new model when the number plates changed. Neither Lisa nor Big Danny ever mentioned him though, and so Annie and Maria didn't either. He seemed to have a sixth sense and always seemed to visit when the girls were out, other than one time a few years back when Faith was at the Other Home so Lisa could instruct her how she was to chaperone Little Danny and Charity while Lisa and Big Danny went out one night.

Little Danny had grown into a handsome lad, but despite many of the local girls giving him the glad eye as he'd matured, it had only ever been Charity in his sights as far as he was concerned, and his greatest stroke of luck was that she felt exactly the same about him.

Generally, it was the girls' attitude to their schoolwork that warmed the hearts of Annie and Maria the most.

To see the strong young women the three girls were promising to be, and the way they would take over the kitchen after tea to do their homework, Radio One playing softly in the background as they wrote their essays and practised their French vocab, was always heartening for Annie and Maria to see.

Annie and Maria both regretted they had each had their own education cut short as it had limited their opportunities so much. Maria's girls understood, clearly, that if they worked hard at their schoolbooks, then whatever they wanted to do was subsequently going to be so much easier to achieve.

Annie and Maria thought about this often on their nights standing on draughty street corners, when all they wanted to do was go home.

And the determination to give Faith, Hope and Charity the very best that they could usually kept mother and grandmother standing there long after other brasses would have called it a day.

It hadn't been easy over the years, but they were proud that they had managed to remain working independently and they'd slowly built a decent core of loyal regulars whom they trusted, although they never stopped looking out for each other if either of them went with a new john. Maria was thirty-one, and Annie forty-seven.

Joyce, now in her early sixties but incredibly well-preserved, and still as fond of her backcombing and her leopard print as ever, had begun to wind down some of her work up west.

She joked that at the flat these days she more frequently made cups of tea for her men, most of whom she'd had on her books for years, having a natter with them as they drank their tea instead of having sex with them, as they seemed to favour the former.

She tried to get Annie to go in with her, and begin working in the West End flat.

'It's a doddle, Annie, really it is, and if you came in with me now, it would enable you to take things easier, and I could pass on some of my punters over to you, so you'd be quids in,' said Joyce. 'None of us are getting any younger, you know, and there's no need to be freezing your arse off in the winter nights, not any longer. And I 'ave a maid who'd be 'appy to look after yer too – she's very reasonable – so you wouldn't need to lift a finger in the flat to keep things clean and shipshape.'

'It's so tempting, Joyce, really it is, but I can't,' said Annie, despite the fact that she would love to go and work in the way her friend described. 'Maria needs me to look out for 'er – and the men that want to go with 'er aren't the sort who'd be tempted to visit a nice flat in the West End. I'd never get a moment's peace if I wasn't close by to where Maria is, and you know that she'd never want to work too far away from where her girls are, in case they need 'er. She feels they'll be leaving 'ome before too long, and even now they're big, she likes to be with them each evening until they've done their 'omework.'

Joyce smiled at Annie, and patted her arm as she said, 'I thought you'd say that, but I 'ad to ask. I've never met better mums than you two. People think brasses don't care, but that only goes to show they 'aven't met you and Maria.'

'We just try and do our best,' said Annie. 'There's nothing special about that.'

Joyce knew this wasn't true.

CHAPTER NINETEEN

Joyce was still in touch now and again with Ted Walton.

After Maria had her face slashed so heartlessly in the illegal drinking den, Joyce said she would cut all ties with Ted.

But Annie knew that Joyce and Ted went back a long way, and she begged her not to do that, saying that Joyce could be useful in misdirecting his attentions away from Annie and Maria's actual whereabouts, should Ted or his brother Frank ever ask Joyce where they might be now.

Joyce had understood what Annie was saying, and told her that she would continue to check in with Ted now and again, and that if ever he asked anything about where Gary's family might live, she would say she'd lost touch in recent years but the last thing she'd heard was that Annie and Maria had moved to Dublin, but she did know that Fred's baby had died at birth.

As time passed over the years, Annie learned from Joyce that Ted and Frank had diversified into supplying slot machines that had been altered so that they were even more profitable to the arcades where they were installed than they were legally allowed to be, and the brothers had made a lot of money from this. Consequently they had opened a couple of casinos in the north of England.

And there was still a lot of illegal stuff going on under the table apparently – hiring out guns and ammunition for jobs, extortion of small businesses to pay protection money, their stable of escorts and brasses, illegal dog fights and all the other things one would expect of the Waltons.

They were, Joyce had heard, exploring the supply of drugs to council estates in ice cream vans, but rumour had it that this hadn't been the money-spinner they'd expected as they'd tried to muscle in on dealers who'd already established themselves in their territory with exactly this means of supply, and who were none too keen to share a lucrative market with the Waltons.

Although the Waltons liked to wash as much money as possible so that it looked clean and as if it had come from profitable legal businesses, predictably there had been some problems with the taxman over the years, and for a while it looked like this might bring their business empire down.

But they'd weathered that particular storm, as they had also dealt with Ted's son Fred's knack of getting into one scrape after another – the very Fred who had so badly hurt Maria.

A few years after Annie and Maria had arrived in London, Joyce dared to bring up the subject of Fred with Annie.

'After you and Maria left,' Joyce said, 'Ted sent Fred away, supposedly for a year, after what 'e'd done to Maria, Ted telling 'im it was to knock some sense into his stupid 'ead, as money was money, and Fred's actions badly 'it Ted in the pocket, as it had cost the family the services of you, Annie, who had been so popular with clients and making the family a lot of regular money.

'Fred was sent to Ted's connections in Glasgow, but it wasn't even six months before 'e was back with Ted again for acting recklessly and drawing the attention of the police to the rackets going on. The straw that broke the camel's back was 'im using a flick knife at a football match, and this couldn't be brushed under the carpet in the way that Maria was as there were too many who witnessed it, and so Fred had had to be smuggled back to Wakefield before the law came calling. And apparently things haven't improved since then, and Ted is always having to make amends after something stupid Fred does.'

Each time Fred was talked about by Joyce, Annie couldn't prevent a wince at the first time Joyce would say his name. But then Annie wouldn't allow herself to be hurt by the thought of him further. He had ruined Maria's face, and now Annie was determined that the mere idea of him wouldn't be allowed to contaminate and ruin a second more of her own thoughts if she could possibly help it.

This was easier to say than to do, but Annie surprised herself by how readily she could excise Fred from her thoughts, once she'd decided to do so.

'I don't want to know any more, Joyce,' Annie would say. ''E's just scum.'

''E is,' Joyce agreed. 'But yer need to know what the Waltons are about. Fer Maria's sake.'

Then one day, Joyce arrived with shocking news from Wakefield – Annie's husband Gary had died.

There'd been a fight in a bookie's that Ted now owned, Joyce said, and one of the staff had got a bit fist-happy and had decked Gary, who'd been knocked to the ground, his bad back not allowing him to duck out of the way in time. His face had scuffed across the filthy nylon carpet, resulting in carpet burns across his cheek.

''E didn't go to 'ospital to have the grazes properly cleaned and so within a few days 'e'd got a bad infection, and although the 'ospital did their best, it was too late and 'is body just gave up,' explained Joyce to Annie and Maria, as they and the girls sat in the living room on a Sunday afternoon. 'Ted told me it was an 'orrible death and very painful, and Gary knew exactly what was 'appening, right up to the end. 'E kept asking, why him? And Ted said he told him it was because 'e were a bastard, and 'e always 'ad been.'

'Good riddance to bad rubbish,' said Annie with an uncharacteristic fervour she'd never let surface before. 'I 'ope 'e suffered every second, and that when 'e died, 'e was thinking about 'ow 'e'd done me wrong. If I'd never met 'im, we wouldn't be as we are now. You know that technically we're still married, Joyce – and this means at last I can feel free of 'im. I've waited fer this a long, long time.'

'Mummy!' Maria was shocked, her eyes huge, with pupils almost the size of her irises and black as coal. 'What cruel things to say. That's my father you're talking about, remember. And 'e wasn't perfect, but 'e wasn't a monster. 'E never laid a finger on me, and 'e could 'ave 'is moments of kindness.'

Annie gave a snort of disbelief, and then said, 'You've got selective memory, my girl! Gary *was* a monster and 'e beat me black and blue nearly every day that I lived with 'im. Yer wouldn't treat a dog in the way 'e treated me.'

'I'm not defending everything 'e did, not by any means,' Maria cried. 'And I know all too well what 'appened between the two of you, Mummy – I'd lie on my bed with the door locked and a pillow over my ears to drown out the sound, don't forget. But he was my daddy all the same and it feels a wrench, and I can't 'elp that – I wish I could lie to you that it means nothing, but I can't. This news is a shock and, as far as I'm concerned, while I'm not sad as such, it just feels odd not to 'ave a dad any longer, even if 'e wasn't up to much in the long run, and although 'e's not been in my life for years. Most of all, I don't like to hear that sort of 'ate coming from yer mouth, when yer normally so kind and always look for the good – it feels wrong. I think yer better than that.'

Annie's voice was harsh as she snapped back at her daughter, 'Oh, fer goodness' sake, get a grip, Maria! You'll be saying next that Faith's lucky to 'ave Fred Walton as 'er father at this rate.'

Faith had never been told who her father was, no matter how many times she'd asked, and Annie clamped a hand to her mouth as immediately she and Maria and Joyce all glanced anxiously towards Faith.

They hadn't wanted her to know who her father was in case she got some hare-brained idea about seeking him out, and all three women were pretty certain, if that happened, then Fred would pick a time to seek out Maria and Annie just so that he could kick them around a bit.

But aside from a distinct narrowing of the eyes, Faith didn't look up from the book she was reading, and so nobody could tell if she'd heard or not, and of course they couldn't ask her, as if she hadn't heard then this would be tantamount to making an official announcement.

And then Hope said, 'Well, at least Faith *has* a father. Me and Charity could 'ave ours as any one of a thousand men, and that's a real bitch to get yer 'ead around.'

But before Maria or Annie could think of anything to say to this in their defence, aside from Maria merely chastising her daughter with 'Language, Hope,' Charity interrupted with, 'Well, us three *all* 'ave a father, just not in the biological sense. If anybody in this room feels Big Danny 'asn't looked out for us in the way a real father would, then I don't know what you're thinking and I'll be ashamed of you. He's cared when we've been ill or out of sorts, and 'e's been better at taking care of us than anyone who'd be rutting away for a couple of minutes and then walking out of yer lives. And if yer can't see that, it's a disgrace, and you've all got shit fer brains.'

Nobody spoke, the ticking of the kitchen clock marking time passing, as everyone thought about Charity's comments, trying to ignore the 'shit fer brains' that they knew she'd thrown in just to get a rise from them.

And then they looked from one to another to acknowledge there was a lot of truth in what had just been said about Big Danny.

*

Faith was the only one who didn't respond, and this was because she was lost in her own world as she stared unseeing at the pages of her book. For, at long last, she had a name for her father. This was something she had yearned for since she could remember.

Fred Walton.

Fred Walton.

She didn't know who he was, or anything about him, and Faith and her sisters had long ago stopped registering their mother's cruelly damaged face.

But Fred Walton was a nice enough name, wasn't it, Faith thought. And why should Annie think so strongly that she was unlucky to have him as her father?

Although Faith had never heard of Fred before, the surname Walton was familiar, as several times Faith had heard Joyce and her granny talk about the Waltons.

Indeed Faith had heard enough that she'd been able to work out already that they were a high-stakes criminal family who lived in Wakefield.

She remembered Joyce mentioning a drinking den, and cards, and glamorous dresses, and even guns.

Once she'd even heard Annie admitting sheepishly that there had been times when she'd thought longingly of the posh frocks she'd left behind, and this had made Faith feel that whatever the Waltons stood for sounded very exciting, although she couldn't quite see what Annie and Maria's connection to the family had been.

Once, a long time ago, Faith had dared to ask Maria about the Waltons and why she never spoke of them.

But with cheeks darkening by a slash of crimson, her mother had only been able to give a small grunt of acknowledgement that she'd heard Faith's question, before abruptly throwing down her knife and fork, and then she'd pushed her chair back with a teeth-jangling scrape on the kitchen lino and gone to stand in the yard for quite a while even though it was raining heavily and she'd been just about to begin her lunch.

Faith had gone to the window to look at her mother. She turned to Annie and began to ask what was going on, but Annie had a steely smile on her face as she talked over Faith's words with a cheery, 'I 'eard something very funny at the newsagent's yesterday, shall I tell yer all what it was?'

And then Annie described something very dull and not the slightest bit funny. It was only later as Faith lay in bed that she realised Annie's voice hadn't been cheery, but desperate.

Faith thought about all of this now, and she decided that one didn't have to be a genius to conclude her conception hadn't been one that had arisen through love, not that she ever really thought it had.

Fred Walton.

What sort of man might he be, Faith wondered.

And then she realised that he would be eating, or drinking, or playing pool, or any manner of other things, right at that very moment. It hardly mattered what he was doing, just that he was alive with his blood pumping through his veins.

Exactly as she was living and breathing.

Fred Walton wouldn't recognise her on the street, and she wouldn't know him from Adam either, should she pass him by.

But it didn't matter. They were inextricably linked by blood.

They were family, whether they liked it or not.

And deep inside, Faith could feel a spark within her had been ignited. She wasn't sure what this meant yet, but she was sure it meant *something*.

CHAPTER TWENTY

It was a surprise to no one that the inevitable happened on the night of Hope and Charity's sixteenth birthday at a big family dinner at a local Italian restaurant that Lisa and Big Danny were treating them all to, in part as it was Little Danny's birthday too.

After the candles on the two cakes had been blown out and wishes made, and the slices of cake had been finished, Big Danny tapped a teaspoon against his wine glass for some quiet.

Looking very serious, Little Danny stood up and gave a self-conscious smile.

Then he got down on one knee before Charity, and pulled out a small ring box from his trouser pocket. He opened it and said, 'I love you, and it's only ever been you, and can only ever be you, Charity. Will you do me the honour of marrying me?'

She just beamed at him and nodded, and everybody cheered and clapped as he slipped the ring on to the third finger of her left hand.

Maria looked intently at her daughter's hand.

Something about that ring was familiar.

The penny dropped, and Maria then glanced across at Lisa, saying, 'Isn't that the ring of yours Little Danny stole from yer jewellery box all those years ago when 'e was nowt but a cheeky young thing, and 'e'd asked Charity to marry 'im?'

Lisa smiled and said, 'Yes, it is! It was my engagement ring, but Charity is like a daughter to me, yer know, and I wanted 'er to 'ave it when Little Danny finally got around to asking me about it, as it were clear which way 'is thoughts were going. So I wore it especially when Big Danny took me out fer *our* last wedding anniversary, and then we had it cleaned in Hatton Garden and sized fer Charity, asking the jeweller to make a special job of it. And now it feels as if it's finishing the circle and it's meant to be 'ers.'

'Charity is a very *lucky* girl,' said Maria. 'But please don't let 'er 'ave it if it makes you uncomfortable or yer miss it, Lisa, or if yer'll feel odd seeing 'er wear it. She'll almost certainly never take it off, given 'alf a chance.'

'Yer Charity's a very *lovely* girl,' Lisa echoed, 'and I think they'll be really content with each other. Me and Big Danny 'ave been so 'appy in our marriage that this ring stood fer, but now 'e and I know neither of us is going anywhere away from each other, and so it's time the new generation 'as a go. And I can't think of anywhere that ring's going to get better use than with these two. They're meant to be, and 'ave been since the day they clapped eyes on each other.'

Maria thought so too, although she wouldn't have talked about it as romantically as Lisa described.

But nobody had ever denied that Charity and Little Danny had always fitted one another perfectly, and Maria couldn't remember a single time they'd even had raised words with one another or had so much as glanced at anybody else. And while in theory she didn't approve of someone as young as Charity getting hitched, it seemed fitting and inevitable with these two.

Maria pulled Lisa into a hug and said, 'Hello there, sister-in-law,' and then Maria saw that Lisa had to wipe a tear from under her eye and blink rapidly before she could reply a slightly damp 'Hello, you' back.

'Technically it's mother-in-law, of course,' said Maria to allow Lisa time to recover herself.

'Give over,' Lisa replied, 'we're much too young for that.'

Being still at school, in the final year before they could leave, Charity and Little Danny decided they'd have an engagement knees-up the first Saturday of the summer holidays once their exams had finished, with the wedding planned for the following Easter, as Father O'Reilly was able to fit them in then following a cancellation.

Big Danny hired a room at the Peacock for, as he called it, 'the grand engagement shindig'.

There would be a DJ and a comedian, and a photographer so everyone should dress up. The food and drink were going to be free-flowing, Big Danny insisted, and even though he described it as a small do, there were a lot of young people going to be there who would be well below the legal age for drinking in pubs.

Big Danny assured everyone that nobody need worry as he'd had a word in a few people's ears and the result was an official blind eye was going to be turned and there wasn't going to be any trouble about this from the law. And of course he would be on hand throughout the evening to make sure things didn't get too lively.

Maria wasn't certain how reassuring the parents of friends the same age as the happy couple were going to find this, bearing in mind how wild teenagers could get.

Big Danny's view of what 'too lively' constituted was likely to be a lot more lax than where some of the other parents would draw the line, Maria was pretty certain. But she didn't think anyone would argue with Big Danny that perhaps such free licence wasn't appropriate. And she was quite right in this, as they didn't.

Hoping that Big Danny garnered enough respect locally that none of the youngsters would risk stepping too far out of line, Maria gave her daughters some money to go to the West End to treat themselves to new clothes and shoes for the engagement party, and they came back laden with shopping bags.

Immediately they ran upstairs to change, and then they paraded their new togs for Annie and Maria to admire, with each having bought exactly what Maria would have expected them to pick.

Faith's outfit was sober and sensible, with prim low-heeled court shoes, all in a deep green, and although really the outfit and her hairstyle were far too old and staid for her, she looked every inch as if she was giving a trial run to the clothes she hoped one day to be wearing under her barrister's gown.

Hope obviously thought so too. 'You look ridiculous,' she told Faith, 'as if you're forty years old going on fifty, and working in Citizens Advice. And in any case, who'll see what you'll wear down the line, hidden under those court gubbings when you're wearing that hideous wig.'

'No shame in working for Citizens Advice, so I'm not even going to go *there* with you on that,' said a prissy Faith, her voice increasingly cut-glass these days from all those elocution lessons. Her eyes darkened as she added, 'But at least I have ambition, Hope. And FYI, that wig barristers wear is a peruke, and the jabot is . . .'

'Oh, give it a rest, Faith. No one wants to hear it,' interrupted Hope. 'And who said I don't have ambition? I don't know what I want yet, but I definitely have ambitions.'

Faith

Hope was dressed head to toe in black, the legs of the trousers connected by bondage straps and with black winkle-pickers on her feet, and an X-Ray Spex T-shirt tucked into the trousers, a combination that perfectly matched the blue-black dye she'd recently put on her naturally blonde hair and her red-black lipstick. She'd been too young to have dressed punkily at the time it was most fashionable, but punk was clearly the main influence of this look, with none of the current New Wave softening about it. She had used a lot of black eyeshadow and her nails were inky. She looked formidable.

In contrast, Charity's outfit was bright-neon Day-Glo and very girlie, all fluff and sparkle and shoulder pads, and her blonde hair with its frosted tips candy-flossed into a voluminous cascade flanked by huge silver hoop earrings, and her lips bubble-gum pink.

'Do you think I'll stand out at my party, Mum?' Charity asked, not having paid either sister any attention.

'I should say so, Charity! You look wonderful, and very, er, bright, and exactly as if you are getting ready for being 'itched,' said Maria. 'In fact you all look extremely special, and you make me proud. In your, um, very . . . er, *different* ways.'

The sisters grinned at their mother. Clearly Maria had managed to say the correct thing at precisely the right moment.

'Well done there,' Annie said, as the girls disappeared back to their bedroom to take off their new outfits.

209

'Extremely, shall we say, tactful. The only thing that hints at them being sisters is their figures, which they've inherited from you.'

Maria caught her mother's eye and then they couldn't help laughing, Maria saying, 'What a sight! The daft buggers.'

'We definitely must get a picture of the three of them together,' said Annie, 'as they won't believe it in ten years unless there's proof.'

At the party, the sisters' contrasting outfits, hair and make-up were indeed a talking point, and the photographer used up several rolls of film taking shots of them both together and individually.

But their contrasting styles weren't as much of a talking point as how happy Charity and Little Danny looked together, although Maria noticed several people check Charity's enviably flat belly to see if this was a shotgun wedding.

She understood why these guests did it, but she couldn't pretend this didn't make her feel a little uncomfortable, bearing in mind her and Annie's history.

She didn't know if Charity and Little Danny had had sex yet, but Maria assumed they probably had. Still, if so, it looked like they understood the need for precautions, and for that, Maria could only be grateful.

Maria could definitely see the irony in her attitude to sex. For, in spite of what she and Annie did for a living, neither of them could ever be comfortable talking about sex or the facts of life, even with each other. And Maria had never veered into this territory when speaking with any of her girls, which really wasn't great of her, she knew, but somehow she could never bring herself to do it.

Sex with men was a distasteful part of her life she didn't like to think about, not even when she was actually doing it. She couldn't imagine ever doing it for pleasure, nor wanting to spend time with any man.

As Maria studied Charity at her engagement party, she thought her daughter's confident demeanour suggested she had learned from her mother and grandmother's past mistakes, and had at the least taken care not to let herself fall pregnant when she was hardly more than a child herself.

Faith and Hope were still to show even the slightest interest in the opposite sex, and so Maria hoped they were late starters on the actually-having-sex front, and perhaps this indicated that she had done something right in her mothering of all three girls.

As people at the party moved on to their second and third drinks and the volume of the chit-chat rose, Charity and Little Danny lapped up the attention everyone showered upon them.

Maria knew she'd have hated being in the limelight like this, but Charity was clearly in her element as she constantly held out her left hand on which the diamond ring was now sitting proudly so that everyone could get a good look.

Maria had put her foot down about Charity wearing the ring to school, saying it was far too valuable to risk getting lost in a classroom. Charity had seen the sense in that and so this was the first time she'd been able to show it off to her pals.

Little Danny looked on proudly, an arm protectively round his fiancée's waist.

'Little Danny's very good with 'er,' Maria said to Lisa. 'There's not many young lads that would be happy to be bombarded with talk about rings and dresses as 'e's putting up with right now.'

Lisa studied her son almost as if she had never really seen him before. ''E's going into these summer 'olidays with something of the boy still about 'im, but by the time they walk down the aisle at Easter, 'e'll be a man,' said Lisa. 'I see 'im changing every day – and Charity is good fer 'im as she pulls 'im back from being too much, and through 'er, 'e's gaining a bit of confidence as 'e's shyer than 'e likes us to think.'

At the back of the room Annie and Joyce were sitting at a table as they watched what was going on.

Annie laughed, and said, 'Not the small do then that Big Danny said it would be.'

'It's not. And there's a large range of people 'ere too,' Joyce pointed out. 'Big Danny's clearly pulled out all the stops. This'll be his way of thanking a few people for favours and fer reminding others they shouldn't mess with 'im. That table over there is a family that runs a protection racket to do with local pawnbrokers, fer instance; those on the other side are something to do with backhanders to the council, I've heard. They're in tarmac, and have won a big contract through greasing the right palms. So I'm told.'

'And he's a copper,' said Annie, nodding towards the Rover-driving man she had occasionally seen at Other Home, who was sitting at another table.

'That table's all the law,' said Joyce, and she and Annie watched a man carrying a tray of assorted beverages come back from the bar and set it down in front of these drinking-buddy policemen, but not before he'd stopped to drop off to Charity what looked like a gin and tonic and Little Danny a pint.

Annie tried not to dwell on Charity's hangover that would be coming the next morning, and was glad she'd bought some aspirin from the chemist to have in as it looked like these would be needed. Maria had had the conversation that morning with Charity about pacing out the alcohol, but it didn't seem as if Charity had been taking much notice.

Lisa and Big Danny were excellent hosts though, it had to be said. They kept circulating to make sure everyone was happy as they urged people to go to the buffet and fill their plates, reminding anyone who looked a bit uncertain that all the booze was on the house and they ought to go up now as the comedian would be starting in a minute, and the DJ when he'd finished.

Maria came and sat down as she said to Annie and Joyce, 'Big Danny's going to rue the day he said 'e'd run a full bar. Look at how everyone's knocking it back, those coppers especially.'

'Not as much as 'is poker pals over there,' said Joyce. 'Even I'm impressed with 'ow much they're managing to put away.'

At one point Big Danny clapped his hands loudly together for quiet, and asked everyone to raise a glass, but before he got as far as the actual toast, Lisa stopped him with an "Old on, Dan,' and she ran to fetch Maria, ignoring her shaking her head.

Lisa grabbed Maria's arm and dragged her across the room to stand in front of everyone at her side as Big Danny toasted the happy young couple.

'Just what she was dreading,' Annie whispered to Joyce, 'as yer know 'ow Maria hates a fuss, especially in front of anyone outside the family.'

'She shouldn't worry. Everyone's too pie-eyed now to pay much attention,' Joyce murmured back. 'And Faith's gone 'ome already to finish her essay, and 'Ope's 'aving a crafty fag out back, and so it's only you and Charity from 'er own family watching. And nothing's going to get Charity down today, not even 'er mum looking daggers.'

'Maria won't like these strangers staring at her, all the same,' Annie muttered. 'Yer know 'ow self-conscious she feels.'

And Maria's instinct to be cautious over drawing attention to herself wasn't silly, as it turned out.

For when Big Danny went to the gents an hour or so after his toast and was just about to unzip, he overheard the man standing at the urinal next to his, a bookie called Frankie the Fish, giving a grunt of humour and then saying to the man on his other side, 'Oi, did yer see the state of that bint as Dan did the toast? Face bashed and slashed. And that eye! A right scary creature. 'Ideous! Clearly a prossie, but who'd want to go with 'er?'

Big Danny knew from Frankie's tone of voice that he hadn't realised his host was standing right beside him.

And Frankie the Fish's face was horror-struck as Big Danny laid one of his massive hands on his shoulder, and then swung him around to face him.

Big Danny placed his elbow under Frankie's jaw, and menacingly forced him back against the wall where he held Frankie the Fish pinned against it. A final dribble of piss dampened Frankie's knee but neither he nor Big Danny took any notice.

The man Frankie had been talking to took just one quick look at the size of Big Danny up close and his angry face, and quickly made himself scarce, leaving the two men alone as the door to the gents crashed shut behind him with a loud bang.

Big Danny didn't speak for what felt to Frankie the Fish like ages, and then quietly Big Danny demanded, 'Say again what you just said, pal. About the *bash* and the *slash*.'

Frankie gulped. He was too terrified to do anything else.

'Are you deaf?' Big Danny asked, still almost companionably. And with his elbow he leaned hard against the man's windpipe as he hissed in his ear, 'Fucking say out loud what you said. Mate. I won't ask again.'

'I said . . .' Frankie managed to gasp at little more than a whisper once Big Danny released pressure on his windpipe.

'Louder.'

Transfixed, Frankie kept staring at Big Danny, but although he opened and shut his mouth he didn't seem able to speak, and Big Danny could see how he'd got his nickname.

Big Danny stepped back a pace, and quick as a flash with his right hand he slapped Frankie's left cheek hard and then back again the other way with the top of the same hand whipping against Frankie's right cheek, Big Danny's largest gold ring, the one with a flat coin for the face, slicing a shallow path in the skin across the bridge of Frankie's nose.

'I don't like to be violent when it's my boy's big day. You understand that, I'm sure. In fact, I don't agree with violence. If I can 'elp it, that is. But I don't like to hear what yer said about the mother of 'is bride-to-be. So take this, what's 'appening to you, that I'm 'aving to insist on some manners, and it's right and proper I do so.'

Frankie the Fish closed his eyes at these words of Big Danny as if that was going to make him go away.

'Manners!!!' Big Danny bellowed, and Frankie shuddered.

Big Danny's roar of temper opened the sluice gates then, causing Frankie to scream back, 'She's got a bad face and eye, and yer couldn't pay me to go near 'er. That's what I said.'

'You. Will. Never. Talk. Of. Her. Like. That. Again,' said Big Danny, punctuating each word with a punch to the soft part of Frankie's expansive belly. 'Understand? I know yer boss, and I'm going to have a word with 'im, explaining what yer just said and 'ow fucking *rude* yer are. And so if yer want to keep yer job, if ever that *lady* needs a bet, yer'll do it respectful and yer'll do it fer free, do yer 'ear? Yer'll definitely recognise 'er again, won't yer?'

Doubled over in pain from the punches, Frankie gawked up at Big Danny as drops of blood beaded along the length of the graze down his nose.

'Are you stupid? Do yer fucking 'ear me?' If Big Danny had seemed peeved before, he sounded really angry now, and then he added, 'Those jabs were child's play – do yer want to find out 'ow 'ard I can really go?'

Frankie the Fish trembled and then he shook his head, as with a sigh of disgust, Big Danny gave him a firm push that scooted him along the wall and into the condom machine with his shoulder, such force behind the impact that the large metal outer-casing of the machine hit the tiled floor with a deafening clatter.

'And when yer come out of 'ere, yer'll go straight up to 'er and apologise as if yer very life depends on it,' said Big Danny over his shoulder as he went out, adding, 'That's if yer've got any sense. Frankie the Fish.'

Outside the gents, a still obviously cross Big Danny saw Lisa heading his way down the corridor, and when she was by his side she said anxiously, 'What the flipping 'eck is all the noise, Dan? I were going to the bar and it sounded a right ding-dong as I could 'ear it above the DJ, and I knew it were your voice.'

'Forget it, girl. Just shitbag Frankie the Fish getting stupid and letting 'is mouth run away with 'im and disrespecting Maria. So I 'ad to give 'im a little slap.'

Just then Frankie the Fish came barrelling out of the gents, some small pieces of toilet paper dotted on his nose to sop up the spots of blood.

And as Big Danny and Lisa looked on, he rushed past them, taking care not to catch either in the eye, and he went straight up to Maria, who then turned a strange shade of magenta and sat with an open mouth as he leaned down and spoke insistently at her.

'Yer sort 'is runaway mouth?' Lisa said to Big Danny as they watched him.

'Course,' he answered, and Lisa nodded she approved, but then they both stared back at the party, unhappy expressions puckering their brows.

Suddenly Big Danny jumped as a hand was clapped on his back. And he turned to see Taxi Joe, who drove a black cab, with his wife Lissa on his arm.

'Thanks, mate – excellent do, and the two young 'uns look like peaches,' said Taxi Joe. As his own partner Lissa disappeared into the ladies, he linked arms with both Lisa and Big Danny, laughing and saying, 'Honestly, some people. Yer can't credit it! Yer'll never guess what 'appened in the back of my cab this morning . . .'

And by the time Lissa had returned from the ladies and Taxi Joe had finished his funny story, Big Danny and Lisa were all smiles again, determined not to let Frankie the Fish, or anyone else who shared a similar attitude regarding Maria or Annie, cast a pall on proceedings.

'What was that all about?' a puzzled Maria asked Lisa a few minutes later. 'I don't know that geezer from Adam, and there 'e is right in front of me all of a sudden, saying I can 'ave free bets whenever I want, even if it's terrible odds fer 'im. I only 'ave to give 'im the word. I tried to tell 'im that I don't even like betting but 'e wouldn't listen.'

'No idea. That's Frankie the Fish, and 'e probably just wants to get on yer good side, now we're all going to be family,' said Lisa in a reassuring voice. 'Now, I spy Father

O'Reilly sitting there all on 'is lonesome, and I promised 'im a dance, and so I'm going to call it in.'

Maria didn't look convinced by Lisa's explanation as she watched her friend totter away on her sky-high heels towards the priest.

Something had happened, Maria knew, and it seemed whatever it was, Lisa didn't care to elaborate.

Maria glanced towards Big Danny, but he was the epitome of bonhomie as he chatted to the table of coppers as if he hadn't a care in the world, and then roared with laughter as the detective Annie had recognised said something funny, and another popped a giant cigar into the breast pocket on Big Danny's jacket and then patted the pocket a couple of times.

And of Frankie the Fish there was now simply no sign at all that Maria could see.

She watched Joyce and Annie dancing in front of the DJ with a puzzled look on her face, and then Charity and Little Danny found her and asked her to dance with them.

But although this was the very first time ever that Maria had danced, in either private or in public, the sensation was dulled by the inescapable feeling that she had just swerved an unknown threat that wouldn't have done her any favours.

CHAPTER TWENTY-ONE

Stepney, East London, 1981

First thing in the New Year, disaster struck.

Somehow both Big Danny and Little Danny managed to get themselves arrested on the same night, and they were taken to the same police station, one just outside the Stepney borders.

It was a coincidence that they had both been nabbed that night, but it sent everyone into a frenzy as the wedding was going to be on Easter Saturday, which was 18 April, and there was no guarantee that Charity would have anyone to walk her down the aisle as Big Danny was going to do this, or that she was even going to be able to have a bridegroom at her side.

Lisa was an old hand at court appearances, both from the viewing gallery and having appeared in court herself, as she had watched Big Danny being given several prison terms previously, while he'd been found not guilty on a few other occasions. But even Lisa looked worried about the timing of these arrests.

When the news first came through of them both being apprehended, Lisa was less concerned about Big Danny as she knew that he would know the score and probably had favours he could call in, and so she thought he'd handle himself well over at the nick in the immediate aftermath of his arrest.

But Little Danny was another matter, Lisa felt, and so she organised the best brief she could afford to represent both Dannys over their interviews and charges.

Understandably Charity was beside herself when Lisa knocked on the door early one frosty morning during the first week of January to break the bad news.

'Little Danny is at the nick right now. 'E's got 'is brief with 'im, and the brief will ask for bail, and if 'e's charged and taken to court, it'll be at the youth court. It's his first time at the nick, but he was caught in an offie after hours with a wodge of cash, and the brief said although it's a first offence and 'e's young, the fact it was two thousand pounds probably means a custodial sentence, although probably not fer too long,' explained Lisa. 'Yer mustn't fret too much, Charity.'

'But what about the wedding?' bawled Charity all the same, and then she wouldn't be consoled, no matter what anyone said to her.

And when Faith tried to come over all lawyerly and offer her sister advice, Charity looked at her with such a livid expression that Faith, normally immune to her sisters' emotions, stopped speaking immediately.

'Come and sit down, Lisa, and have a cuppa,' said Maria. 'What on earth was he doing? Little Danny was here last night when we left for work, and we didn't go out until about nine.'

'The brief told me just now that 'e got it into his 'ead 'e wanted to buy Charity a flash piece of jewellery as a wedding present, and that 'e thought an off-licence would likely 'ave a lot of money on the premises after Christmas and everyone seeing the New Year in. And Little Danny wasn't wrong in that. But 'is mistake was that 'e didn't do it on Big Danny's safe patch, and so when 'e were nicked, there were no way our Little Danny could avoid getting 'auled off,' Lisa explained. 'But the brief says the fact Little Danny waited until gone midnight, deliberately choosing when no one was on the premises, will 'elp 'im in court.'

'What about Big Danny?' Maria asked.

'And as luck would have it, 'e were doing a favour for a mate by delivering a car from Tower Hill to out Wanstead way, but it was an E-type Jag, and the police were looking fer it as it'd been stolen to order, although not by Big Danny as 'e's not into lifting vehicles. Anyway, uniform stopped 'im, and the brief says that 'e probably won't get bail as the car is said to be worth thirty thousand pounds, and of course 'e 'as a record. I know Big Danny won't say who put 'im up for the job, and as it were Whitechapel police who nicked 'im, they won't make it go away.'

'Oh Lisa!' cried Annie. 'That's a shocker. Are you OK?'

'Don't worry, I'm fine. Dan and I always expect that 'e'll serve a bit of time every five years or so, and 'e were only saying over Christmas that 'e's 'ad a good run fer 'is money, as it's been fourteen years since the last time. And Little Danny knows the drill in theory now 'e's been working full-time for 'is dad since leaving school, although the brief's going to argue leniency for a first offence in his case,' said Lisa. 'The real issue is the wedding . . .'

And at the word 'wedding' Charity let out another anguished wail.

Nobody could work out whether the wedding should be cancelled or not, and so they decided to sit tight for a while, and wait to see how the next steps unfolded.

Father O'Reilly's lack of surprise or censure suggested to Annie and Maria that he'd been in similar situations with other members of his congregation many times before. He advised everybody not to let silly thoughts run away with them that might have no basis in reality, and instead they should pray and hope for the best, and so that's what they all did.

The brief had a word with Big Danny's friendly police buddies, who were able to pull a few strings and get the cases scheduled pronto.

Little Danny was allowed bail, and then when he pleaded guilty in youth court four weeks after his arrest, he was sentenced to four months in Borstal, the judge saying that the sentence would ordinarily be longer because of the size of the theft, but that because he had been so remorseful, there was no suggestion violence had been planned, and seeing as he had a settled future lined up with his marriage and a secure job, the judge was happy to give a shorter sentence than he might otherwise have done.

With time off for good behaviour, Lisa calculated Little Danny should manage to get a release date a fortnight before the wedding.

'This means no fighting or giving any lip,' said Lisa, 'and keeping yer nose clean, no matter what. You 'ear me, Danny? No getting into trouble . . .'

Everyone had been allowed to see Little Danny in a cell beneath the court as he waited for the transportation to Borstal.

Little Danny nodded that he understood his mother's instructions.

'I'll wait for you!' Charity cried dramatically when an official came in to tell them they had to go.

'Babe!' was the only thing Little Danny could say, his eyes welling up.

'Charity, he'll be out in eight weeks,' groaned Faith with a sigh. 'Get over yourself. It's not long, and he's only being sent to Kent.'

'It feels like it's for ever,' sobbed Charity. 'And where 'e'll be in Rochester is *miles* away – I don't know how I'll bear it.'

Faith and Hope caught each other's eyes and shook their heads in embarrassment at their sister.

Big Danny appeared at the local magistrates court, and the magistrates promptly referred the case to the crown court to deal with, the district judge saying the case was too serious for his court as they took a very dim view of expensive vehicles being stolen to order by a big car-theft ring, and that consequently Big Danny would be held on remand until it came back to court.

It felt very odd and unsettling to the two Senrab Street households to suddenly have both Big Danny and Little Danny absent.

Big Danny pleaded guilty in mid-March at the crown court, and was sentenced to six months in prison. But Lisa worked out that, provided nothing untoward happened, with time already served, he'd be out two days before the wedding.

It was a tight squeak, but he should be out in time.

It looked like there was a fighting chance the wedding would go ahead. Everyone knew though that should Big Danny not get the release date that Lisa thought he would, there would be a postponement of the ceremony as nobody would want the wedding to go ahead without Big Danny there and walking Charity down the aisle.

The prison Big Danny was sent to was in Nottingham, and Lisa said, as prisons go, this one was rumoured not to be too bad and so Big Danny would feel he'd done OK.

The plan previously had been that Charity would move into Other Home full-time once the wedding ring was on her finger, but to keep Lisa company she moved in the evening that Little Danny was sentenced, although she would sleep at home for the couple of weeks before the wedding once Little Danny was back with his mother again.

The minute Charity said that taking her things next door was what she wanted to do, and Maria had agreed to the plan, with indecent haste Faith and Hope set to re-organising the bedroom the three of them had shared for all those years. It had come to feel oppressively cramped in recent years.

Indeed, Faith and Hope were so eager to divvy up the space that Charity's narrow single bed had taken up, that they even helped carry Charity's clothes and bits and pieces next door. Then her bed was dismantled and squeezed into the loft. Charity would have to sleep on the sofa in the living room in the final run-up to the wedding, and she said she was very happy to do this.

Maria and Annie didn't work for the first couple of nights that Charity was no longer there – they realised that it felt oddly quiet not having her in their house, and so they just couldn't face the idea of being out on the streets, especially as the country was caught in a cold snap of weather that felt like winter's last gasp.

Faith and Hope didn't share their mother and grandmother's sense of upset, and they didn't seem to miss Charity at all.

Instead they were very obviously delighted to have the shared bedroom to themselves and, although Maria knew their room had always been snug on space for the three sisters, she couldn't help but be rather taken aback by just how self-interested Faith and Hope had shown themselves to be.

While she and Annie had always been content to cling closely to one another, and although her three girls clearly loved their family, Faith and Hope seemed to be much more forceful about embracing their own futures than Maria could ever have imagined being, clearly yearning for their own independence and doing what they could to achieve it.

Maria felt torn about this.

It was good to see her girls determined not to settle as she had, but she couldn't help wishing they embraced a bit more the warmth of the love and support she had always had with Annie. She wondered if they would be the losers in the long run, and she crossed her fingers that they wouldn't be.

CHAPTER TWENTY-TWO

Taxi Joe was waiting outside HMP Nottingham with the engine running, along with Lisa and a cool-box of treats on the black cab's back seat on the day of Big Danny's release, all ready for the happy couple to enjoy a bottle of bubbly and some smoked salmon and cream cheese bagels from Whitechapel as they were whisked on the long drive all the way back to Stepney.

Annie and Maria ran outside to give Big Danny a hug when the taxi pulled into Senrab Street and drew up outside the house. Taxi Joe gave a thumbs up to show everything had gone to plan.

This didn't stop the two women and Big Danny and Lisa all looking at each other seriously for a moment, and then they burst out laughing, as it meant the wedding could go ahead after all exactly as planned.

Charity had been over on Commercial Road getting her nails done, and as she came home she squealed with joy when she saw Big Danny standing in the street, running towards him with the heels of her white pixie boots frantically click-clacking along the pavement.

Then a car pulled up, and Big Danny leaned in for a quick chat with the driver, who was the mate he'd done the favour for over the E-type Jaguar that had led to him being banged up, Big Danny never having breathed a word about who it had been.

'Lisa, you'll never believe this,' said Big Danny as he stood up to put an arm around his wife as together they then watched the car drive off. ''E's only just said the newlyweds can 'ave two weeks at his own expense in his timeshare in Marbella as a honeymoon thank you for me not dropping 'im in it. And, 'e says, why don't 'e and I start a new business?'

'What sort of business?' asked Lisa.

'A lucrative one, 'e says,' Big Danny answered.

The wedding went off without a hitch, and a little over a month later Little Danny and Charity set off for their fortnight in Marbella once their passports had come through.

Neither Annie nor Maria had been abroad before, nor flown in an aeroplane, as all summer trips and holidays as the girls grew up had been spent in a caravan in Southend in Essex, where the inevitable rain on the caravan's roof would sound deafening. All the same, they weren't sure whether to be envious or not.

'Remind me, where are they off to?' Joyce had asked when she came round for a fish and chip supper the night before Charity and Little Danny left.

'Marbella,' Maria said. 'They'll be staying in a villa. Apparently there's a swimming pool they can use, and lots of bars nearby.'

'Ah yes, you did say. Very grand. Lots of criminals there in Marbella,' Joyce replied. 'The Sunday red-tops always call it the Costa del Crime instead of the Costa del Sol.'

'Our two shall feel right at home then!' said Annie, and the three women looked at each other and then laughed.

'All grown up now. Times change,' said Annie to Maria, the next morning as at the crack of dawn they waved off the newlyweds in the back of Taxi Joe's cab, as he was taking them to Heathrow to catch their flight.

'Thank God that they do,' Maria said.

'Let's hope the times are on the up for all of us,' said Annie. 'I can't help feeling we deserve it.'

Maria would have liked to think this could be the case, but she wasn't optimistic. Life had shown her how very hard just getting from day to day could be.

Still, even Maria in her most gloomy moments had to admit that things in Senrab Street did seem the best they ever had.

The three girls appeared to be the happiest Maria had ever known them, and within a couple of months it was clear that Big Danny's new business venture definitely was taking off.

It seemed to involve regularly driving a Transit van down to Dover, getting the ferry across to Calais where it would be loaded up with cheap fags and booze, which would then be sold on the sly under the counter to a string of pubs, clubs, off-licences and corner shops back in London. There'd be a surreptitious drop-off from each delivery back to Stepney to a detective in an unmarked car to ensure that blind eyes would be turned.

And as the weeks flew by, it wasn't long before there was a second Transit, and Little Danny was mugging up on his Highway Code to get his driving licence, and soon afterwards a third and a fourth Transit were acquired.

In fact Big Danny had to take on a small and decidedly scruffy warehouse to store all that was brought back, with a large outside space to park the fleet of vans.

It was on the Isle of Dogs, and two Alsatians – Wolfie and Simba – roamed loose around the yard to deter thieves.

'Daft creatures who just want their bellies rubbed,' Charity called the dogs. 'They look tough enough, but they'd lick somebody to death rather than bite them.'

Fortunately Wolfie and Simba were never put to the test, which told Annie and Maria a lot about the growth of Big Danny's reputation since his stint in HMP Nottingham, as clearly he'd been promoted amongst his peers to the realm of being a person nobody should mess with, even if they didn't already know him personally. Previously it had seemed Big Danny garnered respect, but that seemed to have come from a much smaller circle than now.

It was a side to him that Annie and Maria didn't care to ponder too deeply as they felt their heartbeats quicken at the mere idea of any sort of violence, whether against a man or a woman. The way the Waltons had gone on had showed them that career criminals might not be too discriminating in this.

And while Big Danny had only treated them with the utmost respect, that dreadful first day aside, they couldn't see that he would get the obedience he did if it wasn't widely believed he would turn vicious if crossed.

Instead, Annie and Maria concentrated on thinking of Big Danny as the kind and amusing next-door man-mountain of a neighbour they always saw, the person who always had their backs.

And they took care never to enquire too deeply with either Lisa or Charity into the intricacies of his business.

So, in theory, the selling-on of illicit smokes and drink was a simple idea.

But such a lucrative one, all the signs seemed to say.

Best of all, it seemed the perfect victimless crime, and who didn't like that?

Or at least, that is what Annie and Maria told each other, only wondering perhaps in the darkest hours in the middle of the night if it might not be as simple as what they were trying to believe.

PART FIVE

CHAPTER TWENTY-THREE

Stepney, East London, 1990

'Sod it, sod it, sod it,' grumbled Lisa as she banged the telephone handset back into its cradle.

Charity didn't say anything to her mother-in-law but she pressed her knee against Lisa's as a gesture of support, and, after a few seconds, Lisa casually pressed her own knee back against Charity's.

They were sitting side by side on hard wooden chairs in a small, stuffy room, done up in their posh togs and both reeking of eye-watering amounts of Dior's Poison perfume.

Lisa always insisted on fine clothes and handbags, tottering high heels and swathes of real gold jewellery, and not much conversation, when she and Charity worked up west.

They needed to blend in at the best establishments and they couldn't risk standing out too much by casually displaying their East End accents or looking like the sort of people who couldn't afford to get taxis everywhere.

Charity could see that Lisa was cross with herself for having taken a silly risk by first following all of her own rules but then, on a whim, suddenly hoisting a slim but expensive clutch when she had already successfully sneaked a fabulous and ruinously expensive silk top into her bag.

And now Lisa had just found out that the brief who normally looked after the family was on holiday, and there wasn't anyone else in the practice who could immediately come to attend them.

The smartly dressed Harvey Nichols store detective had stopped the two women as they'd pushed open the heavy glass doors and were making their way out to the busy Knightsbridge thoroughfare outside.

They hadn't tried to argue, but instead meekly followed the store detective to a private room presumably kept for just this sort of purpose.

Charity had long wondered what it would feel like to be approached by a uniformed police officer or a store detective. She'd been kiting with Lisa for a long while now, Lisa and her keeping the pick of what they stole, and Lisa selling on the rest to specialist contacts who would then find their own buyers for the high-end goods. But so far they had never encountered any sort of problem, and so Charity supposed that she and Lisa had become over-confident.

At times Charity had had vivid imaginings of various dramatic scenarios of being stopped, usually including her own accelerating heartbeat, before she was thrown hurriedly to the ground as people shouted in her ear, and then her hearing the clicks of the handcuffs being slapped around her wrists.

The reality of the quiet 'Excuse me, madams, but I think you might have made a mistake and not paid for all the items in your bags, and so will you accompany me please so that we can sort it out?' had therefore felt to Charity very much an anti-climax.

She'd peered up and down the street for the Black Maria waiting to cart them away, but there wasn't one. Instead there was a doorman looking on, his legs apart as if he were ready to lunge at them should they try to make a break for it, but nobody else was paying any attention. It was all handled in an exceptionally discreet manner.

Once they were out of sight of any customers, Lisa sweet-talked the store detective into letting her make a telephone call, even though this hadn't come to anything at the legal practice, and then Lisa's suggestion that she be allowed a second call had been refused.

Now, as the store detective telephoned the local police station to request a uniformed officer come over, she gave Charity and Maria the sort of stern look that told them she'd seen it all before.

Recognising that they had to see this next bit of the process through, they both leaned back in their chairs with a sigh as they accepted that it wasn't worth making any sort of fuss.

Indeed Charity knew it was only a matter of time before the store detective went through her own handbag, specially chosen because of its sky-high price, which gave her the gloss of affluence, and naturally its extremely generous proportions had had a role to play too.

So Charity rummaged at the bag's bottom and then retrieved the pair of gold sandals she'd filched from upstairs. She gently placed them on the surprisingly shabby table in the cramped room that was such a far cry from the luxurious gleam of the swanky store's nearby shiny-marbled sales floors.

The store detective moved the shoes over to her side of the table and studied their unworn soles and heels, and then she looked pointedly at the store's bag that remained at Charity's feet. Charity passed it across, lifting out the sales receipt, which was immediately matched with the shoe box inside the carrier and the box's contents, everything then handed back with a, 'For now, madam, but don't get your hopes up.'

Lisa raised an eyebrow so slightly and pinched her lips fleetingly. Charity knew this was Lisa acknowledging that Charity had done well to take the first pair of sandals without even Lisa being aware of what her protégé had just accomplished.

Charity responded with the tiniest shrug of acknow-ledgement, and she knew that later on their way home she'd enjoy telling Lisa it had been simple distraction that had won the day.

She had confused the assistant by trying on multiple pairs of sandals, making sure the boxes and unwanted shoes were scattered well about her as she'd strutted up and down in front of various mirrors, before she had got up to pay for the pair she was legitimately buying.

A casual push of the empty box towards a pile of boxes building up close to another equally demanding customer was the sublime finishing touch, a deft nudge with a heel as she went by obscuring the box in the midst of the others.

Charity's kiting skills were now on the verge of surpassing those of Lisa, her very skilled teacher, they would probably both agree.

After waiting a while to make her request to make the store detective a bit more amenable, Charity was allowed to telephone Faith. Faith would be cross with her, but she would help, Charity was sure. Family was family, when all was said and done.

Faith was *very* cross about it all as it turned out, as she said once she'd heard her sister out, 'For fuck's sake, Charity, what on earth were you thinking? You should just have bought the effing shoes, or gone without. It's not like you don't have shoes up to your ears at home. And you should have phoned someone else to help you. Lisa must have a telephone directory of crooked solicitors just waiting for her to ring them.'

Charity knew that because Faith had sworn, and was being mean about Lisa, she was definitely peeved.

Normally these days, Faith spoke at all times in the modulated manner that sounded just like all the other highly educated, upper-middle-class people with whom she worked in chambers. And the fact that just for a moment while at work she'd forgotten herself enough to allow her roots to show through her carefully curated work veneer definitely signified a flash of temper, probably as she was big these days on obviously distancing herself from the criminal leanings of those in Senrab Street.

She wouldn't take kindly to this clear reminder that while she might be squeaky clean in her own behaviour, the same couldn't be said for the rest of the Wills family, or the household next door to which the Wills clan were inextricably linked.

'I know, Faith. You're right, of course. But, well, me and Little Danny, we're back to Marbella for a quick week in a fortnight, and I couldn't make my mind up over the shoes as I got silver for our last visit, but really wanted the gold this time. And I did *buy* the cheaper ones,' explained Charity, as if that made everything better.

'Ach, Charity! Big mistake. Not a word from now, and I'll find a solicitor I can send over to deal with you two. I'll make sure it will be the most expensive one I can track down, and it goes without saying that the bill shall rest with you and Lisa,' said Faith drily, and she hung up before Charity could say anything else.

*

Sitting with Annie, Maria and her sisters that evening to tell them all about it, Charity showed off the sandals she had bought legitimately, and after they had been dutifully admired, she explained that once the police officer had arrived, then she and Lisa had been separated.

Charity had ended up with a mere slap on the wrists in the form of a caution as it was her first offence and she claimed with the most innocent expression on her face that she could muster that she had never done anything like this before. She had no idea at all what had come over her all of a sudden, and she was really sorry. She had managed to squeeze out a tear or two as the icing on the cake. A pack of lies, all of it, but the upshot was that the caution meant she wouldn't need to go to court.

She had waited for Lisa, who was eventually bailed, the solicitor Faith sent over having said that in view of Lisa's record of shoplifting convictions, Lisa should expect this time around to have a prison sentence when it came to court.

Lisa's record of previous suspended prison sentences and fines could be argued by the prosecution not to have worked as a deterrent to her behaviour, the solicitor had explained, and so now the courts would likely deem it time Lisa faced a more severe punishment.

In theory the maximum sentence for theft that she could be given was seven years in prison, but Lisa would almost certainly end up with a much shorter sentence than that as the judges were told in judges' rules not to give any more than a three-year sentence for shoplifting convictions.

Lisa had expected to hear exactly this, apparently, and was much more irritated at being caught, rather than concerned about a looming prison stint, Charity said to her family.

She added, 'The worst of it is that my bloody sandals were on sale, it turned out, and so I wouldn't have wanted them if I'd known that. The flipping cheek of Harvey Nicks, they even asked me if I wanted to buy them after all the fuss. And then as we got a taxi home, Lisa said to me she told the brief she'd do a list of 'er other 'oists so she can wipe the slate clean and therefore won't 'ave to do that much more time. She told 'im it would likely mean in excess of a further thirty or so offences to be taken into consideration at around this level of haul, and 'e looked quite shocked when 'e found out 'ow much the store was charging for the top and the bag.'

Charity laughed in a way that said she was giving respect where respect was due in terms of Lisa being a career kiter.

She added, 'What that brief doesn't know is that Lisa is only going to go back the last four years, she said to me, and the true figure would likely be four or five times what she is going to say! She says that courts like it when previous offences are taken into consideration as it indicates a sense of drawing a line under bad behaviour, and the police love TICs too as it makes their clear-up rates look good.'

'I suppose it's a good thing she can get it all – more or less – dealt with at one time, and begin again with a clean slate. Though why Lisa keeps on doing it when Big Danny is coining it in as 'e is, is anybody's guess,' said Maria, a puzzled kink to her brow. 'I can't say I approve of 'ow you two go on, and yer know that. But those in glass 'ouses shouldn't throw stones, and so I'll bite it back.'

Charity ignored her mother's last comment, explaining instead, 'Lisa says she needs to keep 'er 'and in, as she could end up the breadwinner for a long while if Big Danny gets arrested again as 'e'd serve a good stretch next time around, most probably. The turnover 'e 'as these days is really big business. Nearly all illegal, but of course 'e wants to 'ave more of it legit.'

'True, from what I've seen,' said Hope. ''E'll need to diversify soon to spread 'is risk, and I've told 'im so.'

Words like turnover and diversify almost made it sound as if it were all above board, Maria thought. And she didn't doubt that there was a lot of money sloshing around at Other Home, to judge by the number of weeks Little Danny and Charity spent in Marbella each year, so much so that Charity had pretty much a year-round tan of which she was very proud and was always keen to show off, rarely wearing tights to cover her brown legs, even in the depths of mid-winter.

While Maria didn't approve of the casual attitude next door to the law, she was pleased Charity and Danny seemed as happy in their marriage still as they had been when they tied the knot. Little Danny, like his father, had proved to be a very good husband, and Charity looked to be thriving, although there was still no sign of any kiddies. Recently Maria had noticed Little Danny's hairline was already thinning slightly at his temples, not that she'd ever have pointed this out, but of course Little Danny was edging towards his late twenties now, with he and Charity celebrating their tenth wedding anniversary next time around.

Maria looked across the kitchen table towards her other daughters.

Hope had stopped her formal education after her A levels – she got straight As – and eventually she had trained as an accountant, although since qualifying she had never joined an accountancy firm nor indeed had any sort of proper nine-to-five job.

Maria thought Hope had taken the accountancy exams simply to prove to her sisters and her mother that she could do them, rather than having any intention of actually working in the field in any sort of formal way.

Instead Hope seemed happy to live quite cheaply at home with Annie and Maria as she considered her next moves, helped by the fact she hardly ever spent anything as she favoured interchangeable black clothing and make-up without much regard for fashion trends, and she rarely went out at night. Maria wasn't quite sure how Hope spent a lot of her time as she was usually upstairs listening to her Walkman, but she never seemed to be bored or frustrated with her lot.

Hope had never signed on and instead when she could be bothered she made a little cash by running an eye through the accounts for Big Danny and some of his mates to make sure that nobody was ripping them off, and then sometimes helping them wash some of their money clean in a legal-looking way. Big Danny now part-owned some launderettes and video rental stores.

Presumably the fact that Hope had had sight of Big Danny's books was why she felt qualified to tell him that he needed to diversify. And the interesting thing, Maria thought, was that Hope had decided to mention this to her family.

Meanwhile, Joyce had suggested to Annie, who had promptly relayed the news to Maria, that the rumour was that occasionally Hope worked the books for a few more dubious businesses than Big Danny would countenance, ranging from chemists to massage parlours, all of which seemed to be running illegal sidelines of one sort or another. Maria worried that Hope didn't seem to share Big Danny's moral code about what was acceptable (jump-ups, and knock-off goods), and what wasn't (selling on legal pharmaceuticals obtained illegally, or all manner of practices that came up under the banner 'sex').

Once, Lisa said to Maria that Big Danny thought Hope very talented, and she could go far, should she put a bit more backbone into her work.

Maria had no idea if Big Danny had any idea about the other people Hope worked for – should Joyce's grapevine gossip be correct, which Maria thought it almost certainly was – other than those who were already acquainted with him business-wise.

But Maria wasn't about to risk rocking anything by blabbing to Lisa about Hope and her other clients for her book-work skills.

Still, Maria couldn't resist passing on to her daughter what Lisa had said about Big Danny thinking her very talented but, in effect, that she didn't work hard enough.

Hope ignored the bit about being talented, and about her lack of work ethic; she just scoffed, 'As if.'

Maria was left uncertain how to respond.

There was something tough and unyielding about Hope, she felt, and she doubted she was alone in this opinion.

But this quality to her daughter's personality told Maria that Hope was probably very good at looking after herself. And so Maria had long ago forced herself to give up wondering what Hope was ideally suited for when it came to supporting herself; not least as Hope would let out an unsympathetic huff should Maria ever dare to hint that sometimes she worried about her.

Probably the sensible thing to do, which wouldn't cause upset, Maria decided, was to say nothing further to Hope on any subject as she was bound to get it wrong as far as Hope was concerned.

She looked at her eldest daughter.

Faith was a quite different matter as she was all too ready to talk about her career and plans, in fact so much so that her family rarely broached the subject with her as it could end up as a very long conversation on something about which only Faith had any real idea.

She kept a base at the family home in Senrab Street, although she didn't seem to be there that often, and even when she was, like her sister Hope, nobody tended to see her much, other than at meal times. She was often studying in libraries at the Inns of Court until late at night, and she also had a desk in Annie's room so that she could work quietly when back in Senrab Street.

Faith's extreme focus right from her very first day at primary school had never wavered.

She had sailed through her law degree at Oxford, exactly as Faith had insisted she would, and subsequently she had completed her vocational training with the Bar Professional Training Course, followed by the 'first six' non-practising period, and she was now well into the 'second six' pupillage part of her barrister's qualification.

And provided she was subsequently called to the bar, something not guaranteed apparently, Faith would then be self-employed, and it would be likely that at first a lot of the work the clerk at her chambers would dole out to her would involve travelling to crown courts around the country to represent defendants in criminal cases of all sorts.

Faith had explained to Maria over supper one night a while back that it was only when she was more experienced that she would be increasingly allocated to cases in London, and a while beyond that before she would be able to up her earnings with any real sense of confidence. And, Faith declared, it would be at that point that she could make her own living arrangements, although if Maria and Annie wanted her to move out permanently before that, then of course that wouldn't be a problem.

Maria had had no idea prior to this discussion that, for many barristers, their earning power was, in their early years professionally, so erratic and actually quite small.

Hope had been amused when Faith had first explained how the pupillage system worked, laughing that Faith had worked very hard over the years but the rewards promised to be surprising slight. 'I could easily earn more than you, should I want to,' Hope finished by saying.

'I expect you could, right now. But you won't be saying that when I'm a QC one day. And of course by then you'll be paying my exorbitant fees when I have to represent you in crown court,' Faith snapped back, 'as I'm sure that whatever you do, it will *never* be legal. You doing the books for that brothel down Commercial Road that you've been boasting about at the Peacock, being a case in point, Hope. Oh sorry, *massage parlour*, I meant.'

Hope opened her mouth to retort, but Annie cut her off with a, 'Girls, please.'

'Faith, you'll always 'ave a bed 'ere,' said Maria, not drawing attention to the Commercial Road brothel comment as this was the first she'd heard of it and Maria was uncertain what she thought about the mere idea of it. 'And so will you, 'Ope. Remember, family comes first, and there's not a single thing I wouldn't do for any of yer in order to keep everybody safe and to give yer the best opportunities,' Maria went on.

Faith and Hope looked at each other, and then Faith said, 'I know that, Mummy. But I'm not going to reach thirty and still be sharing a room with my little sister, that I promise.'

'Yer should be so lucky,' said Hope. 'Yer'll be 'ooked up with some chinless 'Ooray 'Enry by then.'

'Hooray Henry,' corrected Faith as she emphasised the Hs, determined as always that she should have the last word.

Annie and Maria exchanged a look.

Hope always emphasised her Stepney accent when talking to Faith, and Faith never seemed to realise that this was Hope baiting her.

Recently Maria had tried to stop Hope doing this but, unrepentant, Hope had replied, 'Just keeping it real for 'er, Ma. Somebody's got to remind Faith of 'er roots, and that'll be me.'

'Yer can see why she's gone into the law,' Annie said now to Maria with a small toss of her head towards Faith. Annie couldn't help smiling at Hope's intimidating sideways look towards her sister with eyes slyly half-closed, and Faith's studied response of turning her head to look out of the kitchen window as she lifted up her hand as if she were intent on studying her nails.

'Hmmn,' Maria replied, almost as if she wished she couldn't see why all her daughters had turned out to be exactly the sort of people one could have guessed they were going to be, even as children.

Naturally Maria was very proud that each of her girls was extremely clever and had had the brains to embrace an excellent education.

Even Charity was like this. And although she had left school at sixteen, she'd taken ten O levels and got top grades in every single one. Still, Little Danny's results had been poor, and he'd only scraped three passes at minimum grades, and so nobody talked O level results with either of them.

Both Annie and Maria had wondered occasionally how exams might have gone for themselves, had neither of them become pregnant so early. Nobody would ever know for sure, but they each had a strong sense that they had very much missed out on what might have proved to be a golden opportunity.

But so far it was only Faith who had properly embraced the further education that Annie and Maria would have loved to have themselves.

Maria wished Hope and Charity had pushed themselves harder and had been keener to succeed in the everyday world. But there seemed something deep inside the twins that kept pulling them towards the criminal way of doing things, a secret place that ran according to rules every bit as strict as those ordinary people lived by.

Perhaps it wasn't so surprising after all, as what had the girls grown up knowing? If true, possibly this meant that it was Faith who was the cuckoo in the family nest.

CHAPTER TWENTY-FOUR

Meanwhile, both Annie and Maria were still out working on the streets at night, although not as much as they used to, not now that they hadn't had Charity at home for a long time, and with Hope and Faith each occasionally contributing a small amount to the housekeeping.

Money remained tight, but provided nothing too untoward cropped up, they could manage.

Annie was closer to sixty than fifty these days, and Maria had recently turned forty-one.

Both women had taken as good care of their health as they could over the years, and neither smoked or drank, and so – aside from the scars on Maria's face – their looks didn't betray the lives they led. This was probably aided by the legacy Gary and Fred Walton had left both women with: their highly developed sixth sense about dangerous men, and so they'd become adept at avoiding them.

Joyce was nearly seventy, and these days was a maid at the flat in Soho where she'd once been a brass. Both Annie and Maria had noticed her hacking cough when she'd come over these past few months, and they'd made Joyce promise them to cut back on her beloved ciggies.

'I wish you'd come and work as a maid with me,' wheezed Joyce to Annie. 'You deserve a warm and safe place to work.'

'You know why I can't,' said Annie.

'Maria,' the two friends said in unison.

'Well, maybe there'll come a time when Maria won't want to be working under the arches much longer,' said Joyce.

'I'd love to think that,' said Annie.

She and Maria had found over the last couple of years that they'd done better by moving most of their business to the arches between Wapping and Limehouse, where the old London docks and the River Thames rubbed shoulders.

The rise of container ships, which needed deep water dockside to import and export their various goods, had led to the closure of the docks as working ports nearly ten years earlier as the river-bed level hadn't been dropped. And although the shallow-water river trade had subsequently declined too, there was still opportunity there for people like Annie and Maria, and their punters.

It was an area known for its shadows and private corners, and little police attention, and it was this sense of no boundaries that drew the shadier members of society there.

And although gentrification of the area's property and the development of previously derelict plots of land was already well under way, with the result during the day that the sound of building cranes and construction could constantly be heard, when it was dark, it felt that all of this was yet to take a strong hold.

For now, it suited them to patrol this area, Maria especially, as she liked that when she was standing in the lee of the arches she couldn't see clearly many of her clients. And this meant, she knew, that if she couldn't see properly who grunted away as they groped and fondled her, then neither could they see her poor face.

Quite often as a client laboured away, Maria would look up and stare at the red night lights high up on the huge cranes on the building sites.

For some reason these lights instilled in her a sense of both liberty and control, and there'd come a point where she'd barely notice what the men were paying her for.

Then, out of the blue, two things happened to Faith.

She represented her first defendant in London. And she was asked out on a date by a Flying Squad police officer from Peckham.

Everybody went down to Snaresbrook Crown Court to watch Faith in action for the first time on their home ground.

It was a case of domestic abuse, where a woman subjected to years of violence at the hands of her husband had suddenly snapped and knocked him unconscious by throwing an empty saucepan at his head as he came for her.

He'd gone down like a skittle, out cold, and the defendant had immediately called for an ambulance, and she had even rung the police herself.

The husband had recovered quickly in hospital, aside from a lasting dent on his temple, but this hadn't prevented the police charging the woman with two offences, the more serious one of causing grievous bodily harm, and the milder of causing actual bodily harm. Faith and the woman's solicitor agreed pleas of not guilty should be entered on both charges as there were mitigating circumstances.

At Faith's instruction, Annie and Maria dressed in sober clothing Faith thought appropriate for them sitting in a courtroom gallery, while Hope and Charity dressed as they always did, as did Little Danny, Lisa and Big Danny.

Faith didn't glance once at the public seating area as she stood tall in her black robe and white wig alongside the barrister for the prosecution, as the circuit judge in his robes edged with violet entered and sat down with a flourish to make sure that everyone was aware how important he was.

And then once the jury had been called in and settled, the clerk of the court put the charges to the defendant, who was standing nervously in the dock, flanked by two court officers. She pleaded not guilty to both charges.

'She doesn't look overwhelmed by all this pomp and circumstance,' Annie whispered.

'Who? Faith? No, not at all,' Maria hissed back. 'The poor woman in the dock looks terrified though.'

The judge gave them an austere look, and they could see Faith frown although she didn't turn her head their way.

Annie and Maria didn't dare say another word as they were scared that if they did so the judge could ask them to leave his court.

The prosecuting barrister outlined the case, and the evidence against the defendant sounded damning and as if she would definitely end up getting a long prison term.

Faith had told her mother and grandmother that the case would proceed in this manner as it was just a sign of a barrister doing their job. This meant that depending on which side was holding the attention of the court, it would very probably seem as if the case were going that way, and Annie and Maria weren't to read too much into this as it might never become clear to a casual observer whether it was the prosecution or the defence who had the upper hand before the judge summed up and the jury began their deliberations.

But when it was time for the defendant's husband to be called to the witness box to give his side of the story, he was so oafish, boastful and contradictory in what he said that by the time Faith was about to stand up to start her cross-examination of him, a note was being passed to the prosecuting barrister from someone behind him, and consequently the prosecution barrister stood up again and asked if he could approach the bench. There was a whispered conversation between him and the judge, and then the court had to rise while the judge and both barristers left the court, the jury were escorted back to their room and the defendant led from the dock.

Thirty minutes later everyone was back in court, and Annie and Maria watched in confusion as the clerk put the two charges to the defendant again, and this time she pleaded not guilty to the charge of GBH, but guilty to the ABH. The jury was excused and the case adjourned to another day to wait for reports, with bail granted.

Outside the court, the woman who had been in the dock only a few minutes earlier was whisked away by her family, who'd been in the row in front of Faith's family and friends.

And then the Senrab Street group watched while the defendant's boorish husband was arrested on the court steps, him making a lot of fuss about it.

'The 'Eavy Mob 'ave got him now, so 'e'll be wanted for some serious robbing,' explained Big Danny knowingly.

Later that evening, once Faith was home, Maria asked her, 'What was that all about today? Why didn't you get to speak?'

'The husband was such a bad witness on the stand that the Crown Prosecution Service thought they'd never get a conviction by the jury on either of the charges and so they took what we call "a view", helped by the CPS knowing the Flying Squad were waiting outside to arrest the husband on an unrelated matter. And so to cut court costs, horse trading was done, and this meant that the wife pleaded guilty to the lesser charge and the more serious charge was dropped, on the agreement that she will get a short suspended sentence at most once the Social Services reports are done, as there is compelling hospital evidence of his violence against her going back for years,' Faith explained.

'I could have argued that we should still have pleaded not guilty to the lesser charge, but juries can be unpredictable and if they'd – long shot, I know, but a risk all the same – found her guilty, then she'd definitely have got a more severe punishment than what was currently being offered to her. I set before the defendant both options, and she decided to plead to the ABH, saying a suspended sentence wasn't likely to make much difference to her as she was getting divorced and was unlikely to re-offend, and she knew she wasn't going to lose her job over having a conviction for violence.'

Annie thought about what Faith had told them, and then she said, 'But what I don't really get, is if the violence at 'ome 'ad been going on for years, 'ow come it wasn't the husband in the dock?'

Maria instantly thought of how Gary had treated Annie for years, and so was surprised by her mother's question.

'Well, the wife kept going back to the husband, and although in the technical sense the police should prosecute once they know about a violent relationship, the reality is that it's very difficult if they know the wife won't actually get into the witness box, even as a hostile witness, and so they won't waste time and money by pursuing,' said Faith. 'This woman – the defendant – flipped one day, and ended up in court purely as she reported herself to the police; essentially she's a decent character who tried to do the right thing once she'd hurt her waste-of-space husband. If she'd kept quiet and hadn't involved anyone, the likelihood is that he'd have come around at some point with a sore head, and she wouldn't have ended up in the dock.'

Faith looked at them all seriously, and then added, 'It really gets to me that the legal system is much harder on the women who stand up for themselves than it ever is on the violent men around them. They are so vulnerable, but look what happens to them in the legal system time and time again. Men do what they want meanwhile.'

Annie and Maria nodded at each other.

While it wasn't as simple as Faith was currently making out, they felt, the reality was that Gary had got away with ruling the family home with violence for years.

And even though Fred Walton had gone too far with slashing Maria's face, if he'd held back a little and just given her a thump or two, both women could easily imagine a scenario where Maria would still have married him, with

Annie's blessing, as the pull to capitalise on a comfortable financial future and the prevention of Faith being born a bastard would very likely have overridden the concerns about Fred's tendency to be fist-happy.

Faith caught the significance of their shared look, and said, 'I know what you're thinking. You managed to escape, I know. But look at what had to happen first!'

'Don't we know it,' agreed Annie, and Maria let out a slow but tense breath as if words were beyond what she was feeling.

Suddenly Hope cut into the conversation by yelling from the living room, 'Faith, FAITH! There's a detective inspector on the blower who wants to speak to you. DI Tom Jarrett, 'e says.'

Faith blushed a deep shade of crimson and went to take her call, firmly pushing Hope out of the living room and shutting the door in her face to stop any eavesdropping.

'That's not a work call,' said Hope to Maria a second later. 'She never gets work calls at 'ome. And 'e sounded way too matey for it to be anything to do with work.'

'No, I don't think it's a work call either,' said an astonished Maria, who had never seen Faith blush, let alone rush to speak to any man. 'But 'Ope, do me a favour and don't ask about it. She'll tell us when she's ready.'

Hope looked as if she was about to make a smart comment, but when she saw her mother's solemn expression, she changed her mind and said instead, 'OK, but only because it looks like it means so much to you.'

Not half an hour later Faith had changed and run outside when a horn purped, the car speeding away before any of the family had time get to the window to see who the man was who'd made Faith colour up so quickly.

What none of the family knew was that while Faith had been talking to Maria and Annie about what had happened in court earlier in the day, something had shifted in Faith's head as she stared at the deep scars on her mother's cheek and her increasingly cloudy eye with the drooping lid.

It felt to Faith almost as if she were seeing Maria's injuries for the first time ever. And she realised fully at long last exactly how awful it must have been for Maria back when she was first hurt, and how very brave her mother had had to be every single day of her life since then.

A new respect for her mother washed over and through Faith, and she felt changed as a person.

As a woman.

And as a daughter.

If she focused her career towards helping battered women, Faith realised, then she would be able to do a lot of good in the world by helping protect them and their new lives.

And if that was where she was heading, then Faith felt that she owed it to Maria at some point to seek out Fred Walton and at the very least ask him why he had never publicly atoned to Maria for what he had done.

Faith had known his name for a long time, of course. And for many years that had been enough, even though at first she had felt almost desperate that she should engineer a meeting with him.

Fortunately, that impulsive feeling had soon given way to Faith feeling cautious about her father and his role in all of their lives.

Annie and Maria were both solid, sensible women, and if they had excised Fred Walton from their existence, he had to be bad news. Joyce was tight-lipped about him too. None of this boded well, Faith concluded.

And so by the time Faith opened the car door to the passenger seat for her very first date, she felt that aside from possibly having caught the eye of a glamorous detective, this might turn out to be a very apposite meeting should at some point DI Tom Jarrett be amenable to helping her find out more about Fred Walton.

She'd have to take it slowly and suss Tom out, of course, especially as she didn't want to make him probe too much into her own background. Goodness knows what can of worms that might potentially open. Faith gave a small shudder at the thought.

And realistically, Faith understood, Tom might not want to see her again after this date, as she was reading a huge amount into what might be just a fleeting situation.

But Tom Jarrett *might* prove to be keen on her, Faith told herself, and in that case perhaps he could turn out to be the asset she hadn't realised she needed in her life until then. And if so, DI Tom Jarrett might end up the catalyst who'd engineer her actually meeting her own father face to face for the very first time.

'Bevy at the Peacock, and then an Indian?' Tom Jarrett said as he braked and knocked up the indicator to turn out of Senrab Street.

'You bet, Tom,' said Faith, flashing her best smile. 'Thank goodness it's not a school night tonight.'

'Good gal,' he replied. 'I'm liking the sound of this.'

CHAPTER TWENTY-FIVE

A fortnight later, they all went back to court, Knights-bridge Crown Court this time, for Lisa's appearance over the Harvey Nicks shoplifting offence. The judge, Big Danny claimed, was known for being relatively lenient for shoplifting sentences; he was very tough on any drugs crimes though.

'If that judge doesn't end up taking the case, the brief is going to ask for an adjournment,' Big Danny said as they waited for their taxis to pick them up from Senrab Street. 'But with a bit of luck it will all work out in Lisa's favour.'

Hearing this, Maria thought that even the legal system that everyone was judged by seemed open to many biases, which few people were likely ever to mention.

She supposed this was the way of the world, but it seemed odd all the same and yet another thing she had mixed feelings about.

That wasn't to say she didn't like Lisa or want her to receive the shortest possible term in prison, but more that it made her feel uncomfortable that those who didn't know the system or didn't have friends in high places necessarily had the odds stacked against them from the get-go.

Maria knew that she and Annie had been very lucky never to have been arrested for soliciting as they had really bucked the odds, considering how long they had been on the game.

And suddenly Maria understood in a flash that, without a shadow of doubt, Big Danny for many years must have been calling in favours with the police he was friendly with, and that he'd been looking out for them, with these favours offering in effect a lot of protection to herself and Annie. It was good of him certainly, but it made the relationship between the adjacent households that bit more complicated.

It was all so interwoven and hazy, sighed Maria. What seemed to be set in stone or looked on the surface to be perfect, rarely was. Each of her daughters seemed to have been born with this knowledge deep inside them, but somehow she and Annie seemed naturally to be innocent of the ways of the world. And now Maria couldn't tell who were the winners and losers here.

They made their way into Knightsbridge Crown Court, Faith absent from the family group as she was working up in Manchester that day, but everyone else was there.

Lisa stood in the dock, looking calm and unperturbed, and it was the first time Maria had seen her without her gold jewellery, and with her make-up muted and her normally bouncy hair slicked back into a business-like ponytail. She was wearing a crisp white shirt under a navy suit, its pencil skirt that showed off her curves and tight jacket with extravagant shoulder pads being the only hint towards Lisa's usual flamboyant way of dressing.

Joyce was with them this time, and Annie couldn't help but notice a tremble to Joyce's left hand that hadn't been there previously. She looked at her dear friend, and Joyce smiled at her and then linked her arm through Annie's. They'd been through a lot together, the gesture seemed to say.

The theft of the two items from Harvey Nicks was put to Lisa as one charge, to which Lisa pleaded guilty.

Soon, the court heard that the defendant was asking for a further thirty-seven shoplifting cases to be taken into consideration.

There seemed to be a ripple of electricity through the courtroom at Lisa's audacity when it became clear how much the goods she had taken were worth, and in response Maria could see that Lisa was trying not to look proud of how long she'd escaped detection. Her serious expression looked convincing when her eyes were downcast, but when Lisa looked at the judge directly, there was a defiant twinkle beneath her eyelashes that were dark with mascara.

The judge read the Social Services report in silence after the prosecution and defence barristers had set out the facts of the case and the mitigating circumstances, and, as he turned the pages, Maria heard someone cheerfully whisper behind her to a companion, 'All those TICs are going to make somebody's weekly clear-up figures look good,' and a small snigger in reply from whoever the speaker was talking to.

Lisa was asked to stand, and after the judge spoke for a while about her poor history as regards shoplifting and the extraordinarily high value of her thefts, he said then that the situation was partly moderated by her guilty plea, her obvious desire to help the police with accountability for past offences and there never having been any thefts from other than large stores nor had there ever been any hint of violence. Consequently, the total sentence he would impose on Lisa would be fifteen months' imprisonment.

'It's a win! She'll be out in seven months,' Big Danny announced happily as Lisa was escorted from the dock. 'Could 'ave been much worse – she'll be very pleased with that, and so am I. Brief said she'll probably go to 'Olloway.'

Annie and Maria caught each other's eyes, and they raised their eyebrows conspiratorially.

While those at Other Home took prison terms as part and parcel of their chosen way of life, Annie and Maria were signalling to each other that they couldn't imagine anything worse than being sent to prison.

*

Until, that is, Maria made the biggest mistake of her life.

This happened a few weeks later, on 27 December.

The day had started so well too.

Maria and Annie had taken a break over Christmas, and Maria was feeling all the better for it.

This mood had been helped by none of the girls arguing over Christmas, and Big Danny paying for them all on Christmas Day to go en masse for a lavish traditional lunch with all the trimmings at a local restaurant they could walk to, so that everyone could have a rest and enjoy a bevvy or two without somebody having to be the designated driver.

Glasses were raised to toast Lisa's health, and then Faith had a message that Tom was waiting for her outside and off she went, leaving everyone else to crack open another bottle of champagne, champagne that naturally Big Danny had sold to the restaurant.

Boxing Day passed in a feast of television and too much chocolate, and the day after that began with a huge fry-up of eggs and bubble and squeak, and everybody was relaxed and happy.

But by lunchtime, it was clear that Annie and Joyce had both been struck down with bad colds and needed to retreat to rest up in bed, and so this was how that evening became the first time for many months that Maria had worked on her own.

Annie urged her to stay at home for another night but Maria thought that if she did this, then money worries would likely mean Annie refusing to stay lying down for long enough to get properly better, and Maria wanted her to recuperate until she was fully well, secure in the comfort that Maria had taken care of things and in the knowledge that she, Annie, must concentrate on getting well rather than worrying about household expenditure.

Well-intentioned thoughts, but once Maria was outside in her winter coat, she discovered the weather was thoroughly nasty, being cold and alternating between sleeting and driving rain.

But she told herself there'd probably be a break in the weather and, in any case, she'd find shelter at the arches, and off she plodded in the direction of Wapping.

It was depressing that nearer to the river the weather felt even worse as now the strong winds seemed to be blowing the cold and wet towards wherever Maria was standing.

It wasn't a surprise that there weren't really any punters about, which aside from most probably not wanting to go out for a thoroughly dispiriting soaking, she supposed was because too many of them had spent up in the run-up to Christmas and were now feeling the pinch of festive spending and were very light of pocket.

Maria felt similarly poor, and that she was only there as she'd hoped to bump up her own coffers by working tonight, so it just didn't seem fair.

She stared upwards at such a dark low night sky that only promised more of the same grim weather, and Maria felt cross with herself that in her determination to do the right thing, she hadn't banked on the inhospitable weather or the post-Christmas gloominess, and so she couldn't stop her spirits plunging.

As her saturated collar from the damp weather began to funnel icy water down her backbone, Maria began to shiver.

She realised she had a thumping headache and that she felt somehow simultaneously too hot and too cold, making her think she may well have picked up whatever it was that had forced Annie to her bed.

Maria gazed about. It was quiet, and she couldn't hear or see anyone else around. In fact, all she could hear was the rainwater swirling into the metal drain she was standing near.

There didn't seem any point in staying out any longer, and as she began to trek back towards Commercial Road, Maria gave a tight-lipped smile at the thought of the giant mug of strong builders' tea she would be treating herself to the moment she got in, and the short work she would make of a round of hot buttered toast.

Suddenly a hand snaked out of an unlit doorway and caught her elbow, jerking Maria to an abrupt halt.

'Doing business?' the man growled.

'Yes. Yes. Um, I mean, no, I'm not,' said a flustered Maria.

His grip tightened on her arm, and he stepped out of the doorway to stand directly in front of her in a threatening way at the precise second the weather broke enough for a full moon to move out from behind a cloud.

Even in the imperfect light of the moon, Maria was horrified by what she saw.

Her prospective client looked as if he'd not had a bath for weeks, and his wispy long hair was lank and greasy. The worst thing of all though was the way he smelled, which was a gagging mix of lack of personal hygiene and the rancid smell of a long-term alcoholic who had clearly been topping himself up with copious amounts of whiskey earlier in the day.

He stumbled slightly as he continued to grasp her arm, his head suddenly swinging towards hers and his foul breath hot in Maria's face, even though she tried to turn away. Clearly drunk, he leered at her and Maria saw the terrible state of his teeth, brown and furry with plaque.

He was holding her arm so tightly that it hurt, and Maria didn't see how she could get away from him easily.

She needed to buy some time while she worked out what to do.

'Nice Christmas?' she asked.

'Not so as you'd noticed,' he replied sourly. 'We were still in the North Sea. I only landed this morning.'

He burped, and Maria had a gust of putrid breath blasted in her direction.

Goodness knows what he was doing here, Maria thought, assuming he was either a sailor or a fisherman who'd have disembarked miles away.

'Twenty pounds,' she said, hoping she'd said enough to put him off.

He looked as if he didn't have two pennies to rub together, and Maria really hoped that this was the case.

'Afterwards,' he said, and very roughly he pulled her into the doorway, Maria's head hitting the bricks painfully, the man firmly pushing his knee between her legs as he twisted her in front of him, forcing them wide apart.

As always happened if anyone tried to manhandle her, Maria found herself beginning to freeze, and she thought perhaps the best thing to do was to just go with what he wanted. Then she could get her money and it would all be over and done with very quickly.

She tried to shake his grasp loose but he wouldn't let up on his grip, and this was making Maria's pain in her head feel excruciating.

She told him he'd need to stop holding her arm like that, and then in a chink of moonlight falling on his lower half, she saw the worst thing. This was that he wasn't yet hard, and the soft nub of the head of his penis was poking an inch out of his undone flies.

This was the worst situation, as if a punter couldn't perform, it could quickly turn into a situation that was very unpredictable.

The man pulled her coat apart and began roughly to paw at her breasts. And then he moved a hand to her cheek. His fingertips and knuckles were rough and calloused, and smelt disgusting.

But the minute he discovered the undulations of scars on Maria's cheek, he said in a complete change of voice, 'You beaut,' and as he ran his horned knuckles over the deep grooves of her face and sighed with pleasure, to her horror Maria realised he was certainly not flaccid any longer.

And for the first time ever, she snapped. She hated that he'd been aroused by touching the scars on her face, and she loathed it that he hadn't cared whether she wanted their commercial transaction or not.

Enough was enough, Maria thought, as a new resolve swept through her.

She had an idea.

'Here, let me help you,' she said as seductively as she could, as she reached for his belt.

He relaxed his hold on her arm and gave the most hideous throaty laugh as clearly he thought Maria was about to give him oral sex.

Instead Maria rolled him, forcing his trousers and underpants down, the pants stiff with the filth of weeks, so that they bunched around his ankles.

Although she was vulnerable leaning down before him with her head and neck exposed in a way that she couldn't protect should this client want to attack her, he still hadn't cottoned on and instead he put out his hands to support himself against the wall in anticipation of what he thought Maria was about to do.

Quickly Maria squeezed both of his trouser front pockets and in one she felt something solid.

She reached in and grabbed it, and then she ducked away from under his arm and began to run as fast as she could up towards Commercial Road.

Her rolling of him had taken mere seconds.

The man let out a howl of pure rage.

Maria was by no means a speedy mover, and even though this man was drunk, somehow he managed to yank up his pants and trousers to set off in pursuit.

'You fucking WHORE,' Maria could hear he was yelling as he ran after her.

There was no one around to help Maria, and she knew he'd at the least beat her black and blue if he caught her.

She heard the rasp of his breaths, and the pounding of his steel-capped boots getting closer.

'Fucker,' he screamed. 'FUCKER!'

She despaired.

She was certain now he would kill her given a chance.

Maria had never thought she'd live a long life, but she didn't want to die on a cold, wet road with nobody around and at the hands of the most repulsive person she'd ever seen.

Faith

Then Maria saw in front of her the orange light of a free taxi cab swinging around a nearby corner and she ran right out in front of it, waving her hands in the air.

The taxi's brakes were jammed on, the vehicle squealing to a stop about an inch away from her, Maria's hands on its bonnet and her eyes fastened on those of the horrified driver.

He gave a quick nod.

Hastily, she ran around and clambered into the back.

It wasn't a moment too soon as the revolting man was wrenching open the passenger door on the other side to hoick her out, but Maria lunged for the inside handle and she held on to it with all of her might, even though she was now lying on the floor of the passenger bit of the cab with her feet jammed against the seat to give her leverage.

And the taxi driver drove away so fast that the man was shaken off.

The last sight Maria had of him as she sprang up and on to the back seat to look out of the rear window, and just as the taxi swung around a junction, was a black bundle of clothes lying in the road.

There was a screech of brakes from the car that had been following the taxi as the vehicle's driver tried to avoid running Maria's assailant over.

'Where to, missus?' cried the flustered cabbie, who turned in his seat to look at her.

11

11
11

11

11

'Senrab Street,' Maria managed to stutter, feeling most light-headed. She realised she had been holding her breath, and she took a huge gasp. 'I can't thank you enough – I think you've just saved my life,' she said squeakily, her voice not yet sounding like hers at all. And then she gave in to shoulder-heaving sobs.

''E looked like a right fucker, excuse my French,' the cabbie told her as he stopped outside Maria's front door a couple of minutes later. 'Yer take good care of yerself. And there'll be no charge.'

At this kindness, Maria's sobs became howls as she just stood on the pavement with the cab door still open as the rain turned heavy again, and the cabbie jumped out of the taxi and knocked at Maria's front door.

Annie answered it, and the cabbie helped a distraught Maria stumble to her.

Alerted by the noise outside, Big Danny poked his head out of the door of Other Home. He took one look at Maria and the now worried look on the cabbie's face and, stepping close to him, he reached into his pocket for two twenty-pound notes that he pressed into the cabbie's hand with a, 'For yer trouble. You get off now, and I'll take it from here.'

The cabbie clearly knew who Big Danny was as he said, 'Right, boss,' and promptly made himself scarce before Big Danny had any chance to start to wonder whether the cabbie might have had anything to do with what had made Maria so upset.

In the kitchen, Annie made Maria some strong, sweet tea as Big Danny helped her out of her sodden coat and then gently guided her to a chair. Maria was gasping and crying at the same time, and didn't seem able to catch her breath.

'Whatever were yer doing out working tonight, girl?' Big Danny said kindly as he crouched beside her, the coat discarded on the floor. 'Yer should have been enjoying yourself up the Peacock with Little Danny and your three, as they're all there 'aving a good time and playing darts.'

'Thank goodness they are. None of them need to see this,' said a husky-voiced Annie as she placed the mug beside Maria along with two paracetamol, and knelt down to rub Maria's damp legs with a towel. 'I told yer it wasn't worth yer going out tonight, Maria. Yer should 'ave listened to me, love.'

Then Annie glimpsed something. 'What's that you're 'olding on to so tightly there?' she asked.

'Holding on to?' said her daughter in confusion, her knuckles white and her pupils large.

Maria was clearly in shock.

Annie slowly prised open Maria's hand. 'Why, it's a bundle of money. Whatever 'as 'appened, Maria?'

Annie counted the wad of cash, and then added in an awed voice, 'Lordy. There's nearly two thousand pounds 'ere!'

Maria looked down as she gave in to new tears, silent this time, and Big Danny ran home for a few moments to get a bottle of brandy, pouring Maria a generous slug on his return.

Annie put a blanket around Maria's shoulders, and eventually she was able to get herself back under control.

She drank the brandy, and then the tea – suddenly she was very thirsty – and then, haltingly, Maria told Annie and Big Danny every detail.

'I feel so ashamed, and such an idiot,' Maria finished, wiping new tears from beneath her eyes. 'It's so crackers. Daft! I've never even thought for a second before about rolling a punter. I don't know whatever I was thinking. But 'e was so 'orrible, and I needed to get away. I was terrified of 'im as I ran away. I think he would have killed me. The taxi was a gift from 'eaven.'

'Oh, Maria,' said Annie, pale too at the thought of how badly this could have ended.

Maria sat there taking huge gulpy breaths as one emotion after another hit home.

'Don't take on so, girl,' said Big Danny, as he placed a second large brandy in her hands, then gave one to Annie too. 'Drink up now. And, Maria, you think about what sort of man would lean out of a doorway and then act as he did. You might be a brass, but yer deserve respect, and 'e weren't being respectful, was 'e? No, not in the slight-est, and yer remember that. And what self-respecting man would go down to them arches on a night like this and not expect to get rolled? None of this is yer own fault, yer must know that, Maria. I'm telling yer, the fault is all 'is, and if 'e's lost all his wages, as it looks like, well then 'e only 'as 'imself to blame.'

Maria didn't see it as Big Danny did. Instead she con-sidered herself very much to blame for what had happened, although she appreciated that Big Danny was trying hard to make her feel better.

She felt that, without a shadow of doubt, she had done something very wrong, and the knowledge that she had it in her to stoop so low that she could behave in this way made her feel extremely uncomfortable.

'And, Maria,' Annie said, trying to make the best of a bad situation, 'try not to take on so. Surely it's much better that money has ended up in yer 'and, rather than one belonging to some slimy pimp that beats 'is brasses for every last penny, don't yer think? Yer'll use it well, and a pimp never would.'

Joyce said as much the next day, having forced herself out of her sickbed to come to comfort Maria, insisting that she should stop berating herself and not give the vile man another thought.

Joyce must have been on the blower to Father O'Reilly as he arrived soon after Joyce had left.

Maria did feel better after she and the Father had had a long chat, although once he had gone, after she had pressed into his hand forty pounds for the collection box, she couldn't help but dwell on his final words to her.

'Best you keep a low profile for a while and stay inside,' Father O'Reilly had warned. 'A man as you describe is very likely to come seeking revenge.'

'You think?' said Maria.

'Well, of course I can't say for sure, but if you stay tucked up inside and out of harm's way for a month or two, well, that would just be sensible, wouldn't it?' Father O'Reilly told her.

CHAPTER TWENTY-SIX

One good thing about the unexpected windfall of money was that it gave Maria and Annie some breathing space in the financial sense, and so to keep Maria company at home, Annie didn't work either.

Faith, Hope and Charity were all white-faced with shock when they came home to the news of what had occurred, even though for many years they had had to live with the continual anxiety of what might happen to their mother or grandmother should things go arse over tit with a punter.

Jointly though, they took the decision not to give even the smallest hint that possibly this was the writing on the wall suggesting the time was drawing near when both Annie and Maria should chuck the towel in on their street-corner brassing days. This was because none of the girls wanted to cause an argument or make either woman feel even more anxious than they already were about how they brought their money in, or make them feel that they were getting past it.

Instead, the three girls made sure they each spent more time with their mother. While they were in agreement with this, it didn't mean the sisters were in total harmony.

'Mummy needs our support now,' said Charity to her sisters.

'She does,' said Faith. 'But if this isn't a lesson that she needs to get off the streets, then I don't know what would be. If she didn't work, then it would mean Gran wouldn't either. And then that would make Mummy happier too. They need to find something else to do.'

'Yeah,' said Hope disparagingly. 'That's very well and all that, Faith. But yer forgetting that they like to eat, and this is how they pay their way. They're both too old to do anything else. Maybe yer should just let them alone, and allow them to lead their own lives without the benefit of yer opinion. Something they've been doing for years perfectly well on their own. You have yer way, and yer'll be taking away their independence. And that's dangerous fer them too.'

'Oh, just shut up, Hope,' snapped Faith. 'If you don't have anything good or constructive to say, then don't say anything at all.'

'No, *you* shut up, Faith, you sanctimonious cow,' Hope replied.

Charity tried to put an end to it with, 'I've an idea – you both shut up.'

'Fuck off, Charity,' Faith and Hope said in unison, and it was the first time they'd agreed on anything since they'd left the Peacock.

Despite the sniping between the sisters, the upshot was that over the coming days Maria couldn't remember a time when she had felt so loved and cosseted by her family, even if Faith was very keen that the rumour mill outside of Senrab Street was clamped down as much as possible so that her Flying Squad boyfriend didn't get to hear of what had happened to Maria.

For Tom Jarrett and Faith were getting on rather well, albeit in a low-key manner, and the last thing Faith wanted to do was advertise so clearly that she came from a family of brasses who lived next door to some local criminals who seemed increasingly well-known to the law these days.

Faith was still trying to suss out the lay of the land and whether there was even the slightest possibility that at some point DI Tom Jarrett might be able to help her with her questions about Fred Walton, but now certainly didn't feel the time to so much as think for a second that anything like this should be imminent.

As the days passed, and she began to feel less frightened, Maria thought for a long while about how she should best spend the money from the rolling. Eventually she decided to use some of the cash for a new television for the living room, this one with an infra-red remote control, as everyone could get the benefit of this.

And this meant the ancient black and white set could be connected to the aerial with a new cable that could be fed into Annie's bedroom. It made Maria feel warm inside, the thought of doing something nice for her mother. Annie had rarely been spoilt, and now Maria was delighted that she could make her feel special.

And the rickety double bed that had cost seven and six from a second-hand shop in Whitechapel over twenty years earlier could go. It had clearly been well past its best all those years ago and it had been shared by Faith and Hope ever since, Charity having had a small single bed against the window when she was still living at home as she tended to windmill her legs about while she slept.

The double was replaced by two spanking new single beds and mattresses, Hope's with an angular wooden frame and exceptionally hard mattress and austere thin pillow, and Faith's more comfortable and adorned with a luxurious silk-covered headboard and deep feather pillows.

Father O'Reilly arranged for the collection of the double, and also Charity's old bed, which was taken down from the loft, as he knew a family who'd be delighted with them both.

Everybody told Maria that she should buy herself something nice as a little treat too, but she couldn't bring herself to do so.

She was glad to make the lives of her mother and daughters a little more comfortable, but she felt it would be a travesty of justice and morality should she do the same for herself. She shouldn't have done what she had, Maria believed, and absolutely she didn't deserve to benefit in a personal way.

Faith

It was only as Annie watched the television alone in her bedroom for the first time that a thought struck her.

She realised she had got the wish she'd voiced to Joyce a while back about longing for Maria not to be out on the streets, although this had happened in a terrifying way, and not at all how Annie had hoped.

Perhaps there was some truth in the old saying 'be careful what you wish for', she thought, as the spell of January wet weather continued to sheet in gusts against her window pane.

And she found that she had to pull up her bedclothes, right to her chin, to keep warm as the room suddenly felt very chill.

CHAPTER TWENTY-SEVEN

Stepney, East London, 1991

The financial windfall didn't last for ever, of course, no matter how many jacket potatoes or plates of beans on toast the family existed on to eke out the funds, and the result was that, by Easter, Annie and Maria had to go back to work.

Since they were last there, they noticed a big difference down near the Wapping and Limehouse arches as new buildings had sprung up apace during their absence, and Charity told them it was incredible what was being planned for the Isle of Dogs, with New York-style skyscrapers and a new railway line.

'I don't care what they say, but I still don't think they'll get the yuppies moving in,' said Maria as she stared about her the first day back on the job, and she wiped her finger on the cracked windowsill of a derelict building and then held up the grubby tip for Annie to see as if this backed up her words. 'Nor the big businesses. There's nothing for them to come 'ere for,' she added.

'I'm not so sure,' said Annie. 'I know we've always seen it as a poor part of London, but that's just our thinking and that of other local people like us who've lived here for a while. But Maria, just look around – there's money being poured in. A lot of money. In fact, Lisa told me when I went to see 'er at 'Olloway last Friday that Big Danny's only gone ahead and purchased the land where 'is warehouse is on the Isle of Dogs, and the parking there, plus the lot next door, and I doubt 'e'd 'ave put 'is 'and in 'is pocket like that if he didn't think 'e'd be making a tidy profit from it at some point.'

'I'm not seeing it, all the same. Or next, yer'll be saying that Lisa and Big Danny will want to buy somewhere else to live,' Maria said. 'And it'd be 'orrible if we didn't 'ave our Charity next door.'

Annie quickly tried to reassure Maria. 'Oh, they'll sit tight for a while yet, Lisa says, now they've bought Other 'Ome under the Right to Buy. They'd been there for such a long time, it was a good deal, and they're waiting to see if the value increases. And yer know that Big Danny doesn't like to show any conspicuous wealth unnecessarily that might interest the taxman, and so it suits them to stay in Senrab Street.'

Annie and Maria had also been eligible to buy their house from the council, but the thirty-thousand-pound valuation of the property was well beyond what they could afford, even if they had been able to get a mortgage. But of course the reality was that they couldn't even apply for a mortgage, seeing that they had no declared earnings, and didn't have bank or building society accounts, or savings.

The security of home ownership seemed a pipe dream for the likes of them, and although it gave them a pang of longing as they would love to have the added security of their own bricks and mortar, neither woman could see that changing and so they told themselves they should make the best of what they had and their ability to pay their rent to Tower Hamlets Council.

'No conspicuous wealth at Other 'Ome, apart from Lisa's wardrobe, yer mean,' said Maria naughtily.

'Well, there is that,' laughed Annie. 'But everybody now knows she didn't pay for most of it.'

Lisa was due out of prison in two and a half months, provided nothing stopped her having time off for good behaviour. Somehow neither Annie nor Maria believed for a moment that Lisa wouldn't go back to regular kiting almost immediately. It was what she knew, and what she did. And that would be that.

For the next six weeks or so, Annie and Maria remained very cautious when they were working, but as time passed they began to relax a little. They didn't come up against any trouble and all their regulars seemed glad to see them.

And then, one fine summer's evening, Annie was running late after helping Father O'Reilly and Joyce organise a jumble collection for a sale at the church at the weekend.

Back in Senrab Street, Maria had already left the house for the arches as she had arranged to meet up with a regular, and Annie was just sitting at the kitchen table with her feet up and resting on the seat of the opposite chair for a few minutes as she enjoyed a cuppa before going to join Maria, when she heard the sound of hurrying and then Joyce furiously rattling the front door handle as she gasped hoarsely for Annie to let her in.

Instantly Annie felt sick. Whatever had happened couldn't be good news, she was certain.

She'd only left Joyce not ten minutes previously, and everything had been fine then, other than Joyce looking peaky, not that this had stopped her lighting ciggie after ciggie as they'd talked about Saturday's jumble sale.

Annie ran to the door, and pulled it open to see Joyce clinging to one side of its frame.

'What on earth's 'appened to you?' cried Annie in concern as she went to help her friend inside.

'No, no, it's not me,' Joyce told her, 'it's yer Maria! It's bad, Annie, it's very bad.'

And it was.

Joyce described to Annie how she'd been heading home when an old regular of hers stopped her in the street. His son had just told him that Maria was in trouble down at the arches. There was a man who had been asking about Maria and her whereabouts for nearly a week now, and apparently nobody had liked the look of him, with there being murmurs that the way this man was so insistent on tracking Maria down was too much.

Linda Calvey

And, the lad said to his dad, his mate had told him that Maria had been seen walking to where he was, and nothing about this felt other than really bad news . . .

Annie trusted the instincts of the man's son – one didn't live for years in this area without getting an extra sense for when things were about to go wrong, and this lad had been spooked enough to find his father to warn him.

That was enough for Annie.

She asked Joyce where the lad had seen Maria, and then told her to ring the police.

'What are yer going to do?' said Joyce through the phlegmy rattle of her chest.

Annie gave Joyce a look that said she was going to protect her daughter.

And then she set off to find Maria, running towards the arches as if her life depended on it.

For Maria's did, she was convinced.

Although some punters sought Maria out because of her scars, there was something about the description of this man that sounded too obsessive and definitely a red flag, and this son of Joyce's friend had clearly thought so too.

It hardly bore thinking about.

Annie's blood ran cold.

She forced herself to run faster.

292

CHAPTER TWENTY-EIGHT

Maria had finished with the regular she'd arranged to meet, and she was keeping an eye out for Annie's arrival as she stood in a patch of sunlight, enjoying the warmth on her face.

She hadn't suspected a thing at first.

The man was wearing a grey suit and a white shirt, and spoke politely enough when he came up to her.

Maria didn't particularly want to service another john so soon, but he was making it very easy for her to agree with what he wanted, not least as he offered her twice as much as she usually charged and he even gave her the money up front.

She could see from its slight fraying that his shirt's collar and cuffs had seen better days, and that the fit of the only slightly grubby suit suggested it had almost certainly come from a charity shop and had been bought initially by somebody shorter and fatter. The man's shoes were a bit scuffed, but generally he seemed to be exactly like fifty per cent of her clients, not that she ever looked at them closely these days.

She'd seen so many men over the years that she'd lost interest in knowing what they looked like.

But in spite of this, Maria's first impressions were that the man was cleanly shaven and had recently had a decent haircut. He'd even used some aftershave, and although it wasn't very nice and caught in the back of her throat, this gave her a jolt as she realised that she'd never had a man previously make any special effort to seem attractive to her.

This was going to be easy money, she thought, as she led him to a secluded bit of brick wall so they could have sex as she leaned against it, Maria feeling happy that then she and Annie could go home early as Maria would have earned enough that Annie didn't need to work too.

It was only as the man ran his gnarly knuckles down the side of her scarred cheek as he climaxed with the hiss of the word 'beaut' oozing out from his mouth that Maria realised who he was.

He was the man she had rolled back that dreadful night at Christmas.

Oh no.

How could it be?

Why had she been so stupid to let her guard down, and not pay a bit more attention?

This was a nightmare, brought to life.

And as Maria stood motionless and stared at him in abject dumbstruck horror, his penis still inside her, the man moved his hand to the back of her head and painfully grabbed a handful of hair, and then he gave it a firm yank.

He snarled and Maria remembered the sight of every single tombstone tooth in his fetid mouth.

'Yeah, that's right, bitch,' he sighed in menace as he leaned against her heavily now, his lips so close to her ear on the scarred side of her face as he rubbed his cheek against hers, and she felt him growing hard inside her again at the renewed touch of his flesh against the roughened skin of her cheek. 'You know me now, whore. I made myself look presentable so you didn't go running, and now here we are,' he said and he licked the scars of her cheek, and then he gave himself over to frantic thrusting.

'Here we are,' he repeated, and Maria recognised every ounce of threat in those simple words.

This time it was rape.

She tried to push him away but he was too strong.

'Stop, stop, please,' cried Maria. 'I don't want to.'

He took no notice.

As he banged away he chanted, 'Whore, slag, hooker, tart, pervert, THIEF!' And then he'd go back to the beginning and say it all again.

Maria had never been raped before.

She'd had punters who liked it a little rough, but nothing that compared to this. She'd always felt that those johns were living out a fantasy, and that they would have stopped what they were doing if she'd asked them to. This was very different.

He was pulling her hair with both hands now as hard as he could, and when the tears began to spurt from her eyes, he did it all the more.

'I've looked for you for months, and I thought about you all the time. How sweet it would be when I made you pay. And pay you will over what you did to me. What you fucking did to *me*! You took my money, and you made me a fool. A fucking fool,' he said. 'And when I'm done, I'm going to kill you. Do you hear me? You're about to die, bitch!'

'Please,' pleaded Maria, who didn't doubt he would do exactly what he said, 'I know I did wrong and I shouldn't have rolled you. I can make it up to you. I promise I can.'

He guffawed nastily and then he lifted his head away from Maria. And they looked into each other's eyes.

'If only it were that simple,' he said.

And then he put his head back before nutting Maria on the bridge of her nose with his forehead.

The force with which he connected with her was so much that she heard the crunch of her nose shattering, and saw a spray of blood speckle his face, some of this blood dappling his hideous teeth.

He ran his tongue over his teeth with a smirk, and then he pulled her head to one side and nutted her good cheek, and Maria felt her cheekbone pulverise and some of her own teeth shatter on that side of her face.

And then he took one hand from her hair, leaving the other still entwined in a way that meant she couldn't untangle herself from him, and he reached into his trouser belt at the back to pull out a knife that he held up for her to see.

Still pounding at her with his penis, he lifted the tip of the knife to her unscarred cheek and pressed it in. And as Maria felt the point penetrate her flesh, he climaxed a second time with a groan.

Maria shut her eyes as she expected her throat to be cut, but instead she heard a whump and then to her surprise he lurched back from her a little.

Instantly she felt light and as if she might float up into the air now that his weight was pulling back from her chest.

There was a terrible din going on, but Maria couldn't for a moment make sense of it, and as the sight from her eyes began to tip one way and then the other, she realised she was probably concussed.

Then she began to realise what was going on.

The racket was Annie screaming, 'Yer leave 'er alone!', as she hit the man again and again on the back of his head with an old brick in one hand and a heavy metal scaffolding coupler she must have found lying on the road with her other hand.

Although he was swaying precariously, the man managed to turn around to face Annie.

And then Maria saw the glint of the knife blade as he drove it into Annie's stomach, once, twice and then in a frenzy.

The force he used was so hard that Annie had to take a step backwards each time.

Blood was pumping furiously from her belly as she stood there and her eyes sought Maria's, and Maria stared back at her mother in abject terror at what she'd just seen.

The man teetered a few paces away from Annie, and then tried to turn back towards Maria to give her some of the same, but his knees gave way and he crashed unconscious to the ground as the head wound from the scaffolding coupler began to bleed, the knife falling from his hand and skittering away to rest in the gutter.

Maria forgot her own injuries as she flung herself forward to catch the now tottering Annie and then lower her crumpling body carefully to the ground, the pair ending up on the pavement with Annie's chest and head on Maria's lap as she cradled her mother.

Maria's blood from her cheek and nose began to drip on to Annie, as she pulled her mother as close to her breast as she could and began to rock her.

Maria tried not to look at the spread of red beneath Annie, signifying the seriousness of the injuries to her stomach.

As Annie gasped and then took her final breaths in Maria's arms, the pair of them drenched in gore, mother and daughter never took their eyes off each other.

'I love you, Mummy, and I could never 'ave 'ad a better mother than you, not in the whole wide world, and I want yer to know yer've been amazing,' were the last words Annie ever heard, even though Maria's voice was cracking with so much emotion she could barely speak.

Annie managed to mouth silently 'love' to Maria and then she died.

As the light faded from Annie's eyes and her body gave a final tremor, Maria's shriek of anguish was ear-splitting.

Suddenly Joyce arrived on the scene, and as she tried and failed to catch her breath, her hand clasped between her breasts, she tried to indicate to Maria with her other hand that she should let Annie go so she could move to safety in case the man came around.

Joyce held up his bloodied knife, which she had just snatched up from the gutter, but this didn't mean they were both safe yet as Maria and Joyce both knew the injured man could rally and suddenly stand up. And he might have more weapons on him or choose to attack them with his bare hands.

But he lay unmoving as his head wounds bled across the tarmac, his folded body insignificant now and his crabby shrunken genitals on display through the slit of his open trousers. A puddle of urine pooled beneath his hips.

Maria wouldn't stopping clasping her mother tightly despite Joyce's frantic beckonings, and then Joyce sank to the ground herself right beside them as she began to cough and cough, her whole body racked with the effort, and Maria found an arm to put around Joyce and she held the frail and bird-thin woman close to her and Annie.

Joyce's tiny hand found Maria's, and then Joyce put her other hand to Annie's half-closed eyes and, soft as a feather, she brushed her friend's eyelids closed.

Totally spent now and far beyond mere words, all Maria and Joyce could do was take solace in feeling each other's hearts beating so near together as they both sat, drained and still, staring down at Annie and the vivid rips in her blue cotton dress where the knife had repeatedly plunged through.

Blue flashing lights heralded the arrival of a police car and immediately a uniformed officer saw what he was dealing with and he used his handset to contact the station.

Soon another two police cars were there and then an ambulance. A few minutes later another three ambulances arrived.

Joyce had foamy blood running freely now from her mouth into Maria's lap, but Maria didn't know this.

Indeed she could no longer comfort Joyce as the world around her was shrinking and becoming slowly dark at its edges and increasingly remote, with the sound of the police radios distorting and the flashing lights of their cars making her dizzy, and then her head sank forward as she passed out, still sitting up and holding tightly these two women she adored and who had done so much for her.

Joyce was taken away in the first ambulance, and then Maria, and finally the man.

Forensic technicians were called and the area cordoned
off as a scene-of-crime.

Annie's body was left lying on the ground for a long
time once a doctor had pronounced death. Her corpse
looked very undignified, and it took a uniformed woman
police officer to pull her skirt down a little so that Annie's
knickers weren't on display.

It was well past midnight and Annie's skin was cold to the
touch, although still sticky with the congealing blood that
coated her, before her body was placed in a plastic zip-up
body bag and then placed inside the fourth ambulance to
go to the mortuary, the shoes of the medics and the forensic
people making strange sounds as their soles got constantly
sucked by the gummy blood thick on the ground.

'What a shit-show. A total bloodbath, eh?' said one of
the uniformed police officers, closing his notebook as he
got ready to get back in the patrol car.

His fellow officer, who'd held it in for a long time after
he'd first seen the four people, all slick with bodily fluids,
was now too busy vomiting under the next arch to hear
what his colleague was saying.

But that's what it had been.

A bloodbath.

CHAPTER TWENTY-NINE

The girls and Big and Little Danny spent all night at the hospital. They were shell-shocked.

Maria was put under sedation and given strong painkillers, and then she had her face X-rayed, as the doctors were concerned her eye above her shattered cheek might be badly damaged. An MRI scan showed bleeding on the brain too. She needed to be operated on first thing in the morning.

Maria's family saw her lying on a gurney as she waited to have her scan. Her face was swollen and black and blue with bruising. Her previously good cheek now had a nasty incision, which had been taped together.

She looked ghastly, very poorly and possibly at death's door.

'Oh, I'd never have recognised her,' said Charity. The silence of everyone else confirmed this feeling was mutual among them all. 'Mummy, don't give in – don't let that bastard win,' Charity said then, and Maria blinked at her to show that she'd heard what her daughter was saying.

A nurse ushered them back to a waiting room where they sat in silence, plastic cups of tea and coffee from the vending machine in the corner of the room before them.

Annie's body was down in the mortuary now, and the girls would be making a formal identification to the police in the morning.

They could hear the first early morning signs of the hospital starting to rouse itself for the coming day, and there seemed to be a change of staff to judge by the increased footfall outside the door. A doctor came in and said Maria's injuries were severe but unlikely to be life-threatening, although she would need to have some extensive dental work at some point in the future.

She had had police photographs taken and her body examined for forensic evidence, and was being taken to theatre now, the doctor told them, and they should assume she would remain on a ward for at least three or four days after she had come around following the operation.

The doctor went out, and then another doctor entered and told them Joyce was very poorly, and she wasn't expected to live more than a few days. They had been treating her at the hospital for a while as she had terminal inoperable lung cancer, but she had suffered severe haemorrhages in both lungs the previous evening, and was now refusing to have a blood transfusion or to have the painkilling drugs she needed to make her comfortable.

Joyce was lucid though and asking for Faith, Hope and Charity, and they would be able to see her once the police had finished taking her statement, the doctor said, and Joyce had given permission for him to share her medical details with them all.

When the doctor had left, Hope said, 'Joyce must have had that lung cancer for a while. I'm sure she never said anything to Gran, as I think she would have said something to us. But whatever happened at the arches must have been too much for her.'

Everyone sat in silence after that, deep in their own thoughts. There didn't seem to be anything worth saying.

Eventually a ward sister went to the waiting room and said she would allow Joyce to have her visitors now that the police had finished, but she needed to explain that they mustn't be shocked at how Joyce looked or be surprised if Joyce started to ramble as it could get like that when someone was nearing the end of their life.

Should anything happen with Maria meanwhile, the sister would come and get them, she promised, but for now Maria was still in theatre and then she would be put into in a chemically induced sleep in the intensive care unit until she was comfortable and had steady vital signs.

'Your mother won't know if you are there or not when she first comes out of the recovery room and we won't want you all crashing around ICU until we have her settled. My advice would be to concentrate on your friend instead, as she is so anxious to speak to you and we can't get her to have the other drugs she needs until she has had a word,' the sister said. 'Time isn't on your side, as she could go at any minute. And in any case she might not be able or care to speak tomorrow, and once we give her morphine you might not get much sense out of her from then on anyway, all of which is a long way of saying that I don't think you should wait around.'

The group of Senrab Street residents looked at each other sadly as Joyce had been such a consistent part of their lives ever since they'd been there, always warm and wise, and a huge support to them all.

Joyce had been put in a small private room, and had spent nearly two hours speaking to two plain-clothes policemen. As the sister led the way to her room, Father O'Reilly came up and tagged along at the back, saying he had found out that the man who'd caused this chaos was still in surgery, and when he came out he would be kept under a constant police guard.

Faith looked at the priest in a rather dazed way as things were happening so shockingly and so quickly that she couldn't fully comprehend what was going on. She saw him mouth 'touch and go' to Big Danny about the condition of the man who had attacked Annie and Maria. Faith didn't know if she wanted the man to die, or to recover enough so that he could stand trial for what he'd done.

In actual fact, none of them knew yet any of the details of what had actually happened beneath the arches, but they were all convinced that it had most definitely all been this dreadful man's fault.

'Poppycock,' said Joyce to Father O'Reilly, when he said to her that they'd only stay a minute as she must rest. 'I'll 'ave time enough to do that later. Resting is the last thing I want.'

The girls were glad the sister had warned them Joyce wouldn't look herself.

She had been mostly cleaned up although there was dried blood under her nails and around her hairline, while the blonde beehive that she'd been very loyal to for many years was matted and filthy, which they knew she'd hate.

Joyce seemed to have shrunk almost to nothing in the past few hours, and there was already a livid dark bruise on the back of her hand where a canula had been inserted so that she could be attached to a drip. Her skin everywhere had turned a disturbing shade of yellow and she was skeleton-thin. Now they knew she had terminal cancer, it was very obvious, and the three girls exchanged a look between them.

'Now let me speak and don't interrupt as there are things I must make clear and we might not get another chance,' Joyce told them. Her voice was weak, but somehow steely and determined. 'It's been a terrible, terrible thing. But nothing can bring Annie back, and we must pray for Maria. I've given a detailed interview to the police over what 'appened, telling them about what took place back at Christmas with this bastard, although I said it must have been a dipper who took his money in the boozer but 'e accused Maria of 'aving done that, when she didn't. If that story doesn't stick, then you are to say that it must 'ave been Annie who grabbed the money when Maria took his trousers down at Christmas, as I don't think Maria needs anyone asking too much about 'er and the rolling, should that bastard ever come around.'

'Right,' said Hope.

Joyce wasn't yet finished. 'And I told them what I thought probably 'appened today. That I said I was certain Maria 'adn't attacked the man, and his 'ead injuries must have been caused by Annie, who'd been acting in self-defence on behalf of both of them. I told the police about my friend and his son telling me the man was looking fer Maria – and this then means there's at least two witnesses that will back up the story of what a bastard 'e is. Now I wasn't close enough to see all of how it came down, but Annie going for him seems what I saw, as I can't see why he'd 'ave stabbed Annie if she 'adn't gone for him. Remember always that Annie loved you all very much, and she wouldn't want 'er death to be in vain. I know there'll be scientific evidence that might disagree with my version, but a good brief can probably put a different spin on that, should it ever come to court.

'So the *really* important thing is that you tell Maria the moment she wakes up what the story is that I said, make her learn it, as the police will question her, and you must one 'undred per cent make sure that she sticks to it word for word: she never took 'is damned money, and she never 'urt the man. That poor woman has been through so much that you must look after 'er. Agreed?'

Maria's daughters nodded their heads. They knew Annie would want to sacrifice her own reputation in order to protect Maria. And they each felt very strongly there was nothing they could do to bring Annie back, and although Maria would probably want to be honest with the police in a way that was likely to get them asking more questions rather than putting the case to bed, the wisest thing would be for Maria to do exactly as Joyce instructed.

The worst thing that could happen would be that Maria would be arrested and sent to court to stand trial, and if throwing Annie's reputation under the bus was a way to stop this happening, then none of the girls would give it a second thought.

'Right, now yer've got that on board, the next thing is that yer must all insist that Maria is to take over my job as the maid at the gentlemen's 'ouse in Soho,' Joyce said next. 'I was going to make sure that Annie took it on, but now it's obvious Maria should do it. It's safe and warm, and she won't have to do any sort of business no longer.

She just needs to keep the rooms clean and tidy for the other girls, and go to the flat door to let the johns in – it's really easy, the punters know to be respectful and well behaved, and the pay is good.' Joyce gave details of who Faith needed to speak to about this.

Hope went to say something, but Joyce interrupted with, "Ope, please, I'm not done yet. The last thing I want to say is that yer all know I 'ave no family of my own, and over the years I've come to think of you three girls as the family I would 'ave 'ad myself, should my life have turned out different. I love each one of yer very much, and always 'ave done. A few years back I made a will, and aside from a bequest fer the church that Father O'Reilly will 'andle – he's got my solicitor's details and is executor of the will – the rest of my estate goes to you three girls in its entirety, to be divided equally between you all. I've got some savings and premium bonds, and my house. There's some jewellery too. I can't think of a better home for everything I have than you three. And yer must use it as yer will. I know I'm dying and so it gives me comfort to know you three are all right.'

Faith, Hope and Charity just stared at Joyce. None of them had expected her to say anything like this.

Joyce's voice was faded and wobbly as she said then, 'I'm spent. Now, can one of you please get that nurse as I'd like the morphine she promised?'

Faith told Joyce how amazing she was, and she reached into her pocket and then pushed a tiny stuffed toy leopard into Joyce's hand.

Faith had been in Hamleys on Regent Street recently buying a present for a friend who'd just had a baby, and she had come across the leopard. She'd never seen Joyce without at least one item of leopard print on, and usually she was dressed head to toe in it, one of her favourite expression being 'more is more', and so Faith had bought the toy to pop in a drawer and save for Joyce's Christmas present.

But now it seemed as if Joyce wouldn't be with them those months later at Christmas, and so Faith had brought the leopard to the hospital. With glistening eyes, she pointed out to Joyce the label she had written and tied around its neck with a scrap of ribbon.

'More is definitely more' the label said, and although exhausted and desperately poorly, Joyce found the energy to smile. And Faith had to work very hard at making sure she was smiling back with only the very slightest wobble to her lips.

Big Danny went out of the room to get help and then the sister came in to administer the medicine Joyce needed, and before it knocked Joyce out, there were hugs and thank-yous and I-love-yous and tears before Joyce slipped asleep with everyone gathered around, with Faith and Charity holding her hands, and Father O'Reilly saying a prayer.

Faith

Back in the waiting room, Father O'Reilly wrestled with the drinks machine to get everyone something warm to keep their energy up as they waited for news of Maria.

As the machine ate the Father's coins but refused to give out the drinks, Faith looked at her sisters and said, 'I have an idea . . .'

CHAPTER THIRTY

Joyce passed away the following evening without ever regaining consciousness.

It was as if once she had tried to look after her dear friends Annie and Maria, and then said everything she needed to from her hospital bed, she had decided it was time for her to let go and die, and so that's what she'd done.

Faith pushed aside the fleeting thought she had had over whether Big Danny had somehow convinced the sister to give Joyce something that would end her life peacefully and that had meant Joyce would be in no danger of suffering any longer over her last hours. She knew she would never ask Big Danny whether he had done this or not, but she hoped that he had.

An hour after Joyce died, the drugs keeping Maria in an induced coma were reduced.

The girls were at her bedside when Maria came to and it wasn't long before she had been told about Joyce.

Faith

Although Maria's face was too numb for her to speak or move it, salty water slid from her puffy eyes.

The sight of their mother weeping like this set her three daughters off again as they all huddled together to mourn the deaths of Annie and Joyce, and how Maria had had such violence wreaked on her once again at the hands of a man.

The tears of the girls flowed freely even though Faith, Hope and Charity each felt they had already cried all they possibly could.

There was nobody in the world to care a jot when the horrible man died the next morning, without coming-to from when he crashed down unconscious to lie in the road in the shadow of the arches.

Not a single tear was shed, and nor did anyone mourn him.

The police traced his family and he turned out to have been a Catholic, but Father O'Reilly refused to allow his funeral to happen at his church.

And after the police had told the man's family what it seemed had happened and his vindictive part in it, his family disowned him and said they wouldn't be party to any funeral or remembrance of him.

When Maria and the girls heard of this, it felt like a victory. A small one, but a victory all the same.

*

Three weeks later a joint funeral for Annie and Joyce took place.

It was a grand affair.

The previous afternoon, two coffins had been moved from the undertaker's to the house in Senrab Street where Annie had lived.

The curtains were drawn shut in the front room and the furniture placed in the backyard to free up some space. Candles were lit on the mantelpiece and the hard chairs from the kitchen brought in.

Annie and Joyce's coffins stood side by side on trestles, and were never left alone for even a moment, the family taking it in turns to keep vigil right through the night.

There had been an option to have the coffins open but Maria had requested the lids be screwed shut, as she wanted everyone to remember both women in their prime rather than being reminded of how ravaged they had each looked at their ends.

Maria was out of hospital now and her wounds were healing, although her face was badly swollen. She was still suffering headaches from the bleed on the brain, and she could only eat soft food because her broken teeth hadn't yet been attended to. She was under strict instructions from her doctor that she wasn't to overdo things.

Maria had agreed to a wheelchair for the graveside burials, the plots being next to each other with Annie's being dug especially deep as one day Maria wanted to be buried in the same grave.

But she let everyone know very firmly that she would be walking unaided into the church and sitting in a pew and not the wheelchair for Father O'Reilly's service.

Annie and Joyce would be transported to the church in ornate glass-sided horse-drawn hearse carriages, the matching two pairs of horses that pulled each carriage a shiny black and the same height, replete with old-fashioned funeral livery and with extravagant dyed-black plumes of ostrich feathers jauntily waving at their polls.

Floral tributes in white roses would be in each hearse, placed so that they could be read through its glass sides, Annie's saying 'MOTHER' on one side of her coffin and 'HEROINE' on the other, and Joyce's 'DEAR FRIEND' and 'HEROINE'.

A demure outfit had been purchased for Annie to be dressed in as Maria thought that would be how she would have chosen to meet her maker.

Meanwhile, the small toy leopard Faith had given her had been placed in Joyce's coffin, clasped between her newly manicured hands, the nails a vibrant scarlet, and Maria had gone through Joyce's wardrobe to find her most outrageous outfit of animal print to be buried in, while Joyce's hairdresser had set her hair into its trademark beehive. And then Joyce's face had been made up exactly as she had done it every day, with her heavy eyeliner and pale lips, and finally her favourite heavy round earrings with the big fake pearls at their centre had been clipped to her earlobes.

The sound of the horses' hooves on the tarmac brought the undertakers out from sitting in the black cars parked a way back in Senrab Street, and, as the hearses were pulled to a halt outside the front door, the undertakers went inside to collect the coffins. It wasn't an easy job to manoeuvre the coffins down the narrow hallway, and then out into the road before they were tenderly slid into and secured in the hearses, but the undertakers managed it without mishap.

Everyone was dressed in sombre black, although Faith hadn't been able to resist saying to Hope, 'So just a normal day for you then,' and Hope, smiling back at her, had taken Faith's words in the slightly playful spirit they'd been meant.

The girls had all made efforts not to argue in the past weeks. This had been good for them as it had reminded everyone how much they liked each other and how sometimes previously they'd been a bit quick to argue and take umbrage with one another, which in the big scheme of things now felt childish and ridiculous in the light of the yawning loss of Annie and Joyce, and the shocking attack on Maria.

Faith's boyfriend Tom Jarrett was working up in Newcastle, Faith thought he had said, and so he wasn't going to be in attendance.

She was secretly relieved about this as she still hadn't introduced him to her family, and she was glad she didn't have to do it on a day like this.

He was working undercover at the moment, and in fact Faith didn't even know if he was definitely in Newcastle or if this was just the cover-story he had given her. They hadn't been in touch since the week before Annie had died, which Faith had been expecting, and so she would tell him what had happened once he got back in touch.

She felt less awkward about her family background now. The floral tributes of 'HEROINE' had been her idea; she thought it applied to Maria too. It made her feel proud that she had such a lineage and she felt now that there was nothing about her background that she should ever feel ashamed of.

Once the coffins were safely secured and the drivers had gathered the horses' reins, Maria and her daughters got into one black car, and Big Danny and Little Danny into the other.

Lisa was there too in the second car, having been released from HMP Holloway first thing that morning, with Taxi Joe driving like the clappers to have her back to Senrab Street in time for a bath and full makeover. It had worked, as Lisa's hair was big and full, and she was slathered in jewellery once more, her bracelets clinking merrily together every time she moved her arm, although she'd said she didn't know if she could last the whole day out on such savage heels as she was so out of practice.

As they toasted Annie and Joyce with large glasses of brandy in Big Danny's best cut-glass tumblers while they waited for the hearses to arrive, Maria thought it was good to see Lisa back to her old self as she'd felt, when visiting her, that her prison garb had made Lisa seem disconcertingly dowdy.

Now, a top-hatted man in a black coat, with a long black length of chiffon material tied around the hat and hanging down his back, got into place. He would be walking in front of the hearses, Annie's going in front of Joyce's, and then Maria and her girls were in the first car that would come next, and those from Other Home in the second car.

The procession made its way slowly down the street, with everyone coming out of their houses to pay their respects.

As the cortège turned the corner at the end of the street, Maria looked back to see an assistant from the undertaker escorting in the caterers who would get the house ready for the wake, and put the food and drink out ready for everyone after the funeral.

The eight horses drawing the two hearses made such a distinctive noise with their metal shoes on the flinty stones in the tarmac that people came out of their houses and shops to see the impressive sight, and it seemed to

Maria that the whole of Stepney ground to a halt as the cortège made its way through to the church.

Strangers bowed their heads in respect, and no car drivers used their horns to speed up the procession.

At the church there were all those who Joyce and Annie knew, and some of their punters too. There were empty pews as it was a large church and it wasn't by any means the largest funeral that Father O'Reilly had conducted, but it was, without a doubt, the most poignant.

Father O'Reilly led the service, and he said he was honoured to count himself among the friends of both extraordinary women.

The pallbearers bore the coffins to the open graves, and standing before the graves, Father O'Reilly said the internment prayers.

The coffins were lowered, and Maria and her daughters led the throwing in of handfuls of earth on the top of each coffin.

Faith looked around and noticed the gravediggers waiting a respectful distance away, ready to heap the earth back into the graves once everyone had moved away.

She looked toward Maria to see if her mother needed anything.

Maria was standing beside the wheelchair, having pointedly refused to get into it at all. And beside her there was a distinguished-looking older man in an expensive suit, with grey, almost white hair, who had a dark mac over his arm and a matching trilby hat in his hand, as he talked quietly with his head close to Maria's.

Her curiosity piqued, Faith tried to remember whether she had seen this man in the church, but she didn't think she had.

Then he stepped back five or six paces from Maria as somebody else was waiting to talk to her.

Faith couldn't read the expression on her mother's face. She had never seen her look like she did at that moment, and it seemed as if Maria wasn't paying any attention to what this new person was saying to her.

How strange, as Maria normally went out of her way to be polite to everybody.

It was impossible to tell if she was pleased or furious.

Faith thought about it and then decided her mother appeared to be thunderstruck more than anything else.

She peered at the man again, and to her surprise he was staring right back at her with rapt attention. Even though she was used to being the centre of attention in the court-room, in her private life this seemed a very different matter.

Faith felt peculiar at being under intense scrutiny like this.

But she refused to look away, and so she held the man's stare.

There was something about his face that caught her attention, but she couldn't tell what it was.

Then he gave her the slightest nod, put the hat on his head and walked away, leaving her feeling hot and agitated.

Back in the living room of Senrab Street, the curtains now fully open to allow the afternoon sunshine in, Maria chugged two large glasses of brandy one after the other before anyone outside the family or Other Home arrived.

Their mother hardly ever drank alcohol, and so, even though this was a difficult day, such extreme behaviour seemed aberrant.

The three girls looked from one to another a bit anxiously as, while wakes could get a bit unruly, everyone knew and always forgave this, they thought Maria would be mortified if she ended up behaving poorly at this chance to celebrate the lives of Annie and Joyce, as she would feel she had been callow and disrespectful should she end up falling down drunk.

And the sisters knew that Faith was going to break some very important news to Maria, and so they wanted their mother not to get too drunk to hear it.

Faith raised her eyebrows in a question, and Hope and Charity nodded that she should go ahead, and promptly they made themselves scarce, closing the living room door firmly so that the two could have a little privacy.

'Come and sit by me on the sofa, Mummy, and we can have a quiet five minutes to ourselves before everyone else gets here,' Faith said, taking the brandy glass from Maria's hand and putting it out of easy reach.

And once she and Maria were settled, Faith asked, 'How are you, Mummy?'

'I'm not sure,' said Maria. 'It feels like the end of an era.'

Faith nodded that this was true. It did feel like that, she had to agree.

'I don't know how we'll manage without them both,' Maria added.

'We *will* manage without them. It won't be the same, but it shall be just as good, I promise. And that's because we have *you*,' Faith told Maria.

She reached for her mother's hand.

'There is something us three girls want you to know, and you will be getting a letter about it soon,' said Faith carefully.

Maria glanced at her with a worried expression.

'No, no, it's not bad news, I promise,' Faith answered quickly, and Maria's expression relaxed a little although she remained looking pensive.

'We've waited until we'd given our instructions to the solicitor and the executor of Joyce's will to say anything to you. You were in hospital and then there was lots to do getting ready for today and we couldn't say anything in case it wasn't going to happen or there was a problem, but now it seems as if everything should be fairly straight forwa—'

'Don't keep me on tenterhooks – just say it,' Maria butted in.

'Well, Joyce left me, Hope and Charity the entirety of her estate, a portion for Father O'Reilly and the church aside. There's some premium bonds, savings, jewellery and her house, and us three girls have equal shares in that. So me and Hope and Charity have had a serious chat together, and we are going to give you everything Joyce has left us, Mummy. This means you can leave Senrab Street if you want and live in your own house . . .'

Maria looked so shocked at this suggestion, that quickly Faith added, 'Or you can rent it out for an income, or do whatever you want with it. The point is that life can become easier for you. That's what Annie would have wanted for you. She always believed that at some time you would have some good luck. She never lost faith there would be better times ahead, and you know that. And Joyce did too – she said to us very firmly in the hospital that you must take her job as the maid in the place she was working at in Soho. You'd be in the flat all the time and just have to keep it tidy and welcoming, and escort the gentlemen in . . . and that's it, Mummy. No more punters, no more business and no more street corners on a winter's night. That's got to be a good thing, no? And us girls don't *need* what Joyce left us – what we need is to see you set up and happy.'

Maria hid her face in her hands as emotion over-whelmed her. She didn't cry or say anything, but when

Faith put an arm around her shoulder, she leaned against her eldest daughter.

Hope and Charity came in and both squeezed on to the sofa to hug their mother, and the situation was only broken up when a knock on the door announced the arrival of the first mourners, and Hope and Charity left to deal with them.

'Mummy, before you get up, I have a question. Who was that man with the white hair and smart suit who talked to you after the burial, with his hat in his hand? What did he say to you?' Faith asked. 'He stared at me in such a strange way, and I'd already seen you looking rattled. But he didn't look aggressive. I couldn't work him out.'

Maria sighed and looked at her daughter in a very solemn way. 'That . . . That was your grandfather who'd come down from Wakefield to pay his respects and tell me how fond he had been of both Annie and Joyce,' Maria managed to say after quite a while, even if her voice was quiet and broken.

A flabbergasted Faith was quite lost for words.

As Lisa came in to take Maria to greet her guests, Faith was left sitting on the sofa.

She scratched her arm as she wondered if she'd heard Maria correctly.

But as Faith stood up to go and help her mother with the hosting duties, she caught sight of herself in the mirror above the fireplace.

And she knew then that what her mother had just said to her was the truth. And it had been why Maria had needed all that brandy to steady her nerves.

For the smartly dressed white-haired man's face was being reflected right back at her as she stared at the mirror, the two candles still burning either side.

Faith could see that without a shadow of doubt she was definitely closely related to him as they looked so similar, as if they were two peas in a pod.

And as they circulated amongst those at the wake, both Maria and Faith felt quite dreamlike and as if it were all very unreal. Neither were certain what this man's presence at the funeral would mean for them.

If anybody noticed that Maria and Faith seemed preoccupied and silent as the wake continued, they probably thought this was because of grief.

Now and again they would glance at each other but, each time they did this, it seemed they were each battling with a maelstrom of emotions and so they then would look away.

Eventually everyone left, and it was just the occupants of the two houses who remained.

A tipsy Big Danny went back to Other Home and returned with three bottles of chilled champagne and some glass flutes.

'It's been a sad day,' he said once he'd popped the cork and put filled glasses in everyone's hands, 'but while we'll never forget our dear Annie and Joyce, it's time that we all look to the future now. And I have a cracker of an announcement to make that I think everyone will like. Now, please raise your glasses for a toast.'

Bemused, everybody did as Big Danny had asked.

'The future!' he said, lifting his champagne flute high.

'The future,' everybody echoed, even if none of them had any idea what it was that they were toasting.

EPILOGUE

Cadogan Terrace, Victoria Park, Hackney, East London, 1992

It had been a real scramble to get everything ready in time, but Father O'Reilly had asked at the end of a Sunday service if builders, decorators, handymen and gardeners were available for double the going rate. And the same for cleaners too.

The result was that Big Danny was able to turn around an impressive but tumbledown house in a mere six weeks. Everybody had told him it couldn't be done, not least as the property was enormous, but he'd remained certain that it could, saying, 'It's going to be the Notting 'Ill Carnival the August bank holiday weekend, and that's when we'll 'ave our own carnival 'ere, although we'll call it an 'ouse-warming so that the Notting 'Ill lot don't get jealous.'

And Big Danny's unshakeable belief carried the day, helped no doubt by the promise of generous bonuses for those that worked on the house should their tasks be completed to an excellent standard and ahead of schedule.

New bathrooms and kitchens were put in and their floors tiled, the roof and guttering were repaired as were all the rickety bannisters; new wooden-framed windows were installed throughout and the Victorian tiles in the impressive hallway restored. Floorboards were replaced where necessary, some then sanded and stained, and the others covered with new fitted carpets, and the final touch was the restoration of the front door, with a specialist found to bring the stained glass up to scratch.

The minute a room had had all its building work finished and the freshly plastered walls were dry enough for emulsion, the decorators arrived en masse. And once they had gone, an army of cleaners moved to make sure everything was spick and span, with house removers bringing over and unpacking everyone's possessions, and seeing all the new furniture that had been ordered into place.

Out in the extensive back garden, a rotavator was used to level the ground, new turf was laid, a wooden gazebo built in the garden, and a deck and patio, with the small front garden being given a thorough spruce-up and all the outside render painted an expensive-looking cream.

On the night of the party, garden torches had been stuck in the ground and lit, and Chinese lanterns were strung to the fences. It looked very pretty, but as the turf was too new to be walked on, Big Danny made sure that the tables for the food and drink were placed by the catering company to form a natural barrier so that the partygoers couldn't stray beyond the patio-paved area.

Maria stood with Charity and Hope on the patio as the white-shirted waiters put the finishing touches to the buffet tables, lighting up the burners under the large metal trays of beef stroganoff and rice. The guests would be arriving in under an hour.

'Feels like a dream, doesn't it?' said Hope. And Charity ran her fingers through her hair to fluff it up as she nodded in agreement.

'I'm speechless,' Maria answered, and she was.

The last year had been the strangest one of Maria's life. Her injuries had taken some getting over, and she didn't think she'd ever properly heal from the loss of Annie and Joyce.

At first she had been unable to think about the house Joyce had bequeathed to the girls, and that in turn they had insisted should be hers.

But at New Year Maria had decided it was time for a new start, and so within a week she and Faith and Hope had moved into Joyce's home, with the keys to their old Senrab Street home being handed back to the council.

But Maria began to have terrible nightmares in Joyce's house, and she knew it was because it was the place she had spent her first hours in London, when she and Annie had fled Wakefield. Visiting Joyce there many times over the years as she had was, Maria discovered, a very different experience from actually living there all the time, when instead of the secure place she'd expected through owning it, it continually brought up distressing memories that haunted her. And because Maria so obviously wasn't happy, neither were Faith nor Hope.

Maria found she enjoyed working as a maid at the Soho flat, just as Joyce thought she would, revelling in the fact that she need never let another man near her in an intimate way. But she found herself dreading going back home to Joyce's house.

And this feeling got worse when the inquest took place into Annie's death and an inquest too into the man who'd killed her, Maria having to speak to the coroner on both occasions. Fortunately Joyce hadn't needed an inquest as she had died in hospital and had been under medical supervision for her terminal cancer before that, and so her death wasn't deemed unexpected.

Maria had supposed she would find this period harrowing, especially following on from the extensive police questioning she'd had to endure when she was well enough to answer questions, but she was surprised that these public inquiries felt emotionally much more taxing than laying Annie and Joyce to rest had been, or when she had so unexpectedly seen Ted Walton. She felt so low, in fact, that when the police told her they wouldn't be putting any sort of charges before her, she couldn't feel even the slightest bit relieved.

'Good God, my girl, whatever's up with yer?' said Lisa one day a couple of months after Maria and the girls had moved, and Lisa had come around for a cup of tea. 'Charity said you weren't too good, and I see what she means. Yer clothes are 'anging off yer, yer've lost so much weight. And it's not as if yer weren't thin as a whippet before then.'

Maria gave a depressed sigh. 'Oh, I guess time and life 'as caught up with me at last. For many reasons this seemed a good move, but the truth of it is that I 'ate the 'ouse, and I miss you and I miss Charity.'

'We miss you too,' agreed Lisa sadly. 'It's awful and it feels as if all the life and laughter 'as been sucked right out of Senrab Street, and Charity is moping about too, no matter 'ow Little Danny tries to make 'er giggle, or 'ow often she 'as 'er nails and 'air done. And because she's down, then Little Danny is down – they're like bears with sore 'eads, and I 'ate to see it. And the new residents at yer old place seem to 'ate each other as they're always screaming and shouting out in the street, and I 'ad to 'ave a right go at them the other day for bringing down the tone of the neighbourhood.'

'I bet they shut up then,' said Maria, who could imagine vividly how this might have gone.

Lisa sniffed. 'Not as you'd notice.'

'You must be losing yer touch, Lisa.' Then Maria added, 'But that's not good with Charity being like that as normally she's so sunny. I thought she'd be made up over her and Little Danny being asked to be directors in Big Danny's new company – I know 'Ope is loving being more involved with helping him go legit,' said Maria. 'Not that she or Faith are liking it now we're all living 'ere any more than I do.'

Big Danny's toast at Annie and Joyce's funeral had been over the setting up of this company as his first serious move towards turning his business clean, and everyone had been very excited. Now it seemed as if the gloss was wearing thin all the way around.

Lisa and Maria had a long hug at Joyce's doorstep when Lisa said it was time she went back to Senrab Street. But later that evening, Big Danny turned up at Maria's to tell her he'd had an idea he thought she might like.

Why didn't the two former Senrab Street households pool their money, and buy a big house that they could divide up for them all to live in?

And so that's what happened, Big Danny asking Hope to get together cash from most of his various interests, and Maria selling Joyce's house.

Maria had taken quite a lot of persuading as she couldn't help feeling she brought bad luck with her wherever she went, but it was amazing how persuasive her three daughters, Lisa and Big Danny turned out to be. And she had found it really difficult not to be next door to Charity and Lisa, and this seemed a perfect way they could all be together again.

Once Maria finally said she was in, they all sat down one evening to draw up a list of what everybody wanted from the new property, and then Charity and Lisa got on to estate agents with the lengthy list of requirements, and they ended up going to see over twenty properties.

It was a five-storey house on the edge of Victoria Park in Hackney, a stone's throw from the canal, that had won them all over in the end. It needed work to make it what they wanted, but they'd made sure to allocate money for that.

Once Big Danny had collected the keys, the lower and upper ground floors were converted into a maisonette for Little Danny and Charity, with the French doors from the lower ground opening to the garden, the assumption being they'd have children and so this made getting them outside easy. The next two floors were Big Danny's and Lisa's, and the top floor was Maria and Hope's, and theirs had tiny roof terraces front and back, two minute bedrooms to the front of the house, and a generous open-plan kitchen and living area that looked out over the garden.

Faith could have had a room in either of the other two flats, or sleep in Hope's room as her bed had a bit under it that you could pull out for a second bed, or on the sofa bed Maria had bought for the living room. But instead she had decided to take a room at the Camberwell home of one of her colleagues at her chambers, drawn there, thought Maria, to be closer to Tom working only a mile away – when he was around, that is, as quite often he seemed not to be. Maria had only met Tom once, and that was when she went to Camberwell to see Faith's new home, and she'd liked him and thought he and Faith a good match for one another. And while she knew she'd miss Faith, out of each of her daughters, Maria thought it was Faith who really needed to live outside of the family unit, for a while at least.

Maria insisted she kept her job as a maid as she didn't want to be a burden to anyone and not pay her way in the new house. The third day she returned there from central London, Maria felt a rush of happiness as she walked up the steps to the front door.

This house felt like home, she realised.

It was the first time she had ever lived anywhere where she felt truly content or that felt properly warm and welcoming to her, and she had to take a minute on the doorstep to catch her breath over how very much this moved her.

The doorbell rang on the night of the house-warming, and Big Danny went to the front door to let the first guests in.

Maria and her daughters stayed out on the patio. Faith was going to stay in Hope's room after the party.

They looked about them, and then Maria said, 'What do you think Annie and Joyce would have made of all this?'

'They'd be really cross at missing a party like this,' said Charity with a laugh. 'Furious, in fact. They'd have bought new clothes and used a can of hairspray each.'

Hope added, 'And Joyce would have discovered that at least six of the guests would be her regulars. They'd be judges and councillors and policemen, all in Big Danny's pocket, and Joyce and the regulars would all have pretended not to know each other and really enjoyed the charade. And Annie would have got flirted with by a neighbour whose wife wouldn't have been best pleased, and she'd have been horrified by him being too presumptuous.'

'They'd have made sure we all had a great time, and drunk too much champagne,' said Faith. 'And at the end of the night, when we were clearing up, they'd have made us drink more champagne, this time to us all believing for all those years that we deserved a better future, and that we have now come a long way from where we started without really any help other than from each other and Other Home.'

'Well, let's drink to Annie and Joyce now then,' said Maria, and held her glass aloft, 'while it's just us here. For without those women, and how they believed in us, we wouldn't be standing here today. To Annie and Joyce!'

'Annie and Joyce,' echoed Faith, Hope and Charity.

*

Maybe Hope was psychic, or just cynical, as indeed Big Danny had asked many influential people to the party, who were all happy to rub shoulders with the shady characters he sometimes did business with. There were indeed a couple of judges there who had been Joyce's clients at the Soho flat, as well as some important businessmen and lawyers and councillors and policemen. Goodness knows what their new neighbours thought of the wide range of guests at the house-warming.

And when Tom Jarrett arrived, and Faith saw a cheery Big Danny throw an arm around his neck, and then Tom said, 'Hello, sir,' to an older man Big Danny had been talking to, whom Hope had just described to Faith as a high-up policeman who owed Big Danny a few favours, Faith realised that she and Tom could never go the course together. It made her feel sad, although only a bit.

She watched as Tom and the judges and a couple of barristers Faith knew by reputation, although not personally, acknowledged each other with a slightly raised brow or a flicker of a wink and she understood that Tom existed in murky waters and was quite happy to do so. He might not be out-and-out bent, but the more Faith stared at him, the more she could see that DI Tom Jarrett wasn't squeaky clean either.

Although Faith liked him, she was too ambitious to risk being brought down herself should any taint attaching to Tom leach across to her. She didn't enjoy his company *that* much. She'd tell him a few days after the party that they needed to cool things down, she decided.

Tom looked at her and smiled, and Faith thought she detected him realising already what she was thinking.

He gave the tiniest shrug as if to say there were no hard feelings, and she gave a similarly small shrug back.

*

As it turned out, that night Faith was in another man's thoughts.

For up in Wakefield, Fred Walton had just overheard two of the girls working at the drinking den talking about their mothers remembering what a wonderful sight Joyce and Annie had been in their heyday, all beehives and tight cocktail dresses that made them wiggle as they walked.

'But they left when there was some trouble,' one said.

'Yeah,' the other replied, 'one of their daughters got into trouble, Ma said, I think. Ted wasn't best pleased about it anyhow as it were very sudden and nobody knew what 'ad 'appened.'

Fred hadn't thought of Maria for many years, but what a beauty she'd been back then, he thought, and how chuffed he'd been in Woolies when she'd agreed to go to the coffee bar with him. Then he remembered how furious he'd been over her pregnancy. Such mad times. Maybe he had gone a little far that night in the bar but once he'd cut her the first time with his right hand it had been hard to stop – certainly Ted had thought he'd overstepped the mark. He and his father had steadfastly refused to mention that night to each other ever since, and Fred had known his father had never thought much of him after that.

And then Fred wondered what had happened to Maria.

Suddenly he felt an overwhelming need to find out.

Then a new thought struck him – maybe he, Fred Walton, had a child out there.

His two marriages had never produced children. And now he was divorced for the second time, and there was no obvious successor to follow in his footsteps to take over the Waltons' empire, while local women steered clear of him if they could possibly help it.

He was only forty-five but his uncle Frank had died of knife wounds when he was fifty-two, and so maybe Fred shouldn't count on a long life.

He didn't know quite why, but Fred felt convinced then that without a shadow of doubt he was a father.

Family was family, after all.

Wasn't it? And, as unconsciously Fred Walton flexed his knuckles and stared at the ring with the razor-blade tip embedded in it that he still wore every day, he decided he needed to do something about this.

*

All the way down in Hackney, Faith felt a cold draught on her neck. It was as if somebody was walking over her grave. She looked about her, but she couldn't see anything or anybody that might have made her feel like this.

She looked at her mother, and her sisters. They seemed to be enjoying themselves as they stood together, three handsome and strong women. She wished she had a camera to mark the moment.

Faith realised that for a long time she hadn't noticed her mother's scars, and for a moment she couldn't quite remember which side of Maria's face was damaged. The puckers to the skin Fred had given her were still red and raised, and always would be. But nobody who knew and loved Maria thought they made her any less beautiful.

Faith had the sensation again.

She didn't understand why, but she knew without a shadow of doubt it didn't augur well . . .

To be continued . . .

ACKNOWLEDGEMENTS

Firstly, a big thank you to my new friend and story right-hand, Jenny Parrot. Jenny has allowed me to explore this amazing new world of drama on the page, and my journey is all the better for it.

I started these books with the help and guidance of my literary agent, Kerr MacRae, and we have watched together as my thoughts and ideas have come to life on the page. He keeps me on the straight and narrow and makes sure we make every right move along the way.

To my publishers, Mountain Leopard Press at Headline, a massive thank-you for all your hard work behind and in front of the scenes. To my editor Beth Wickington for her advice and enthusiasm and to Jenni Edgecombe for editorial support. To Marta Juncosa, Margarida Mendes Ribeiro and Isabelle Wilson for marketing and publicising my books to get them in to readers' hands. Thanks too to Dominic Gribben for creating the wonderful audiobook.

Finally, a big thank-you to you, the readers. Your response to my new-found life has been amazing. The incredible reviews for my stories make it all worthwhile.

ABOUT THE AUTHOR

'The first time I held a gun, I forgot to breathe'

LINDA CALVEY has served eighteen years behind bars, making her one of Britain's longest-serving female prisoners. She moved to fourteen different prisons, doing time with Rose West and Myra Hindley. But prison didn't break her. Since her release, Linda has become a full-time author. Her fascinating memoir, *The Black Widow*, was published in 2019, and her runaway fiction debut, *The Locksmith*, in 2021, with its sequel, *The Game*, coming the following year. *Faith* is the opener to Linda's new series of novels that are set in the seedier side of London's East End.

Don't miss
Linda Calvey
telling her own thrilling story
in this gritty account of prison life

Out now